Loving The Enemy

Mia Faye

Mia Faye

ISBN: 9798720368258

Copyright © 2021 by Mia Faye
Author's note: This is a work of fiction. Some of the names and geographical locations in this book are products of the author's imagination, and do not necessarily correspond with reality.

For all romantics out there

TABLE OF CONTENTS

Prologue

Chapter 1

Chapter 2

Chapter 3

Chapter 4

Chapter 5

Chapter 6

Chapter 7

Chapter 8

Chapter 9

Chapter 10

Chapter 11

Chapter 12

Chapter 13

Chapter 14

Chapter 15

Chapter 16

Chapter 17

Chapter 18

Chapter 19

Chapter 20

Chapter 21

Chapter 22

Chapter 23

Chapter 24

Chapter 25

Chapter 26
Chapter 27
Chapter 28
Chapter 29
Chapter 30
Chapter 31
Chapter 32
Chapter 33
Epilogue

Prologue

Eliza

One Year Ago

The music was pumping - hard, fun, fast. Lights were spinning, but really it might have just been my head; I never drank as much as I did that night. But damn it all to hell, I was throwing caution to the wind. Tired of being Elizabeth Piquel, the boring accountant who did all the sensible things, I needed to party. I was a pretty girl, the kind you'd see on a cereal box selling moderately healthy breakfast foods to equally mildly health-conscious cereal consumers. I was someone you could pass by. Pretty, but not stop the world, end a war, pretty. So, at Ophelia and Asher's Legende Party, a massive bash thrown every year to celebrate their anniversary, I let my crazy fly.

Ophelia had been my roommate for a while before she met the billionaire storage entrepreneur turned club owner, influencer, doting husband, and father. Harper, my best friend and college roommate, had just found her happily ever after with Reid, a local senator, which left little ol' me sitting there drinking that night's specialty cocktail.

"Oh my God, I am so drunk my drunk is drunk. Why did you leave me, Harper? I can't be left alone. See, I make such bad choices." I flopped into the chair beside Harper and Reid in a cozy dark corner of the club.

"You make amazing choices! You just drank too much of the famous Andromeda Fire on the rocks. It has absinthe in it, and that can really sneak up on you. Here, have some water ... drink the whole glass," Harper said as I guzzled the glass before me.

When I absentmindedly finished, it made me feel woozy, like I was in an alternate universe.

"Maybe I should just go home and pass out on the couch," I complained, seeing all the other people in the room paired up.

"Don't. Ophelia slept on that couch for a year; it's a beast." Harper laughed as she tipped the water glass back up to my lips.

"Or, I can sleep in his bed." My eyes wandered over to a tall, sexy man wearing designer jeans tucked into cowboy boots.

It was a weird look for DC, so I figured he wasn't from anywhere local. As soon as Reid got up to shake his hand, my whole body was electrified. He knew the tall, dark stranger.

"Andre," Reid was kind and welcoming. "Join us." He then turned to us at the table. "This is my wife Harper," Reid said, nodding to Harper, who was sitting beside me. "And her friend Pickle." That made both Reid and Tall-Dark-and-Handsome laugh.

"Pickle?" The stranger's face curled into a sexy frown.

"It's actually Piquel, as in Pee-Kale, but everyone thinks it's funny to call me Pickle so it stuck. I'm Eliza, short for Elizabeth." I did my best to stand up and shake his hand, but found when I did the room spun all the more. I realized that instead of shaking my hand, he was gently holding me up. I offered an awkward smile.

"Nice to meet you, Eliza. I'm Andre, short for nothing." His eyes smoldered, and I could feel myself getting wet and instantaneously regretting that I wore thong underwear with a too short, too tight dress.

Nothing about the Eliza Piquel Andre met that night was actually me. I had a heavy slather of makeup on that made me look like a supermodel, my hair had been professionally coiffed, and my clothes were almost painted on. My natural look is big brown eyes, the kind you could get lost in, and a tight, delicious body. I loved to walk as a workout and dance, but seriously I could thank my skinny-ass mom for her rockin' genetics. She was the local beauty pageant winner three years in a row until my dad knocked her up. Boy, I never heard the end of it. I was the reason she was no longer sexy ... whatever. I got her body and my dad's sensible face; the combination made a pretty mix of boring if not gussied up a bit. That night I was gussied up a lot.

Reid made small talk with Andre, but Andre's eyes stayed on me. My whole body was on fire. Nothing felt better than that hot stare. He offered to get us drinks and we let him. Soon I was sitting with another wicked beverage in my hand and the dreamy Andre beside me, fully engaged in conversation. I knew better than to actually drink the dangerous libation before me, so I sipped and interjected my two cents when I had something to share. At one point during the night, which was mostly a euphoric haze of memory, Andre and I started dancing. He smelled like expensive booze and rich cologne. We slow danced even to the faster songs. We didn't talk much, just danced in our quiet corner of the crazy club. I could feel his hardness pressed against my hip as we danced, and soon his arousal and mine were so evident it could no longer be ignored.

"I'm staying at the hotel up the road." He caressed my face and then leaned in and kissed me with such intense passion.

I tasted him as his mouth was upon me, and I found him quite feral and rough under all that beauty. His kiss was hard and passionate, and I could only imagine that his cock would be the same. All I could think about was the fact that I'd been such a good girl all of my life. I played exactly by the rules and never once walked on the wild side, and so, with his tongue in my mouth and his cologne on my clothes, I committed to doing 'it,' whatever it would entail.

"Yes, sure. Let me just tell my friends." I barely breathed as I got my purse and told the girls I was leaving with Andre.

Both gave me rather surprised looks followed by big-sisterly praises for deciding to dance with danger.

"Just text us if you need us," Harper said. "But have fun. Reid says Andre's an upstanding guy, so enjoy your night." Her voice rose three octaves like she was talking to a three-year-old and I sort of cringed, and yet, it was just what I needed to solidify my resolve.

"I will," I sing-songed back at her and rushed to join Andre, who already had his coat on and was paying the concierge to get him a taxi.

He leaned in, kissed my forehead, and brought me in for a hug as if we'd been dating for years. As soon as we slid into the back seat of the taxi, he was on me, kissing again.

"I cannot get enough of you," he confessed as he pulled me onto his lap and we continued to kiss.

My way-too-short skirt rode right up my ass, laying me essentially bare with only my thong panties, so it was pretty much a given that he'd start playing with me the moment I was exposed. He was discreet seeing that we were in a car, and turned me to face him as his hand trailed up my skirt. I'd had sex before, one drunken night at a frat house where I lost my virginity to a guy I couldn't even remember. It was one of those things where I was in a room with a bunch of people all drunk and stoned off their asses. It was the one other time I was wild. I did go in, at twenty-two years old, fully expecting I'd be losing my virginity. In fact, I was on a quest, so the fact that it happened the way I had planned it was a score in my book. I wanted it, I got it, I hardly remembered it, but I proudly handed in my V-card and entered the realm of sexually active adults pretty damn proud of myself.

The only other time was with a guy I dated in college for a minute, we fooled around a lot, a ton in fact, and when it came time for us to make it to home base, he wasn't too thrilling. He was pretty small, pretty unskilled, and that was pretty much the end of it. I wanted to date more but just never found anyone that exciting. I wasn't into any more meaningless stuff; I wanted the real deal but never found it.

I was back to being okay with just sex as I was horny as hell. So, having sexy Andre's fingers lodged deep inside my dripping pussy was like having professional sex. Metaphorically I'd made it to the majors, no more sleazy nightclubs; I was going for the headliner. It was a blissfully short taxi ride, and before I knew it I was trailing behind him, walking through an ornate lobby with a chandelier, brocade chairs, and very good lighting. He swiped his keycard, and voila, we were in his suite with a view of all of DC.

"Can I get you something to drink?" he asked as he started to unbutton his shirt, and my pussy tightened.

"Actually, just some water. I think I should slow down a little on the alcohol." I flashed him a grin as I stood there awkwardly.

He laughed. "Good call." He went to the minibar and got us two cold bottles of water, opening each of them and handing me one. He then continued to take off his shirt and raised the bottle to me. "Bottoms up, then let's hit the sheets."

Shit! Okay.

I chugged my water to the best of my ability and was pretty impressed that I didn't choke on it. We both finished drinking our water at the same time when Andre strolled over to me.

"Do you want to freshen up first?" he asked as his finger grazed over my nipple.

Freshen up? As in powder? Do my pits and bits? What?

"Um ... sure." I shrugged my shoulders, and his look turned feral.

"May I?" he asked as he bent over to lift the hem of my skirt.

"Um ... sure," I said a little quieter as he whipped my dress off, leaving me in my thong underwear and a push-up bra.

"Fuck, I love your tits." He unsnapped my bra off, which clasped in the front, and dove ... literally dove for my breasts.

Perhaps he was a little drunk, too, though I doubted it. He sucked hard on my nipple while pinching the other; he was very enthusiastic like he wanted me bad. He then slapped my ass.

"Come on, let's get in the shower. I gotta wash this DC grime and travel off me before I get to lovin' on you."

He had a fun way of talking, sexy, manly, dominant ... Um, yes, sir! At that point there wasn't much of me left to undress. I stepped out of my thong, and he threw off his jeans, revealing a very hard erection saluting the air. It was thick, long, veiny, and had a hot purpling tip that seemed to be begging for sex. He stroked himself a little, not to harden himself any more because the man was jutting out stick straight, but I think he was rather proud of his package as he stroked himself and laughed.

"You ready for this, darling?" he asked in a sweet tone of voice.

"Wow, I am not sure." And I wasn't.

I'd never seen anything so impressive in my life.

"Don't worry, I'm a good driver ... you're gonna love the feel of this inside of you. Come on, let's get all hot and bothered." He shuttled me into the bathroom, and I just thanked God I'd shaved and trimmed everything.

I was fresh and ready for whatever he had to offer. I was going to go the distance, no turning back. Elizabeth Piquel was having a one-night stand ... gloriously adult and consenting. I had my IUD firmly planted and was ready for a whole night of fun. He shimmied up behind me as he turned on the water and stabbed my ass with his love spear. The idea of it made me laugh as I rounded my hand behind me and grabbed it.

"So are we just divin' in here? I mean, I'm fully consenting to have sex with you," I said, and then asked, "but are you sure you even know my name?"

He kissed my neck and fondled my tits again. "Elizabeth Piquel, but everyone calls you Pickle, and you don't like it, so I'll call you Eliza."

Holy fuck, I was in love. We kissed and fondled but mostly showered in the shower. He lathered and soaped me up, spending a lot of time on my pussy and my ass, and I did the same, spending a ton of time greasing up the gear shift.

"Ah, ah, ah." He stopped my hand's pumping. "Better slow your roll; I don't want to cum in the shower." He took the showerhead off the holder and rinsed us both off. "So let's talk birth control. What are we working with?"

"I'm good. I've got an IUD, and I'm not due for a new one until next year, so um ... you can wear a condom or not."

"I'm free and clear, just had a nice clean bill of health last week so... After you, madam," he said as we stepped out of the shower.

We barely got ourselves dry before we were on the bed kissing, with his hands spreading out my pussy lips so that he could dive his finger into my wetness. His insistent fingers really worked me into a frenzy, but when his thumb pressed hard into my clit, I burst all over him. It was more of a stress orgasm than a euphoric one, but I'd take it. I guess my panting and whining was his cue to ram it on in cause in one hard thrust he was inside me, and my world blew apart.

"Oh my God," I blathered, feeling so full of him with a pinchy ache at the back of my vagina that just needed more of everything. He had a monster cock and everything hurt as it went in, but also felt so damn good.

"I've been dreaming all night of doing that! Fuck, Eliza."

And fuck ... we did.

He had me so rough and so deep I was seeing stars. My legs wrapped around his back as he grunted and came deep inside of me the first time. After that round it was more kissing, but his cock never really deflated. He rolled me onto my tummy and took me from behind, driving his cock into my raw, needy flesh, he lifted himself onto his elbows and pumped me ferociously from behind. I spread my legs out, trying to take as much of him as I could stand, and then he came again, collapsing on me as he did. He dug his fingers into my pussy and pinched my clit, and my sex-crazed brain rocketed to outer space.

After two rough, frenzied fucks we slowed down.

"Damn, Eliza ..." He rolled me back onto him and kissed me again with his wilted cock sandwiched on my hot sweaty belly.

"You're like an animal." I laughed and snuggled into his chest, wanting to be near his warm body. "I hope I can walk in the morning."

I wanted to play with him more, but after two vigorous sessions I couldn't keep my eyes open. I should have at least rinsed all of our crazy love off, but I was just buzzing with him. We both fell asleep pretty fast, and sometime during the middle of the night I got cold and groped for the covers, which I discovered were laying in a heap on the floor. He had his leg flopped over me, and I found it hard to extract myself enough to grab the covers. His body heat was nice, but my ass was freezing. In my attempt to retrieve the comforter he woke up.

"Sorry, I'm cold," I whispered as I pulled the heavy comforter up from the ground and put it over us.

"Right, yes ... me, too." He rolled into me so that I could cover him.

I wanted to snuggle up on him again, so I cuddled into his arms which graciously brought me into his embrace ... but we were up, and neither of us really wanted to go back to sleep.

"I want you again," he confessed in a soft, seductive tone.

"I want you, too, but you've made a pretty big mess down there." I touched myself for emphasis. "I don't think I can take any more apeman, but if you can be nice and do me softly, I'd be down for that. I like you, Andre."

He laughed. "Well, you shouldn't." He leaned into me and kissed me sweetly. "Nobody does."

I should have known then.

After that he did have sex with me gently with lots of kissing my breasts, belly ... And his cock was sweet and lovely as he positioned me so that I was riding him, calling the shots, until we both hit the big O together, collapsed on each other, and that was it for the night.

At god awful o'clock in the morning, he shuffled me off of him. I think I heard the shower, but after fucking him three times that night I wasn't going to get out of bed unless he dragged me out. When I did finally pry myself awake at sunrise, I realized he was gone. There was a note with orange juice and a muffin next to the bed.

Thanks for the fun ... Andre.

That was it. No phone number, no text, I didn't even know where he lived in Texas ... I sort of felt like shit, but that was what I'd signed up for. I thought about staying until he got back, but the note was pretty self-explanatory: thanks for the fun ... and the fun was over.

So, I got dressed, tried to wrangle my hair into something that didn't look just-fucked, and did the ride of shame home.

Chapter 1

Eliza

July twenty-second was just over one year from that infamous night at Legende where I met Andre and had the sexiest sex I'd ever had. I was at Legende again celebrating, but this time I was there for me. It wasn't the annual party that drew out the who's who of, well, just about everyone. No, this was my going away party. I was leaving DC for the time being. I was both scared and excited about my new adventure in graduate school. I planned on going for an MBA because I was completely done being an accountant. It was a good job for some, but watching my friends live the millionaire lifestyle with ambitions of their own, I decided to take my life to the next level. I was able to drag both Harper and Ophelia out of their houses, which was no easy feat as they were mothers of very young children. Ophelia had three little ones, and Harper had a toddler, so a night out on the town was a rare treat, but these were my girls, and they rallied for me - which I appreciated.

I didn't want to admit it, but I was a little jealous of them. They each had such loving and doting husbands and gorgeous children. I'd be lying if I said I didn't want what they had, but I wasn't going to find it in DC, so I had put out my application and picked my dream school, Texas A & M for a Master's in Business Administration. I was planning to focus on environmental ethics.

Deciding on a much tamer beverage than the last time I was at Legende, I chose a simple Sauvignon Blanc and the fresh Tilapia on Quinoa.

"So, did you ever hear from Andre Michelson?" Ophelia asked as soon as our food came.

"Nope, he left me a muffin and orange juice and his stupid note, and that was it. I don't care. He was a jerk, but girl, the sex was so good. I haven't had sex since, but the memories ... are keeping me going."

They all laughed.

"Pickle, you need to go to Texas and find a good man who will love you and treat you right. I'm sure some fine-ass MBA student is going to rock your freakin' world. I'm putting it out there to the universe; Pickle needs some fine-ass, hotter-than-hot fucking sex …"

"And he has to be nice. I've already had hotter than hot sex … and it's overrated when the only thing attached to the dick is an asshole," I chimed in. "Sad part was I thought he was nice."

"Well, Asher says he's not; that's why he didn't push the issue after Andre left," Harper said. "He could have called him and run his mouth at him for what he did to you, but it wouldn't have done any good. Asher found out that Andre Michelson is a real tool. They only know each other from charity stuff and their work on an energy bill. He's got an abysmal reputation … but who knew? Hope you don't run into him in Texas."

"God, I hope not, but Texas is a big state; it's almost impossible to run into someone like that. It's as big as a small country. I'm sure I'll be fine."

"Well, I know you're gonna love being back at a university." Ophelia flashed a dreamy smile. "I'd trade in a day with the kids for a lecture hall anytime," she said with a laugh. "I'd pretty much do anything to trade in the kids."

"Ah, Leah, you say that, but you adore those kids … you'd spend your whole day stressin' over them," I called Ophelia out on her bullshit.

She was the luckiest woman on the planet, and she knew it.

"You're right, but I can dream of a day off …" Ophelia looked away wistfully. "What time does your plane leave?"

I was having so much fun that I had completely forgotten all about the time.

"Nine tonight. Why?" We all looked at our phones. "Shit! It's seven; I've got to go."

I only had two suitcases. My whole life had been pared down to two huge suitcases and a FedEx box that was arriving a week later. The moment had come and it was time for me to start my new life.

"Pickle, I am going to miss you so much!" Harper stood up and threw her arms in the air. "What am I going to do without you?" For a second, I thought that Harper was actually going to cry.

"There's always Zoom, we can Zoom, and I'll be back here every year for the Legende bash. I'm not going to miss that."

"You'd better. I am going to miss you so much," and Harper did cry as she hugged me.

"Me, too," said Ophelia, who was also crying; they were a mess.

Me… I was ready to go. I gave hugs and kisses and last goodbye after last goodbye, and finally, I was in an Uber to the airport. The flight wasn't long, but it was boring. I dozed off a few times and watched part of a bad movie. We landed in the middle of the night, and it was nearly two in the morning when I checked into the motel I'd booked near the airport. The next day I was off to meet my new roommates, register for classes, and begin Eliza's Life 2.0.

Though many of my classes were online, I would have to attend a lecture or two each week. I needed to be near Houston to find a decent job, so I chose to live in a place between Houston and the university and found two girls looking for someone to share a house in Hempstead, Texas. My commutes would be forty-five minutes either way, so I figured I'd find a good podcast and just hunker down for the long drives.

The next morning, I was focused on lugging my stuff up the long driveway to my new home. The house was a huge two-story monstrosity, and my rent was for a song. Dorothy, I was not in DC anymore. I used the key they had mailed me when I signed my contract and gave them my deposit. I walked through the door into a grand foyer with a huge sweeping staircase like you'd see in the movies. The place was pretty old but very spacious, although it smelled weird, like some kind of exotic fragrance.

"Oh my God, you're here!" A gorgeous woman wearing a tank top without a bra and a flowing skirt in vibrantly colored geometric patterns rushed at me with her arms wide open. "Elizabeth!" She zeroed in for a hug, and I braced myself. "I'm Peyton. Welcome home!"

Peyton from California. If I remember correctly, she was living in Texas because she wanted to live in a wide-open space for a while. No other real reason that I could discern other than Los Angeles must have been pretty cramped.

"Hi, Peyton! You can call me Eliza or um ... Pickle, I guess, everyone does." I hated to confess that, but I was used to it. I preferred Eliza to Elizabeth. Boring people were named Elizabeth, and I was doing my best not to be boring.

"Welcome home, Eliza. Let me help you with your things. Genevieve isn't home yet. She works at this greasy spoon a couple of miles away and then has a gig tonight; she's the best singer ever, you are gonna just love her. Okay, your room is on the first floor, and you have the parlor next to it you can use as an office or whatever. This place is so amazing. Your parlor room used to be a proper parlor where people had tea, what fun is that?

The place is like two hundred years old. Fun for parties and stuff, but you have to watch out for mice and other critters. If you see anything, don't worry. Max eventually gets them."

"Max?" I asked, worried there might be more roommates than I'd signed on for. I didn't mind a house full of people, but since I was going to be working and studying, I didn't really want to live with a bunch of conflicting personalities. Meeting Peyton and seeing the size of her big personality was scary enough, not to mention mice!

"Max is the cat. He is one helluva good mouser, so we're golden there. He likes the snakes, too, but doesn't usually finish them off that good. Sometimes we have scary almost-dead snake episodes." Yikes, I was definitely in Texas. "The lizards we leave alone. They eat the crickets and other critters." I was almost on a plane back to DC that first night. "Isn't it all so fun?"

"Um ... uh, yeah. I guess." *NOT! No, critters are not fun!*

"Okay, so here's your room."

I followed Peyton into a massive space that had a big bed, dressed in a very sweet floral quilt that I absolutely hated. There was a hurricane lamp on a bedside table to match the standard antique-style desk, which had an ugly-ass floral upholstered chair, which I remembered seeing in the pictures they showed me.

"It's big," I said, trying to be nice.

"Your bathroom is across the hall. The last girl who was here used the parlor as a dining room. She didn't eat with us, and I think she cooked her meals there. You can do that if you want, but it's better if you chill with us. There's plenty of room in the kitchen for your food and stuff, and we aren't into stealing anything, you know. What's yours is yours. We do cook together sometimes, though, so that's fun. Genevieve and I are on the second floor. Well, she's got the attic, but we share a bathroom, and then there's a living room this way." I followed her toward the living room. "And a separate dining room, and then the back yard is just scary and overgrown. I wouldn't go out there unless you've got a machete and some basic combat training." She laughed at her own joke. "But the porch is nice; we like hanging out there with some wine at night. Do you drink wine?" She looked at me and I wondered if she always talked so much.

"Yes, I love it. Sounds fun ... all of it sounds really fun. So, um, I should unpack and stuff. I want to buy a few things tomorrow. Is there any place within walking distance?"

I knew when I asked the question, the answer would be a big fat resounding, 'no.' We were out in the middle of nowhere, but it was worth a try.

"Sorry to laugh, but we are seriously in bumfuck ... Texas. You're gonna have to get a car. There's nothing around for miles. I can see if we can get Genevieve's brother to hook you up; he's a mechanic in town, and he knows where all the best deals are, until then I've got a car, and I work from home, so I can take you around if you wanna buy some stuff. My commission isn't due until the end of the week. I can chauffeur you just until you find your ride.

"That would be nice, thanks." I wasn't sure what being trapped in a car with her would be like, especially since things were so far away, according to her, but she was so pretty, and her over-bubbly personality sort of fit the picture.

"My pleasure. Well, I'll let you settle in. I thought I'd just order us a pizza for lunch 'cause it's too damn hot to cook." How the hell she stayed so hot and skinny by eating pizza was a mystery, but nothing sounded better than a nice fat glass of wine and a cheesy, delicious slice of pizza.

"Sounds good to me," I said.

"Perfect. It's my treat. So glad you're here, we are going to have so much fun." She smiled and bounded off.

I wasn't sure fun was the way I'd describe graduate school, but she'd definitely keep the adventure entertaining. If I were going to buy a car and a new bed cover and maybe some better decor for my room, I was going to have to get a job pretty quickly as I could see myself blowing through my savings in no time. I decided that after taking a shower and changing clothes, I'd call the headhunter's number Harper had given me and start setting up some interviews.

The next day I met with Margret Etoile of the Temporary Staffing of Houston.

"I have an internship fair on Tuesday where HR personnel from various companies come and interview our pre-screened candidates. I can have you included in that pool if you'd like. You will meet several people in the course of a few hours. We don't tell you the companies' names or what businesses they are in, but we promise to keep them in line with your skills and training. We match the fields you marked on your application to the best of our ability. We keep the companies a secret at this first interview event because we don't want people gossiping or strategizing. We find the interviews go better if the clients meet the candidates in an open forum where they will be giving their honest answers without any idea what the HR recruiter's motivations are. You will be selected for your highest scoring position and will be required to work there for three months before we place you elsewhere if that's what you want." Her pinchy little face smiled.

My first thought was that it was a really weird way to do things, but it did weed out the brown osiers. Since it was an intern assignment, it didn't really matter-the pay was shit but the hours were flexible. And who was I to beg? I probably wouldn't know much about the companies anyway since I'd just arrived on the scene.

"Sounds great; where do I sign up?" I said, and she pushed a stack of papers for me to fill out.

Chapter 2

Andre

I hated intern season almost as much as I hated Christmas. All those newbies walking around asking dumb questions, loitering in the halls. It was a nuisance, and I never really benefited much except getting more work out of my assistants since their mundane tasks were taken over by the incoming grunt workers. The only passing amusement in intern season was that most were young college graduates who were ripe for the picking. Some incredibly sexy women would soon be flooding the halls in their brand new designer suits they couldn't afford, dressed to impress. While my business was clean energy, we did need a lot of marketing because we were about to launch a new product.

As soon as some of the interns discovered this was an energy company, they often dropped off the grid, wanting something more dynamic like the food or music industry. The good thing was I could smell a goner from a mile away. Their perky fresh faces soured pretty quickly when tasked with making calls to chemical companies and labs for lunch meetings or exciting travel to energy conventions. You could sense when one of the sexy interns was in a downward spiral as they'd stop being so sexy and would find clever ways to avoid their mindless tasks. If one were going to strike up a brief sexual interlude, that would be the time, just before they were either fired or quit. I'd had a few exciting adventures with disenchanted interns, and truthfully, they left with a lot more of an education in sex than they did business. I didn't disappoint in that department; women loved fucking me almost as much as I loved fucking ... not necessarily them as 'they' were a parade of sexy faces all morphed into one. There were only a handful of women I remembered, but they'd never know that.

Bill, my business partner and the visionary idealist I had graduated from grad school with, had turned sour as well. No longer the budding financial genius, he was in it to make the most money he could. After marrying his college sweetheart and then ten years later losing his shirt in a messy divorce, Bill Blascoe was all about free pussy. He had really crossed the line a few times, but he was a devilishly handsome man if you like a Ken doll with a smarmy smile. We were both handsome men; it had earned us the reputation of being the sexiest men in science, which made me laugh every time I heard it. That moniker depended on one's definition of sexy, I guessed. He made the women he fucked sign a non-disclosure agreement. He then told them they were there for a physical relationship that 'could' be something more, though the chance of it was as remote as an uncharted island off of Antarctica. A few times his brushes with women definitely danced along the sexual harassment line, but they signed, and so ... 'they knew what they were getting into' he'd say.

Bill handled accounts and big oil businesses, and I was in charge of new technology and innovation. My current project was personal energy storage systems that could store energy gained from wind, water, and solar. We were working on prototypes that could easily connect to one main storage device that would suck off the extra energy and house it. Say if a building had solar panels, a hydro-electric system, and a windmill, each energy system could create energy that would be used during the day, and the overload would be stored when the sun went down, the temperatures dropped, or the wind died. The problem with clean forms of energy was storing it when there was a surplus. In times of cold weather, light wind, and low sunlight, the energy systems failed. My company's goal was to make a storage unit large enough to hold the excess energy for use by individual homes and large complexes but compact enough to be practical. I was obsessed with creating this arm of the company, and so I didn't have much time to be snagging intern pussy, though one would catch my eye from time to time.

I watched them file in, wide-eyed, sharply dressed, and ready to flex their new employee handbooks. Most of them were as expected, fresh-faced young men and women, but one stopped the blood in my veins. She was wearing a black knee-length skirt and a bright orange and white floral blouse, a very bold look for a first day as an intern. Her body was petite, compact, tight, like a runner's body. She had perfectly formed calves and strong hips, a voluptuous set of breasts, and that face ... wait. That sweet face? Suddenly anger bubbled to the surface so hot, I almost marched over and busted through the new intern parade to snatch her away and rail into her. But I breathed through it ... I'd have to keep my cool. She had been an incredible fuck; innocent, sweet, accommodating. She wasn't experienced in the least, but boy, was she delicious. It was the perfect night of passion.

I'd met her about a year ago at DC's famous night club, Legende. Congressman Reid Prentice had just signed an energy bill, and it began our work together. I joined him for drinks, and that drunk little truffle was just ripe for picking. I brought her back to the hotel, and we fucked ourselves dry. In the morning, I couldn't handle her sweet face all curled up with a pillow hugged in her arms. I'd escaped her embrace as she instantaneously morphed into the sweetest looking angel. Most women I'd had one-night stands with just looked well-fucked when I was done with them, but she was sugar and spice, and so I ran. I didn't need complications, and I absolutely didn't need her brand of sweet adorableness in my life. She was in DC, and I was heading back to Texas. I didn't give her my last name; she vaguely knew what I did, and we focused more on fornicating than diving into our life stories.

She certainly could have and probably did grill Reid for my contact information, and here she was in Texas stalking me, the bitch. She couldn't take a hint? When a man leaves you a muffin and a note, it's a nice 'thanks for the fun,' it's not an 'I'll call you later.' Damn, I had to have her fired immediately; there was no way I could work with her around. I broiled and couldn't do anything about it until the end of the workday. I found it really hard to focus on all I had to do that day thinking of how much I hated her for finding me. And what was more distracting was how much I thought about how amazing it would be to taste her again and feel the clenches of her gloriously tight vagina around my cock once more.

"Check out the new batch." Bill came over as he often did during intern season. "That one with the fiery shirt might be something to explore." Bill knew I was the only one he could even dare to talk to that way about his romancing the interns.

"Don't you think you're getting a little old for intern diving, Bill?" I dismissed him, though my neck flushed with heat seeing he was eying my girl.

"Please, Andre, you of all people should know you're never too old for fresh pussy," he leaned in and whispered, "Well, time to go find some filing I need to be done ASAP."

"You get a sexual harassment suit brought against this company, and I will personally roast your balls on an open fire ... trust me."

"Oh, you know I've got that all handled, never fear." The sick look in his eyes made me nauseous, but he brought in tons of money, and he was so handsome no one actually knew what a pig he was.

After he left I forced myself to go back to my office and face the millions of emails until I had the chance to confront Eliza Piquel on my own.

"Alice," I called out of my office to my assistant after failing miserably to think of anything but Eliza.

"Yes, Mr. Michelson." She stood up and walked into my office with her notepad in hand.

She had been my assistant for three years, had just gotten married, and was very kind and efficient, though I treated her like shit. I didn't worry, she'd get herself knocked up in the next year or two, and I'd work my way through another one; they only lasted so long. I was that big of a dick.

"I want you to get Elizabeth Piquel, one of the new interns, and bring her to my office after orientation," I barked out.

"We are assigned to a Henry Wilton. Do you want me to have him reassigned to someone else?" Alice looked confused.

"No, I asked you to have her come to my office, not assign her here."

"Right, sorry to assume. They have about another hour until the orientation meeting is over, and then I'll bring her right out."

"Okay," was all I said as she evaporated out of the office, one of her finer traits, she knew not to linger and was almost invisible.

Fuck, how was I going to keep myself occupied for an entire hour? I looked at my phone, and it was just two hours until the end of the workday. I didn't have much time. To pass the time, I googled Elizabeth Piquel and read what little there was to know about her on the internet. She worked for a high-powered accounting firm and had high praise on LinkedIn. People liked her; that was no shock. There were some tearful goodbyes on Facebook with well wishes and congratulations for her getting into the MBA program at Texas A&M; a shiver sliced up my spine thinking she'd taken very elaborate steps to stalk me. I actually worried about meeting her and thought perhaps I'd have to apply for a restraining order. I then laughed at myself; was I that afraid of commitment?

I took a trip to the men's room and the office kitchen for a cup of coffee I knew I wouldn't drink and wasted enough time so that it was only fifteen minutes more until Alice brought Eliza to my office. I fixed my tie and readied myself to lay into the girl.

"Mr. Michelson," Alice said on the loudspeaker in my office. "I have

Elizabeth Piquel for you."

"Send her in," I said in my deepest monotone. My skin flushed, and I wasn't sure if I wanted to fuck her or throw her out the window.

"What the hell are you doing here?" I asked as soon as she closed the door behind her.

"I'm sorry, what?" Her eyes were big and wide and only got bigger and wider the moment she registered who I was.

"Andre?" she whispered, suddenly looking unsteady on her feet.

"I figured you'd take the hint." I glared at her.

"You mean the muffin?" Her eyebrows raised. "Yes, I took it. Texas is a big state …" she said more to herself than to me. "How the hell?"

"Then why did you go to such extremes to be here? I mean, come on, Eliza? Texas A&M? That's an hour and a half drive from here. What the hell were you thinking?"

"Um … yeah, that's what my dad said. What the hell was I thinking? How am I going to go to grad school and do my internship at the same time? I just worked it out with Margaret in HR, and I think we've whittled it down to a timeline I can manage, and now this bullshit! Did I seriously just start working at your company?" Suddenly she was angry at me, what the hell? "Fuck. I'll just get another job! Damn it!"

"Do you want to explain to me why after a year you are suddenly stalking me?"

"Are you fucking serious? I don't want to be anywhere near you!" she almost screamed. The fire in her eyes was a helluva contrast to the sweet woman I rocked the sheets with a year ago.

Chapter 3

Eliza

What kind of crazy bullshit karma was this? I spent a year licking my wounds after that jerk dumped me like a used condom. I put a lot of work into moving past it, and there he was, standing there, being all smug and accusatory.

"I'm not stalking you. Call HR; I was interviewed at an intern fair, we were hired without knowing what companies we were going to. I got on the bus this morning with a bunch of other interns and ended up here. Yes, you crossed my mind when I saw that this was an energy tech company, but it was a single solitary second of my time. I spent a lot of time getting over the fact that we had absolutely nothing but a night of wild sex. I was hoping for at least a follow-up phone call or a little more than a scribbled note and a pastry, but I figured you must be a complete asshole, so I dodged a bullet. Trust me, the last place on earth I want to be working is here with you. I'll head over to Margaret's office right now and tell her to take me out of the intern pool and look for another job. No need to fire off to 911; I don't want to be here even more than you don't want me here."

"You're not going anywhere. Sit down while I sort this mess out," Andre commanded.

"Seriously, I'm ready to leave. All I need to do is get someone to take me back to the recruiter's office." I was going to stand up to him no matter what; I didn't need a man like Andre Michelson in my life.

"I said, sit down!" he raised his voice, scolding.

He seemed really riled up, so I sat down and just glared at him as he called HR and confirmed that my batch of interns didn't know what company we were going to be working for until that morning. It was a new strategy the recruiting company had employed to stop in-fighting among interns for the high profile jobs. It seemed that since he reiterated everything HR said out loud, my story had cleared.

"Can I go now?" I was irritated, and by the looks of it, so was he.

"No," he quietly said. "I'm sorry. I had an incident about six months ago with a young woman who didn't understand the nature of our relationship, and she made things very difficult for me. I hated calling the police, but I did have her arrested when she trespassed on my property. I didn't even sleep with her; she was just someone who thought I would. So, I want to apologize for jumping to conclusions."

"Forgiven, now can I go?" I was still angry.

"Where are you going?" He already knew the answer, which made me even madder.

"To quit and get reassigned." I glared at him.

"No, I don't want you to quit."

"Well, I don't want to work here, not with you."

"Ha, really, I'm not so bad. But you're right; you shouldn't work with me. That would be a dangerous conflict of interest. No, you'll be working with my partner, Bill. You may or may not even see me as his office is on the floor below this one. So, since I misjudged your character so horribly, I want to make it up to you. The office will be closing in a few minutes, and only those of us with key cards can stay. I'm assuming you haven't gotten a card yet, so I will drive you home after you have dinner with me. It's a peace offering, nothing more." He gave me a big warm smile to show his earnest intention.

"Why?" I cocked my head, confused.

"We have some unfinished business."

'No, no, hell no!' is what I should have said; it's what any respectable woman who had left DC to start a new life would have said. But me, Eliza Piquel? What did I say?

"What unfinished business?"

"I left you because I was only going to be in DC for a week. Now that you're here, maybe we can pick up where we left off?"

"I believe we just had crazy sex; that's all I remember." I stood my ground.

"Well, I'm down for a little more of that. Nothing wrong with a healthy roll in the hay." I think he was teasing.

"So, let me understand you correctly. You call me in here thinking I'm some sort of lunatic stalker, and then you discover that I'm not actually following you, and I might add, had no idea you worked here. So, now you want me to come to your house and engage in some good old-fashioned sex? Because, why not?" My mind was swirling at that point.

"Or just have dinner with me. I'd like to get to know you better. We may not go beyond BBQ ribs and a cold Corona. You'll never know unless you come to my house and let me give you more than a muffin. Come on- you can't pass that up."

God, what did this man think of me? "I'm not going to have sex with you. I'm not like that."

"Let's call it a date. Does that sound better?" He had been leaning against his desk, but suddenly he pushed himself off and made his way toward me, and my heart exploded.

"Um …" Before I had a chance to figure out what I was going to say, he had his lips on mine, and we were kissing, and damn, it felt good.

"Does that persuade you?" He held me, and my eyes darted around the room, looking for windows or ways to see inside.

"Everyone has gone home," he said, reading my mind.

"I'll have dinner with you, but only because I'm starving, and I have no idea where I am and," I looked at my cell phone to confirm. "Yeah," just as I thought. "The intern bus just left." I heaved a big sigh.

"Good, you're mine for the night." He was weirdly giddy. "Give me a minute to tie up a few things here. Go get your things." Was that an order?

I didn't feel like fighting with the man as we were sort of stuck together whether I wanted to be or not. I was at least forty minutes away from home, and my new old, very old, car was at the agency. Most likely it would be locked up in the parking lot after the bus dropped off the interns. During orientation week, we had to take the bus; it was part of their policy. After our internships officially started, the bus would be provided if we wanted it, or we could take our own cars. It was some weird thing the agency did to make sure the interns were a good fit. They sort of kept the reigns nice and tight until they felt comfortable letting us loose. I guess it was how internships in China were done as the recruiting company owner was from Beijing. She used her American husband's money to invest in the company, which was doing great, so yay for her. Anyway, it meant my car was going to be in lockdown, and unless I wanted to take out a mortgage for an Uber ride, I was stuck with Andre, the muffin man.

"Okay, I'll be back in a few." It was nice to get some breathing room to put my thoughts together.

I went to the tiny cubicle I'd been assigned and gathered up my purse and my new employee binder. It all felt so surreal. There were a few people at their cubicles, and many of the managerial offices were still occupied with people busily working. Thank God no one saw him kiss me because he was wrong; there were still a lot of people there after hours. I wondered… if he lied about such a little thing, what else he'd lie about? It didn't really matter- I was going home with him whether I liked it or not, best not to imagine he was a serial killer. The truth was the sound of his voice and his sexy dominance still riled me up. I even jumped a little when I heard his deep sultry rasp behind me.

"Are you ready to go?"

"We probably shouldn't leave together." Always the prudent one, I didn't want to be accused of having a thing with the boss on the first day.

"Trust me, no one will think anything of it," he said, which was strange.

I chose not to argue and followed him into the elevator to the parking garage.

"Why?" I asked as soon as I knew that no one could hear us.

"Why would no one suspect anything if I walked out with you?" The incredulous tone of voice made me a little angry as if I wasn't someone he'd go home with? Was that what he was implying?

"Once you get to know me better you'll understand why," was all he said and seemed like all he planned to say on the subject. "I don't live far from the office. Does BBQ sound good? It's about all I can actually cook."

"Sounds great. I figured a guy like you would have a butler, a cook, a maid …" My fantasy took off a little thinking of a billionaire's life.

"I do, but I invited you for BBQ. Besides, their day ends in fifteen minutes. I try not to pay overtime." He was gruff and to the point.

The elevator dinged on the bottom floor, and I was surprised to see only his car in the parking garage. It was a private subdivision of the parking lot where there were four spaces for cars. A shiny black Maserati sat in the only occupied space. Andre pressed an app on his phone, and the car flared to life.

"Wow, that's cool." I didn't care how dumb I sounded; it was pretty impressive.

"Oh, this will be a fun night if something as pedestrian as Smartstart gets that big of a reaction out of you." The moment he entered the parking lot, there was a complete shift in gears. He was no longer all dominant and in charge, but more lusty and playful like he was the night I'd first met him. "Hop in; I'm hungry."

Sincerely, at that point, I wasn't sure what he was hungry for –

dinner… or me? We listened to music on the drive. I don't think either of us was too interested in conversing though there was a lot for us to say. He flipped around stations till he found a contemporary music station that played overplayed hits. It didn't seem his style, but he also was making concessions for me. Finding a generic music station covered all bases. Actually, I didn't mind. I liked the comfort the overplayed boppy tunes provided. I had a hard time finding my center, so Taylor Swift and Nick Jonas found it for me.

"You're not a vegetarian, are you?" he asked out of the blue.

"Nope, I like my food slaughtered and bloody." Not really, I liked my food sterile and packaged, but I was in the mood to fuck with him since the whole situation was insane.

"We can stop by a butcher if you'd like, or I have some beef patties in the freezer."

"Beef patties sound delightful, Mr. Michelson." Really? What was I doing?

"Okay, you can cut the snarky sarcasm. I get it you're pissed I left you hanging."

So we were having this conversation. "No, you just were exactly as I'd expect you'd be, a complete and total tool. You seduced me, took me to your hotel room, fucked me, and then left me a muffin. What's not to like?"

"You're not wrong. I am an ass, but I did think you were sweet. Maybe I spared you?" He looked at me with heat in his expression.

Damn, if he didn't set off fireworks in my soul.

"Well then, I hope you have a guest room." I glared at him.

"I do, but I hope you won't use it."

"So … beef patties aren't the only meat on the agenda?" *Oh, come on, Eliza, what is wrong with you? No, really?*

That got a laugh out of him. "Are you referring to polska kielbasa? Seasoned sausage? Hot dog on a stick, perhaps?"

"Isn't that a bit childish?" I teased. "I was thinking more along the lines of pulled pork and ground round."

"Maybe we should just skip dinner?" Suddenly his look became dark and lusty.

"No, I'm very hungry." If I could have dove from the car, I would have. Instead, I turned up the radio. "Oh, I love this song." I started humming along.

"Old Town Road?" He looked at me with deep confusion in his eyes.

"It's a classic." I started singing. "Yeah, I'm gonna take my horse to the old town road. I'm gonna ride 'til I can't no more. I'm gonna take my horse to the old town road. I'm gonna ride 'til I can't no more." I was singing and not too badly, I'll admit.

"You know I could say something." He smiled, such a gorgeous smile.

"But you won't." I stopped singing long enough to say.

"I mean, if you want to ride until you can't no more ... that can be arranged." He put his hand on my leg, and I wanted to just hop right on top of him, but I had to win the game.

"Be good to that hand you have on my leg, sir. You'll need to use it later since I'll be sleeping by myself in your guest room." I bucked my chin up.

"I meant I have horses." His smirk was devilish as he drove onto a secluded road without any streetlamps. "Someone's mind is in the gutter this evening."

My heart stopped for a moment as the lingering voice of Lil Nas X filled the air. *Where the hell were we, and what had I gotten myself into?*

Chapter 4

Andre

We drove up to my ranch house, and all went eerily quiet. We were listening to the radio, and for a moment, she was singing. She had a lovely voice, but when we pulled off onto the private road to my estate, she lost most of her gusto. She was a sweet woman. I could tell she'd fired herself up to stay toe to toe with me, but deep down inside she was a good person with a charming face and a rock-solid body. My cock hadn't been so well fucked since I was with her last. She was lean and tight, and the idea of having her again sent chills down my spine. The only problem was, she wasn't just a cute drunk girl in DC anymore. So, what to do with her?

"Do you live out here alone?" she finally asked after the song ended.

"Yes and no. I have a caretaker, Beau, and his wife Jane, who live with their two teenage kids on the back of the property about a ten-minute walk from my ranch house. He's worked with me for twenty years, and his wife does a lot of the cooking and cleaning. The kids get bussed to the local middle school. Outside of them, I live alone. I have a personal assistant, Jeremy. He handles issues with the farm, and I have three farmhands who take care of the garden, livestock, and horses. They all leave at five because I can't be bothered with people. But the town sheriff lives on the ranch we just passed if you're nervous."

"Well, that makes me feel better. I can run there if I have to." She looked at me to gauge my reaction.

"This isn't the Purge; it's dinner and maybe a movie … and then you'll decide." Finally, she laughed.

"Okay, maybe I'm overreacting?" she confessed.

"Ya think?" I said.

We drove into the garage, and I opened her door to let her out.

"This place is stunning," she said, looking at all the plants and trees I'd had landscaped in the front yard.

I like thick green foliage though the Texas weather isn't the most conducive to it. We found plants that would thrive in the oppressively dry heat. I walked toward the front door and opened it. If she liked the outside, she'd probably be blown away by the inside. I didn't bring many women to the ranch. I had a thing about my privacy, but Eliza was a sensible woman; she wouldn't cross boundaries. I was pretty sure bringing her home was a safe bet.

"You should see the back yard," I said, shuttling her forward. "My staff put everything out there that we'd need."

I moved her along as her eyes darted around the space, taking it all in. While most ranch houses were a celebration of farm life, mine was not. I was in Texas because Texas had oil and energy. I didn't necessarily love it there, so I filled my space with art and things I did enjoy, like sculpture. I liked art, most specifically, I liked depictions of the female nude form. I didn't like the females that came in those bodies that often, but boy, playing with them was sure fun.

"I went to the Louvre once," she said as soon as we were outside. "It was full of ancient nude statues. They were spaced out so people didn't crash into each other looking at them, but you definitely have more naked men and women in here than the Louvre. This is a lot of butts, boobs, and penises." She shook her head.

I couldn't help laughing. What could I say? I liked the nude form.

"My statutes are not from antiquity. I actually know all of the models. I commissioned an artist to sculpt them, and I selected each person I wanted to be immortalized by the artist's hand." Perhaps I confessed too much.

"Are they former lovers?" She seemed more intrigued than angered. "I mean, I guess not the men, but the women?"

"Perhaps," is all I gave her.

"Weren't they mad you dumped them?" She craned her head backward to see if she could get a better assessment of the art she'd already passed.

"Not when I paid them what I did for their service. Besides, most of them were happy to leave me."

"That's the second time you've inferred that you're a total dick." She jutted out her hip and smirked.

"Total dick. Hmm. Not sure how to dissect that. I'm well-endowed, as you know, as for my interactions with others? I just don't like people who piss me off." I left it at that. "Now let's BBQ; what's your poison? I have a full bar, and I can mix a mean drink."

"Oh, nothing but water for me. I've played this game before, and it didn't end well."

"Come on; wine never hurt anyone. Or beer, or one cocktail. Don't be a bore." Crap, could she be in rehab? It would be completely tactless if I insinuated drinking made a person interesting.

"I'll have what you're having," is all she said as she sat down on the lounge chair in front of the grill where I was to start cooking.

"So, what brings you to Texas?" I asked with a funny southern drawl, praying still that I wasn't the reason she was there.

"I had to get out of DC. I hated the politics and the commute, though I think I may have jumped from the frying pan into the fire on that one. I'll be driving all over Texas in my shitty new ride.

"I was an accountant, and I'm sure you've forgotten that; I sure wanted to. I want to work in environmental ethics, so I applied to business schools all over the country. I got accepted to three schools, and Texas A & M was the best of them, so here I am. I promise you had nothing to do with my decision. Zero. I was pretty upset for a while by the way things ended between us, but I'm a big girl, and I got over it." It sounded like she had brushed me off as something in her past.

"Well, I hope you're not too over it. As I said, I only left you because I didn't think I'd see you again, and here you are." I made sure to toss her a sultry gaze.

"Eating roasted meat," she said with her own brand of Southern twang.

"One can only hope." I winked at her, and she giggled.

"You're a lot of fun. Whoever said you were a tool probably didn't get a chance to know you," she said, mostly to herself.

"Or they knew me too well," I whispered under my breath. "Okay, vodka martinis coming up. Just keep an eye on the burgers for me while I go to the bar inside and make them. I'll be back in a shake," I said, moving toward the bar.

I knew I was swimming in dangerous water seducing Eliza, but she had a sweetness and grit I found irresistible. The bar was just off the terrace, so I whipped us up some cocktails, being sure to make them extra strong, and returned to Eliza within minutes.

"I used only the finest vodka," I told her, handing her a martini glass. "It should taste smooth and satisfying," I said, playing with the words.

"You should be in advertising; you're obviously in the wrong field," she said, carefully taking the drink from my hands.

"What? You don't find energy storage sexy?"

"I'm studying environmental ethics, energy storage is hella sexy; it's just you have this way of speaking that makes you sound like a billboard." She laughed at herself as she took a sip of her drink.

"Noted." I gruffed.

"So why isn't there a Mrs. Michelson? You're plenty old enough."

She didn't just say that. But she was right. I was at least twenty years her senior.

"Is there a mandatory age for marriage? I must not have gotten the memo. How old do you think I am?"

"I don't know, sixty?" Oh, she had better be playing. "Fifty, maybe? Old enough to be my dad, that's for sure."

"Then you must not be too old for a spanking," I gave her a side-eye, and she shut her mouth quickly. "I'm forty-seven, you?"

"Twenty-six." She glared at me.

"Well then, yes. If I had a child right out of college, you'd be my daughter, and my offer of a spanking still stands."

"Yeah, that's a hard pass for me."

"Don't knock it till you try it." I laughed, thinking of what her firm ass would look like all red and swollen.

I wasn't into BDSM that much. I didn't like pain and suffering, but a little rough stuff was fun, and I found a red and swollen backside made sex that much more thrilling for the recipient. But I had some time before I could explore some of my darker fantasies.

"Sure, any time you want to bend over, I'll give you a wallopin' like you won't forget."

"Is this how you usually get your kicks on Friday nights? Threatening younger women with violence, grandpa?" She must have known what she was doing; it had to have been part of her plan.

"No, I usually get my kicks by throwing interns on my bed and fucking their brains out," I said with a straight face as I handed her a plate with a charbroiled patty on it. "Do you want to eat inside or out? I have the buns and fixings in the fridge, but I can bring them out here if you want."

"It's a nice night," She stretched out her arms and legs. "Let's eat out."

"Fine by me. There's a table just down those steps with a view of the whole ranch. I'll meet you there," I said, handing her the drink she'd set down. "And let me know when you want another one of these." I flashed her an evil grin.

"One will be fine, thank you." She flashed a mimicking grin back.

She'd be a tough nut to crack, which made it all the more fun to be with her. I brought a tray full of food and condiments to the outdoor dining room. It was much more than a table; I had an entire outdoor kitchen, and had I known we'd be throwing this little impromptu dinner party, I would have had my staff stock everything. As it was, there was still some good liquor in the food pantry and a few bottles of wine in the fridge. The BBQ was nearer to the house because on the rare occasions I did throw parties, I had someone up there cooking. I didn't want the smoke to interrupt the party guests.

"This isn't a table; it's like a whole thing," she marveled a little, "Ha!"

"Oh, the things you can do when you have money. I like nice things, and I have the means to have nice things, and so I do. Eat your burger before it gets cold." I didn't mean to instruct her.

"Sorry, Grandpa, I was just enjoying the view."

"Call me Grandpa again, and I'll bend you over my knee right here," I warned, loving the banter.

"You wouldn't."

"Oh, I most certainly would, so don't test me." I gave her a little smile so as not to totally frighten the woman.

She riled me up, though, in a good way. It had been a long time since anyone had done that. She was still wearing her suit from her first day on the job, and I just wanted to fuck the innocence right out of her. Her playful remarks about my age were simply her delicious naivete. It was refreshing since most of the women I'd dated of late were seasoned lovers, people who thought perhaps they'd be the one I'd settle for. Wrong, and in the back of their minds, they knew it, but fun was fun, and sex, in all forms was always fun.

"You're so big and mean, you with your BBQ grill and outdoor dining gazebo, so dark and mysterious." She pretended to shudder.

"I am still the CEO and founder of the company that will be signing your checks. I don't need to be too much more than that," I said calmly.

"So, do you always troll the intern pool?" She loved to push those buttons.

"No, I only do it when I find someone I think needs to get wet."

That shut her up.

Chapter 5

Eliza

I hated him. I loved him. I was afraid of him. I didn't want my clothes on anymore. I was a mess.

I decided to just eat my burger, with his lewd comeback, which had him laughing so seductively, I could hardly keep my panties on. I knew I'd be having sex with him again; there was no stopping me. I was a love-starved woman with a death wish apparently, but at that moment, one vodka martini in, I absolutely didn't care. Fuck those eyes of his, damn him. He had salt and pepper hair, a finely chiseled jawline, and these grey-green eyes that melted you. His pecks were flawless, his cock huge, and everything about him just dripped sex appeal.

"So, let's say I have sex with you tonight." I tried to pull the reins in a little.

"Oh, let's do." He leaned into me, looking so fiercely sexy, I had a hard time finishing my sentence.

"What does that look like for us later?"

"You want a marriage proposal?" He laughed.

"With a prenup. I mean, who doesn't want an outdoor dining room? Hell, I'd marry you for a minute and get a nice fat alimony check after our divorce."

"Cute. No marriage, no prenup, no discussion of extracurricular activities at work, maybe another go at it again sometime in the future, but I'm not promising anything. Mostly this is just because sex is fun. Sex with you was great the last time, and I think you're like me and want a little more of it. That's what this will look like. Sex, and only sex."

"Can I say no?" I was testing him.

"You can, but why would you?"

I just took another bite of my burger, which was delicious, and weighed out the consequences. Sex with him was fun, scary but exhilarating, but I wanted a little more than just a wild ride, and so I went there.

"Okay. Here's the thing. I really had fun with you and felt super duped when you left. But I get why you did it. The thing is, I've known my roommates for a few hours. They aren't really home that often, and I've lived in Texas for all of three days. So technically, you're my oldest friend here. I'm good with some non-committal sex, just be nice ... and though you are older than the hills, if you could at least commit to being my friend, that would make saying yes a whole lot easier. What do you say?" I flashed him a flirty grin hoping he'd say yes.

"Friendship." He smiled. "That's a tall order from such a youngin'." He used a funny old man accent. "But I'll take it, now finish up eating so we can get naked."

"I might be young, but you're the one who's immature."

Having his assurance that he'd be my friend gave me the sense of calm I was seeking. We ate and drank our cocktails. After we'd waved our white flags, I relaxed a little, and things did, in fact, get more fun. He scooted over to my side of the table and sat next to me.

"Okay, this is my favorite time of day." He finished his bite to show me. "If you watch carefully, the sky will turn orange with the setting sun, and on the horizon, you'll see a line of fences. The stark contrast of dark wood to burnt orange sky gives my land a sort of mystical look."

"How long have you lived here?" I asked, suddenly feeling warm and settled.

"My whole life. I was actually born on this ranch, though it wasn't really meant to be that way. We didn't come here on a wagon train." He turned to look at me. "Don't say it - I know you were thinking it."

"Go on." I smiled, not giving my thoughts away.

"My mom actually didn't realize her water had broken. She was in the bathtub when it happened, and when she got out, I was trying to do the same. She delivered me on the bathroom floor with my dad freaking out, according to her, and my grandparents coming in to save the day. I was going to be their one and only."

"You never wanted to leave? And where are they now?" I was so full of questions; I couldn't imagine a man like Andre being raised on a farm.

"I burned the place to the ground when they died. I hated this place but couldn't leave it. My dad was a bastard who I hated, and he died of alcohol poisoning when I was in high school. My mom was everything, and I loved her with all of my heart. She worked hard keeping up the farm after Dad died and didn't go to the doctor so ..." He took a deep breath. "By the time she was diagnosed with cancer, it was too late. When she died, I set the house on fire. I was pretty angry. I wasn't much older than you are at the time. I'd already started making money, so I just ... I couldn't leave, but I didn't want to stay. The house had too many miserable memories. My mom is buried on the property. She loved this place, especially her horses. I stayed here for the horses, for her, and for the millions of dollars' worth of oil I have on the grounds. I had the house rebuilt to my specifications and now it's my house. So, that's me. What's your story?" He finished the last of his cocktail.

"It's pretty run of the mill. My parents are still together and still living in their little three-bedroom bungalow that is bought and paid for. They live in Rhode Island on a little plot of land my mother inherited from her family. My dad owns a convenience store, and my mom is a seamstress. They aren't rich, they aren't very interesting, but they're sweet. I have an older brother with autism who they look after. He's cool, but he doesn't speak. He's a lot of work, but he's also really special." I didn't really want to tell him about Richard but ended up talking about him for some reason.

"That's probably why you're so nice; you learned empathy early on." He had a warm look on his face that was sweet, mesmerizing even, but that all changed the minute he stood up and took our plates. "Okay, enough chitchat. Let's fuck."

I rolled my eyes as I helped him bring our plates inside. "So romantic."

"Just leave the dishes in the sink," he said as he set his dirty dishes down in the pristine white double sink.

I followed suit, and as soon as the clink of the porcelain hit the enamel, he was on me.

"I've been waiting for this all day," he growled as he pounced upon my lips.

He was rough, and his lips were warm and ardent. His five o'clock was scruffy and grazed along my chin, roughing it up a little with his sandpaper texture. His powerful tongue pressed my lips apart and entered my mouth without needing or wanting permission. He then sucked my tongue into his teeth, slicing them along my soft pink tongue, inflaming it with sensation and just a touch of pain.

"I could eat you," he whispered hotly as he slung me into his arms and carried me across the room.

I was completely overwhelmed. My head was swirling with such intense sexual heat, I thought I actually had a fever. He laid me down on a bed. I didn't know if it was his bed or just the bed he fucked on. It had black satin sheets. The room was painted a smoky gray, and there was nothing in it but a statue of a woman bending back into a man's embrace. They weren't clothed, they were just draped in a thin strip of cloth covering both of them, but that was all that was in the room. No dressers, no tables, no chairs, just a bed and the statue.

As soon as he sat me down, he started to rip off his tie and proceeded to indelicately undress.

"I have to ask," I said, propping up on my elbows, enjoying his unraveled behavior. "You aren't a serial killer, are you?"

He snatched his shirt off his back. "If I were, you would already have been dead, don't you think? I mean, you were passed out in the hotel after we fucked three times. Wouldn't that have been a better time than this to murder you?"

"True. But this room only has one sexy statue in it and a bed."

"And?"

"Well, um … it's weird."

"It's a twenty-two-hundred-thousand dollar Vzigon statue. What else do you think a room should have?"

"Jesus, what the hell? Didn't your mom ever teach you how to save money?" I was actually pissed at the price tag.

"My mother taught me how to save money, but she died, so I'm now spending it." His pants dropped to the ground. "Why the hell do you still have clothes on?"

"Just trying to figure out a guy who only has a bed and a statue in his room, that's all. Besides, I'm not a hooker; you want me so badly, you take my clothes off." I splayed out my arms and flopped backward.

He immediately jumped on me and ripped right through my blouse. "No problem."

"What the hell?" I breathed as he shredded my brand new top. "I sure hope you got some change after buying that crazy-ass expensive statue 'cause you're going to have to buy me a new blouse. God, grandpa, simmer down."

"Call me grandpa again!" His eyes were dark and lusty.

"Grandpa …" I whispered.

"I'm not even going to bother with this." He pushed up my skirt, yanked down my panties, kicked off his boxer briefs, and I was facing his massive cock again.

He rolled me onto my back and pushed my legs up over my head so that my ass and pussy were prominently on display. He raked his teeth across my slit, and I nearly came from the intense and feral pain.

"Fuck, Andre!" I leaned my head back, trying to find my center.

"Oh, you will, my dear, you will be fucking Andre all night long."

With that, he dove his tongue straight into me and sucked hard as if he was sucking out my insides. He then slid his tongue in and out of me while intermittently grazing his teeth over my clit, and within moments, literally seconds, I was so wound up and knotted, I came hard shivering and jerking into his mouth. He gave no time to even catch my breath before he was pulsing his fingers in and out of me, rolling me back down so that he could lay on top of me. He then gently licked my lips, having just been inside of me.

"Call me grandpa again," this time the command was dark and heady as he drove three fingers into me.

"I think I'll pass," I said in protest.

He then licked his way down my neck from my chin to my breastbone. He swirled his tongue around each nipple but didn't take them. I arched into him, hoping to offer them to his beastly mouth, but he avoided me as his fingers pulled away and left me hot, wanting, needing, aching …

"Eliza." His voice was still hot and dangerous. "Say my name."

"Andre," I responded, not knowing the game he wanted to play.

He bent down and licked one of my peaked nipples just once, leaving it to cool with his essence glistening on it.

"Beg me to fuck you." He licked the other nipple, doing the same thing.

I stared at him as he pressed his cock close to my pussy but didn't go in. He bent down to one of my breasts and bit it hard. Not hard enough to break the skin, but with enough pressure to make me want more of him.

"I'm not going to beg you," I said, seeing how far this would go. "Grandpa," I said ever so slowly. He bit my other breast, and this time, it was hard enough to hurt. "Ouch. Didn't you get enough dinner?"

He raked his teeth along the nipple he'd just bitten. "I didn't get enough of you."

He bit his way down my stomach back to my dripping wet pussy. "Oh, God, no," I could see where this was going. "No, no … Not there!"

Too late, he nipped at my pussy and zeroed in on my clit. My hands flew to cover my sex, but he fought me, throwing my hands away from myself.

"Beg me, Eliza." He ran his teeth along my clit, making my body scream.

"Oh, my God …"

His tongue followed his teeth, and then he started sucking again, and I could feel myself revving up for another blast-off.

"Don't you want me inside of you?" His tongue dove into where I so badly wanted his cock. "All you have to do is beg me."

I had to get control of him, or he'd dominate me all night, so I grabbed his hair and yanked it hard, angling his face so that he was looking up at me. "Fuck me now! Grandpa!"

"I warned you," is all he said as he flipped me over hard and fast so that my face hit the pillow that smelled like expensive vetiver.

Suddenly his hand came down on my bare ass, and I yelped. Another two blows came hard and fast, and I wiggled away from the assault-flipping myself over onto my back with my legs up ready to fight. He grabbed my ankles and spread my legs apart, and they melted apart like butter and pushed forward until his massive erection was sliding into my dripping wetness.

"Ahh," I cried out, and my head angled back onto the bed.

"Beg …" he said gently as he laid on me harder. "Just beg for me."

"Okay, okay," I breathed with every thought, feeling, and emotion completely filled with my need for him. "Please, Andre …"

That's all he needed as he moved up on me and started thrusting in deep and slow.

"Mmm, you feel so good. You're an angel," he moaned into my neck.

"And you." I gritted my teeth as he stabbed my G-spot and sent stars across my vision. "Are a …"

"Don't say it," Andre cautioned me. "I already know."

With that, he pumped into me hard and fast, putting all of his muscle and weight behind his thrusts, making me crazy for him. He ripped himself out of me and flipped me over so that I was on my knees, and entered me doggy style, grabbing my hips and slamming me onto him until my whole body was electrified with need. He was so big it actually sort of hurt with him diving in deep and hard. Thrust after thrust, I thought he might split me in two, but it was such a good hurt, and I was zeroing in on orgasm number three. One more hard thrust, and we both crumpled onto the bed, and then I felt him grow bigger and twitch inside me.

"You're still on birth control, right?" he barely breathed over his grunting exasperation.

"Yes, yes ... let 'er rip." I was seriously speechless; my mind and body were so tangled, I had no idea what I was saying, but as soon as I felt his warm cum fill me, a sense of calm overtook my body.

I was still in desperate need of another orgasm but knowing he'd cum so hard and fast made everything better. Still, inside of me, he pinched and played with my clit as he sucked a hickey into my neck, and I shattered all over him. Quivering, bucking, gushing, I exploded until we were both a hot mess, literally.

"Boy," I breathed out. "Those two in the corner there are sure gonna have a lot to write home about," I quipped before everything became emotional goo.

Chapter 6

Andre

She did crazy things to me. I hadn't been so unhinged in a long time, perhaps ever. I liked a bit of rough sex now and again, but I was downright animalistic. Bravo for her taking the heat as she did.

"Dear Mom and Dad," I caught my breath as I heard Eliza say breathlessly. "The man whose bedroom we guard just ripped open that poor intern from his office …" Eliza propped herself up onto her elbow, coming back to her senses. "The one who is much too young for him. Send reinforcements, love Fred and Ethel; the bedroom statue."

"Dear Fred and Ethel," I played along. "The intern is the one who was begging for his cock like a sex-starved lunatic," I added with a laugh. "Don't pretend I'm too old for you, Eliza; you can barely take what I give. That was just the beginning; by the time I send you home, you'll be dreaming of my cock day and night."

"Mission accomplished there, bad boy. And bravo for you, you decimated the only clothing I have," she scolded with her cute little turned-up nose reddening in lust, anger, passion? I wasn't sure what was going on in her pretty little head.

"That's not a problem; you don't need clothes for what I've got planned for you."

"Ugh." She flopped back onto the pillow.

Without saying another word, I rolled over to her. "We should get these remnants off of you." I really had shredded her clothing.

It was a little unnerving, even for me. She brought out the best and worst parts of me. I carefully unbuttoned her skirt, which had become twisted around her body in our rabid lovemaking and brought it down her legs. She helped by wiggling out of it, knowing how useless the piece of cloth was at that point. There wasn't much salvageable of her outfit; it was either ripped or wrinkled. So, she extracted herself from all of it.

"I'm not going to walk around naked," she said after she rid herself of her clothes.

"No one else here, why not?" She glared at me, and I deserved it. "Right, let me see what I have for you to put on."

Though I seriously would have been happy to see her hot body walk around naked all night, I did have to show some sense of decency at some point. I got up out of bed, very naked myself and feeling my libido kicking back into gear as I went to my closet to find anything she could put on. She was so much smaller than me that it would have been useless for her to wear my briefs. They'd slip right off her slim, toned body, so she'd be going commando. I found a clean white V-neck T-shirt and tossed it at her, then shut my closet door.

The closet was made to look like the wall. I only needed to kick the baseboard for it to slide open, then kick it again to slide it closed, and it looked like a wall again. My room and house were very minimalistic. I didn't like clutter. My bedroom had only a bed and the statue. I didn't need to sit in my bedroom, I had other spaces in the house for sitting, and there was a chair in my closet for putting on my shoes and socks. I didn't need a television in there; I had a media room. All I did in my bedroom was sleep and fuck, so all I needed was an erotic piece of art and a bed.

"Try that on," I said as I walked back over to her.

"Thanks." She put on the T-shirt, and it dripped off her shoulders just as I'd hoped it would, however, the angry red hickey on her neck was a bit of a worry.

"I think I got a bit carried away," I told her as I swiped my hand over the dark purple bruise.

"Ya think? You went nuts." She rubbed the spot on her neck and shook her head.

"Ha, well, you make me nuts," I countered, enjoying when we sparred with one another.

"So, why does it bother you so much when I call you old?" she asked out of the blue.

"Forty-seven isn't old." For some reason, the age gap did bother me some. It wasn't a mortality thing; I was young at heart, but it was that she was so vibrant and young that it just made me feel not so vibrant and young. She did push my buttons though, which inspired me to act impulsively.

"You're right, it's not old, so when I call you grandpa, you should just laugh." She propped herself up on the headboard and hunkered down for a conversation I didn't want to have with her.

"Or you shouldn't say it." I stayed naked with my cock perking up again.

"You're no fun." She turned to me and grazed her fingernails down my torso to the tuft of hair above my cock.

It was the most spontaneous and erotic thing she'd done. She then tickled her fingers in the hair for a minute as my cock started rising.

"You're playing a dangerous game, Eliza," I warned her.

"Am I?" she asked, moving her hand down to my cock as she slowly pumped it up and down on my rising shaft. "You're the one who wants to fuck all night. This round is on me."

She had guts, that's for sure. As she pumped me to my full length, she licked her fingers slowly with erotic intention and swiped them across her pussy. The act of lubricating herself was bold and presumptuous as she rose to her knees and slung her leg over me to ride my cock.

"I can't guarantee that I won't topple you over at some point," I warned.

"Try me," is all she said as she impaled herself on my erection.

She must have been a little sore because she winced in pain as she slid down my length, taking all of me in one gulp. Still wearing my shirt, she was adorable riding my cock, fully in charge. I wanted to take over but let her lead. She clearly enjoyed some power, and I was willing to give her an inch ... only. Her body lulled forward, and she kissed my lips, just a simple peck at first, but it deepened as she started rolling on my cock, making it pull in and out of her. I grabbed her hair and dove my tongue into her once again gripped by my wild passion once more, but she shimmied away from my kiss, almost extracting her pussy from my cock.

"What's this?" I looked at her surprised.

"You're not going to devour me. I'm not sure how I'm going to cover this hickey at work Monday, so we're doing this my way or no way." She bounced down hard on me for emphasis.

Now, I was fine with being ridden like a fine stallion, and she was doing a great job building the friction needed for a rocketing ejaculation, but seeing her smirk at me as she ground me into ecstasy was too damn inciting. My hands found her hips and impaled her harder, recovering just a fraction of my control as I jutted my hips up into her.

"So, is that how it's gonna be?" Her voice was strangled in passion.

She then laid all of her weight on me, which wasn't much but enough, and imprisoned my cock in her vagina sitting there until I stopped my rutting.

"Gah, you're an infuriating woman!" I roared.

While still pinned on my cock, she bit my belly button making me jump with surprise since I was expecting a kiss or perhaps her tongue. She then proceeded to bite each of my nipples and twirled her hips on me in a rotating motion that ignited my cock just enough for me to want her desperately.

"Fuck this!" I grabbed her under her arms, and with a bolt of all my strength, I careened her onto her back and started jackhammering into her until she came so loudly, I thought she'd crack the plaster on the ceiling.

"Fuck! Andre, NO! Oh my God, oh, God!" Her pussy clamped down on me, and I was toast.

I shot ribbons into the deep caverns of her soul, and by the time we were done rioting in ecstasy, we flopped onto each other, spent, wrung out, and at an impasse.

"Truce?" I breathed into her ear.

Her face craned upward to kiss me. We settled into a delightfully deep kiss, just enjoying the afterglow. When our lips were swollen and raw, she finally said, "truce" and we drifted off to sleep in each other's arms.

***

The next morning as the sun barely rose in the sky, I considered taking her again. My cock was plenty hard, and her sweet naked ass was nicely presented as she slept curled on her side. Everything about her beckoned me, but while I was a lot of nasty things, I wasn't a man who took his pleasure without consent. If I wanted to slip into that sweet pussy of hers, I'd have to ask, and asking meant waking her up. I decided instead to answer emails that had gathered in my inbox. It was much of the same as it was every day, be it Saturday or Monday. The fact that it was Saturday only made it slightly less stressful, though I had a woman in my bed who I wasn't sure I was ready to let loose just yet.

I answered the first emails about the horses; there was another bid on Midnight, a thoroughbred gelding from a famous winning bloodline. His particular temperament and beauty were about to fetch me nearly two million dollars. He was that well sought after, and being of such a pristine and lauded legacy, he had already been used to stud a few of my mares, and so I was willing to part with him for the right price. At the end of the day, I wasn't sentimental; I was a businessman. I had one foal from him, and two other mares were ready to give birth that year, and he'd just bred my last available mare, so that would be four from his bloodline in my collection, and that was enough. If any grew to be as magnificent as he was, I would sell them. I wasn't in a hurry to sell Midnight. I had many offers coming in, and since Christmas was only four months away, I thought I'd hold out for the highest bidder. So, I told the broker to say I was entertaining many offers and to bid realistically as I would take the highest bid.

After that, I answered a few work emails, as my day was never truly over, and the staff had arrived at the house and wanted to know if I wanted breakfast and where. The question also came with an addendum, did I have a guest, and would they be cooking for more than just me? Good question, did I want Eliza to stay the weekend? I could have just let her wake up, grabbed her something suitable enough from my drawers, and have my driver take her home. I did recall she mentioned living an hour and a half away. I didn't have time for a three-hour round trip, but my driver would be discreet. The question was, did I want her to go? I looked at that sweet ass and the puffy little lips that were so sweetly closed under it, wanting me to awaken them. Yep, she was staying.

I texted Beau.

Make breakfast for two. Pastries, coffee, omelets, bacon, juice. Have Midnight and Sunfire saddled, prepare a picnic lunch with plates and utensils, chill several bottles of Chateau Yquem, be on call but not on property. - A. M.

He managed all of those who worked for me. I'd worked with him since he was a teenager, and his father was the groundskeeper for my father. We were roughly the same age; he had just told me that he and his wife were expecting their third child, so he'd be happy to have most of the day off, and I knew when I told him to be off property, he'd clear the place. We'd have the ranch and grounds to ourselves. I was assured that within the hour, the coast would be clear. It was nearly seven in the morning; we hadn't slept much the night before, but she could sleep again after I fucked her if she wanted. I had to have her. I couldn't wait any longer.

I thought about what the best approach might be as we were so antagonistic the night before. I didn't mind a bit of a struggle, it made it all so much hotter for me, but I didn't want to be at odds with her all day. This was the best she'd ever get from me. After our weekend together, she'd see my much darker side. I wanted her to have some fun before I unleashed evil Andre on her. It was my way of keeping the world at arm's distance. I preferred a broad width of personal space, so being considered an asshole suited me fine. But I didn't want to be an asshole to Eliza, at least not on that particular Saturday morning.

I rolled over to her side of the bed and spooned that delicious ass, my jutting erection stabbing her soft skin. I gently moved the mass of hair covering her face and shoulders so that I could lay kisses on her cheeks. I kissed my way to her ear as I felt her stir and moan but not really come to consciousness. I gently nibbled her ear before I slid my lips down to her neck. An angry purple bruise lashed out at me, reminding me how I'd ravaged her. Good thing she was staying the weekend. We wouldn't be bothered by anyone, and she wouldn't have to explain the hickey I'd given her until it had faded some. I coursed my tongue slowly over the injury, rousing her more. Perhaps the tiny prick of pain and pleasure reminded her who she was with.

Her eyes fluttered open as she craned her head back to see me laying behind her, ready to make my entrance again.

"Good morning," I said with hot seduction.

"Wow, morning already?" Her disbelief was probably brought on by the fact that we'd hardly slept the night before.

"I was just looking at this here." I slid my hand over her ass and let my fingers dip into the lips I so wanted to open for me. "And I thought I might have a little bit more before we get up." I gently stroked my finger along her slit, casually as if I wasn't seducing, but rather just awakening it. "You don't have to do anything, just enjoy me."

"Sure," she gave a seductive little smile.

Ooh, she was putty in my hand, which I used to fondle her and flick her little clit that hardened under my touch. She grew wet for me as if on command.

"I'm going to really enjoy this," I said as I positioned my cock at her entrance and slid into heaven.

Chapter 7

Eliza

He was a lot to take on. As soon as his thick, hard erection entered my already sore pussy, take it was just about all I was able to do. I didn't have my wits about me yet. It was early in the morning, too early by my account, but I had heard ranchers were early risers, though I'd hardly classify Andre as a rancher. It did feel amazing having him connected to me again. I knew almost nothing about the man other than he'd lost his family, and he was almost the richest person in Texas, but the person who was giving me a slow morning ride was an enigma I was determined to unravel. At that moment, however, he laid his body weight on me, scooped his arms under my shoulders to hold me in place, and started fucking with determination.

I spread my legs to take more of him and raised my ass feeling him slide into the depths of me. "Ah," I cried out involuntarily as his cock slid in deeper, winding me up in such a torturously delicious way.

"This is how you should be awoken every morning," he growled in my ear as his chest slicked to my back.

What did he mean by that? This was just a weekender, right? He didn't give me any indication that we were starting anything. As he was pounding me hard from behind, I decided not to worry about it all too much. He felt too good. I dug my head into the pillow and just absorbed him ... all of him. I could tell by his heaving breathing and moans that he was close to his climax. Funny, he'd usually try to get me there, too, but this time it was all about him. Since I thought I wouldn't be getting off this round, I inched my hand under me to find my clit and rock my own world, but he batted my hand back.

"Don't touch yourself," he ordered, almost cruelly.

I chalked it up to the fact that he was about to cum, which he did moments later, hot and feral as he pressed himself into me as deep as he would go.

"Fuck, Andre!" The feeling was so intense that it actually cramped me up a little inside.

He continued to grunt until he collapsed, and I could feel his breathing through my spine. He was heavy, so heavy I almost couldn't bear his weight, but after a few minutes getting himself back together again, he lifted off me and withdrew his well-satisfied cock from my still very needy pussy. He then slapped my ass, hard!

"Now, that's how you say good morning!" He seemed very proud of himself.

"Right, if you're you. I'm still hanging here," I complained.

"You won't be hanging for long." He reached over to a small shelf that held only his phone.

He seriously made minimalists look like hoarders. I laid there and just squirmed with my itchy feelings of arousal, and while he was occupied with his phone, I tried to quietly dig my hand through the covers and pleasure myself. While he was tapping away at the screen and not paying attention to me, I heard his gruff voice.

"I said don't touch yourself," he commanded with a taste of anger on his tongue.

"What? Are you a sadist all of a sudden?" Now, I was angry.

He kicked the covers off the bed and onto the floor and spread his legs. "Come here," he commanded a little more softly.

What was this guy's trip? He patted the space between his legs, and as much as I wanted to fume and protest, my pussy pretty much made me get up and crawl between his legs, hoping for enough action to cure the ache. As soon as I settled between his legs, leaning my head on his chest with my ass on his deflated cock, he carefully took each of my legs, one by one, shifting them over his knees, so that I was spread out with my legs over his. He then sat up a little straighter taking me with him and widened his legs just that much farther, so I was really out there. He then brought his arms around me, swiped open his phone with one hand, and placed his other on my wet pussy as he brought the phone to my face.

"I want you to pick something to wear. You can either be naked," he flicked my clit to punctuate his point. "Or dressed in my clothes at home, but when we're out on the estate or in town, you'll need to wear something. I can have anything you pick delivered here in an hour. Here," he handed me the phone as he worked more diligently on my aching center.

"Everything here is way out of my price range," I complained as he dove his middle finger inside of me. "Oh God, that ..." I arched my head back on him.

"Let's not play that game; you know I'll pay for it." He pulled his finger out again. "Now focus on finding something."

I wiggled my pussy and returned to the phone, so he'd put his finger back in. "Fine." I swiped my finger along the screen, and he rewarded me with a hard finger fucking.

It was so hard, in fact, that I could barely focus on picking a sweet pair of jeans, a soft T-shirt, and a beautiful sweater. The entire ensemble cost about two hundred dollars.

"There!" I'd put the items in his cart.

"Now, something sexy for a dinner out," he said as he added a second finger.

As he continued to drive me insane with his fingers, I found a spaghetti strap dress in black that was simple and sexy.

"This," I barely breathed as he revved me up so hard, I was about to explode.

"Yes." He was feeling my desperation as his cock began to harden against my back. "Put it in the cart."

I did, and with a touch of his finger, he'd bought both outfits that were, by the miracle of modern technology, going to appear at the ranch within the hour. As soon as he ordered the clothes, he doubled his efforts, pinching both my clit and my nipple hard while biting my ear and my neck. I came ... in glorious fashion bucking into his hand, calling his name. When I slumped down from Mount Olympus, I was putty. He tossed me to the side, and I was about to go off on him when he scooped me into his arms.

"Time for a shower."

I was so spent from that weird shopping/finger fuck experience that I just let him King Kong me into the shower. When he set me down, I realized his bathroom was just as sparse as everything else. The entire room was a shower. There was no toilet or sink, just a huge tiled room. When he turned the single knob on the wall, the ceiling rained down on us. There was nothing else in the room but a nob, three small shelves wedged into the corner with three silver bottles, and two prongs where a razor had been mounted. The room did have a long tiled bench that could either be sat on ... or anything else, I assumed. He sat me down on that bench, and I saw his cock had come back to life.

Fascinated and drawn to it, I reached out to stroke it, but he backed away. He was so strange. Instead, he bent down and kissed me as the water cascaded down our faces.

"Stay here." He walked to the corner with the three silver bottles, brought them all to the bench, and opened one. He then poured a generous amount on his hands and worked the soap into a lather. "Half," he yelled out, and the water spraying our side of the room stopped as he put the suds in my hair. "I'm going to wash you first." It was so fun and erotic.

He massaged soap into my hair as my body electrified with sensations. Then he used the same soap to lather my body, spending lots of time soaping up my breasts, under my arms, and down my stomach. When he got to my pussy, he sat down next to me and sat me in his lap. He then used another slather of liquid from the bottle and stroked it along himself, sudsing up the hair around his cock and applying a liberal amount to his stiff rod.

"Hop on board," he commanded, slapping my ass.

"I sure hope that's hypo-allergenic," I sort of teased.

"It's derived from completely natural ingredients. Now, ride me!" he ordered. "Full On!" he shouted, and the water came down on us again.

It was sexy and weird. He rinsed the soap out of my hair as I bounced up and down on his stiff pole, loving how he filled me. When the sensations got to be too much, he grabbed my hips and brought me down on him hard and held me there as he jettisoned in and out of me, reaching his second hard climax of the morning. I didn't care that conditioner was running down my face. I was too into him. This time his cock hit my G-spot several times, and I came just after he did. After having two powerful orgasms within an hour of each other, I was totally wrung out. I slipped off him and just laid down on the tiled slab to gather my wits, spreading my legs to let the water wash me clean as Andre filled my vision.

He dipped his face down to kiss me as warm water continued to pelt us. "You're fun," he said softly and then commanded the water to stop. I wasn't sure what we'd do next as I didn't see any towels. "Follow me."

Dripping wet, I followed him, and as we neared the door, he took my hand. At first, I thought it was sweet, and then I realized it was so that I didn't get surprised by the power blowers. Suddenly a burst of warm air hit my body and evaporated up all the wet until I was amazingly dry after only a few minutes. My hair was still wet, but my naked ol' body was dry as a bone. He turned to me and smiled.

"Wow, we aren't in Kansas anymore," I smiled at him.

"We never were," he said. "Okay. There is a changing room across the hall with a vanity and drawers full of things you might need to finish drying your hair. I'll meet you in the kitchen down the hall. I'll leave some clothes for you on the bed until your things arrive."

"Thanks," is all I said to Mr. Efficient.

I went across the hall as he instructed and found a room with a small table, a mirror, and a chest of drawers. Inside the chest of drawers were brand new hairbrushes, combs, and things to style a woman's hair in wrappers. In the drawer below that one, there were gels and leave-in conditioners and products only a woman would use. The sight of such a well-stocked space dedicated clearly to primping and styling a woman made me feel sad. Clearly, he had enough women over to warrant creating a space that was intended for them as they spent time in his home. Knowing what little I did of him and his minimalistic tendencies, this room was an extravagance that showed he had many women in his life.

Feeling overwhelmed by what I saw, I simply combed through the knots, slathered my hair with some leave-in conditioner, and threw it into a ponytail. I didn't spend much time making myself look overly done up as my enthusiasm had started to wane. I walked into his bedroom to find a gray men's dress shirt on the bed and nothing more. Since I didn't know where he kept his clothing, specifically his underwear, I put on the shirt and planned to beg him for some underwear.

I wandered around a little until I found him in the kitchen, setting out dishes on the breakfast bar. It had dishes full of omelets, bacon, sausage, what I assumed were grits, toast, and diced fruit. He turned around and seemed a little startled to see me there.

"Wow, that's quite a spread," I commented, keeping my conversation light, though I wanted to grill him about the lady's powder room he had in his museum-quality ranch house.

"I figured you'd be hungry since we didn't eat much last night." He seemed charming.

"Well, you certainly ate plenty." I laughed, trying to make a joke. "My pussy has never had so much attention." I smiled as I slid into a seat next to him.

"Coffee? Juice? Coffee and juice?" he asked.

"Water." I was so dehydrated the only thing that really sounded good was water.

"Okay." He went to the fridge and pulled out two bottles of cold water. "We should probably hydrate."

After he gave it to me, I guzzled some of the water, then looked at him as he took his seat and started in on his breakfast.

"So, two questions." I began to eat too, feeling completely hungry at that point.

"They are?" he answered as if he was expecting me to ask him to marry me.

"Can I have some underwear? Even huge ones are fine, and why do you have an entire room dedicated to women's beauty products? You're either a serial weekender or secretly a hairdresser." I popped a piece of bacon in my mouth.

"No to the underwear. I want you as naked as I can get you, and yes, that room is for women I sleep with. I have enough space to provide them a place to primp, so why not use it? I'm the only one living here, and I've got more than enough space."

That was what I assumed his answer would be. I couldn't say it hurt exactly, but it did sort of put everything into perspective. I wasn't going to let it ruin me. This was just a weekend, and I knew it.

"That's why you're so good at fucking," I casually mentioned as I continued to eat.

"Yes, I get a lot of practice." He looked at me with an evil glint in his eyes.

What the hell did he have planned?

Chapter 8

Andre

Eliza's questions unnerved me a bit. She was very observant. I did have a vanity space for women to do what they did because I didn't want to yield my bathroom to it. I had the shower room and a private lavatory that I didn't want to be cluttered with makeup, hairbrushes, and other things that the women I had over would use. I converted a guest bedroom to provide them a primping space. But having such a room did give off the impression that I had several women in rotation, and on occasion, I had, but I didn't want Eliza to think she was one of the many who were in and out of my life. I certainly didn't want anything long-lasting, but I was hoping for more than a weekend with her.

I turned to look at her. "So, are you ready to run?" I was sort of teasing.

"I'm trying to decide. I can't run easily. I'd have to call an Uber to get me. I'm wearing nothing but a shirt, and I'd have to pay for an almost two-hour ride home. But I wonder if riding nearly naked might reduce my Uber payment, and that might actually be better than braving you. You did fuck me and leave me once; it's not like I came here to get it on with Prince Charming. I knew what you were about. So … I don't know … it's your call. You are and probably will always be my one and only one or two-night stand, so I'm good if you are."

"I have a nice day planned for us. I'd like you to stay. In fact, will you stay? I'll have my driver take you home tomorrow so that both of us can get ready for work. Sound fair?" I was being very fair.

"Okay." She gave me a big smile.

I know it bothered her that I had other women, but she didn't say anything. I just ate my food. I smiled warmly but didn't engage in small talk, seeing if perhaps she would. She didn't say a thing, just watched the sun over the fields outside of the huge floor to ceiling window. It was awkward, but it was also a test. If the fact that I had numerous other women here were a problem, she'd probably remain silent. If it wasn't a problem or she was working her way through my reality with ease, she'd say something, but she didn't. We ate in a strange and oddly sad silence. When I was done eating, I stood and picked up my plate.

"Are you still eating?" I asked, seeing that she was just pushing pieces of half-eaten food around her plate.

"I think I'm done, thank you." She handed her plate to me, and I put the dishes into the sink.

"It bothers you, doesn't it?" I approached her as I came back. "I waited for you to make small talk, and you didn't," I told her as I sidled up to her and placed myself between her bare legs, watching her flush as I stroked her thighs.

"I'm trying not to care. I don't know you. So, you have a makeup room for women who stay here." She was rationalizing.

"I do." I slid my dress shirt up her legs, exposing her naked pussy.

She had the prettiest pussy. She was a pretty girl overall, sweet, wholesome-looking, but she was tough. I liked that. I could have had her again on the chair and was planning on doing just that before she left the next day. But since we had a fun day ahead of us, I just swiped her slit with my finger and trailed it up her body to her mouth. She flinched a minute, but I quickly replaced the finger with my lips.

"There's so much more for us to explore. Don't get lost in your head." Just at that moment, there was a knock on the door. "That's probably your clothes. I'll just be a minute."

I left her seated at the breakfast bar probably baffled, but I didn't care. I was just as perplexed. I didn't want a relationship with the woman, but she was fun. I enjoyed her company, and I couldn't say that for many people. I ordered her the clothes she'd picked out and was tempted to order her more, but I liked her wearing next to nothing, so I restrained myself. I met the messenger at the door, tipped him, and returned to Eliza.

"Okay, put these on and meet me back here. I have a few calls to make, and then we're heading out to the stables. I want to show you around the place. There's a lot to love about being on a farm. I'm excited to show you things I'm pretty sure you didn't get a chance to see in DC." I gave her a wink, just to mess with her.

"Thanks for these, Andre. It's so nice of you to buy me clothes." She cradled the bag to her chest, still being a little distant, but I was sure our day would erase whatever inner turmoil she was dealing with.

I answered emails before heading to my changing room to get dressed. She'd be seeing a lot of me in my work clothes and hopefully more of me out of them, so I put on a pair of jeans, cowboy boots, and a V-neck. I thought perhaps seeing me in a more casual light would help her let loose a little. When she walked into the room, I was not disappointed with my purchase. I only hoped that the dress she bought made her look as sexy as the jeans and T-shirt she was wearing now. Her top's material was so soft you could see the gentle slope of her breasts through it since she didn't have a bra. I knew what I had done to her panties as well, so after going commando all day, she'd be really ready for me that night.

"You look amazing," I said, approaching her.

"Wow, so do you." I loved the little surprise in her tone. She was barefooted, and the entire picture was arousing. "You think I might borrow some socks? And, um, any chance of finding a clean pair of ladies' underwear? I mean, you being a ladies' man does have its upside if you do." She flashed me a gracious smile.

"I might have some, but I wouldn't let you wear them even if I did." I put my arm around her. "Come on, the stables are out this way."

"You know you're an asshole, right?" she teased. "Bare-assed in jeans isn't the most comfortable."

"I prefer to think of myself as more of a dick," I winked at her again and saw the flush of color dance over her cheeks ... yes, she was really fun. "And feeling my dick on your raw skin will be incredible, trust me. Those jeans will save me a lot of time getting you aroused later ... trust me."

She rolled her eyes at me, and we almost didn't make it out on our little excursion, but I just kept reminding myself I'd have sex with her later.

We walked out to the stables where Midnight and Sunfire were saddled and ready to ride. I had about twenty horses that some of them my staff used to traverse the property, others I bred for the thoroughbred horse trade, and still others were prized racehorses resting off-season.

"So, what do you do here on the ranch? You can't have time for much with all the work you have to do," Eliza asked as we walked.

"Well, surprisingly, a lot of my research for work is done here. I have the prototypes for the energy storage units built here since we have so much space. That large hangar over there is where all the magic happens. I also have horses, which you will see, and I have a small garden for fresh fruits and vegetables that we sell at the local market. That's more my caretaker's business, but we share the profits. And oil. I still harvest oil on the premises and also solar panels and wind turbines, so there's a lot going on. The place I love the most, though, is the lake at the back of my estate. It's peaceful and beautiful. I thought we'd have lunch there later."

"Sounds perfect." There was her beautiful smile again. Whatever drama she was dealing with, she must have worked it out in her head.

"Do you know how to ride a horse?"

"Did you just ask if I had one single riding lesson when I was ten and got spooked by the horse and refused to go back? Because if that's what you asked, then yes, I've ridden a horse before."

"Oh, this should be fun," I pretended to roll my eyes.

"Glad you invited me over yet?" She played along.

"Yes, actually." I took her hand and smiled. "I am."

It was quite a distance to the stables, so we walked hand in hand. I hadn't done that since I was in high school. It was sweet and refreshing. When we got to the stables, she was quite impressed.

"These animals are so beautiful, Andre," she said as she walked past each stall. "Every one of them is gorgeous."

"You should see the two we're riding today. Especially Midnight. He's our star. We're in the middle of negotiating his sale. He's a two-million-dollar horse, so be careful riding him." I didn't mean to caution so callously, but he was a prize stallion.

"I don't have to ride him," she defended herself.

"No, he's the best horse for you."

We walked up on them, and as always, the very sight of Midnight took our breath away. His coat was such rich ebony it looked like black ink. He stood tall and proud as his tail majestically swiped the air. He knew he was the very best of all the horses I'd ever known. With her tawny mane and stately good looks, Sunfire wasn't a bad horse by any stretch of the imagination, but compared to Midnight, she was a cheap whore's donkey.

"Are you kidding me right now?" Eliza stood there impressed. "Andre, these horses …" Her mouth hung wide open.

"The black one is Midnight, the million-dollar stallion. He's the most gentle beast you'll ever know. Sunfire isn't a bad horse, but she's a bit testy, so I'd keep your distance. Here, give me your leg, and I'll help you up. He won't walk until he's told to do so there's nothing to fear."

"I want to be terrified, seriously, but he seems so … I don't know - like he's looking into my soul." With that, Midnight whinnied as if he had heard and understood her, which made Eliza laugh.

"For two million dollars, he may very well be." I put out my hand to help Eliza onto the horse, and as soon as she was in the saddle, she smiled; it felt right.

She looked beautiful sitting up there with the sun glistening through her blonde hair. I loved the sweet look of her like she was designed just for that particular tableau.

She stroked his thick mane. "Thanks, Midnight, for letting me on." She gave him a warm pat on the neck, and again he whinnied in response. "I wish I had two million dollars," she blurted out.

"Why? You planning on running a horse breeding operation?" I asked as I mounted Sunfire.

"No," Eliza dipped her voice. "I just like him."

"Ah, well, if you were the wife of a wealthy man, you'd be in luck, I guess." I clicked my tongue and gave Sunfire a little kick in the side, and she slowly started moving forward.

Without prompting, Midnight followed.

"What do you mean by that?" Eliza asked as Midnight walked abreast of Sunfire as they casually traipsed down the dirt road.

"Well, just what I said, you'd have to marry someone with that kind of money to afford the horse, Eliza." I didn't think there was anything wrong with what I said; there was no way a woman like Eliza could make the kind of money she'd need to own a horse like Midnight; facts were facts.

"And I couldn't make that money without a husband?" she asked, incensed.

All I could do was laugh and click my tongue again, giving a swifter kick to the mare this time, and she took off galloping. Again, Midnight followed. Though he was a tame horse and a very well-mannered one, Eliza found herself being jostled up and down, rising in her seat only to be slammed down again. I could only imagine what horror was being unleashed on her pussy. I had to give her some guidance, or I wouldn't be riding with her again.

"You have to use your thigh muscles to keep from bouncing up and down," I yelled back at her.

With a ferocious look of determination, she doubled her efforts, and her bouncing subsided. She'd still be pretty sore, but that made my plans for the evening just that much more fun. She'd be completely at my mercy.

Chapter 9

Eliza

I tightened my leg muscles as Andre suggested, and it did help with the bouncing, which was causing such a riot in my body. I did everything in my power to keep my pussy from slamming down on the saddle over and over again. Despite my efforts, however, I was pretty sure I was gonna be really sore when the ride was over. We galloped down the dirt drive until we reached the top of a hill. We had come to a part of Andre's property that I couldn't see from the house. Over the ridge was a huge lake that stretched out for miles. I had gone from being impressed to being astonished.

As Midnight came up on Sunfire, I looked to Andre. "Is that all yours?" There was no way the man owned an entire lake.

"It's all mine." He answered in the affirmative as I knew he would, even though I could hardly believe it.

"Why don't you have boat races and like a bed and breakfast out here so people can enjoy this incredible lake?" I just couldn't believe it sat there doing nothing.

"I don't like people, as I mentioned. My caretaker brings his family out here, they enjoy the lake, and we will be enjoying it. There's a picnic and some wine set up down there for us. If you want, we can take a dip in the water, though, with it being early September, I'm pretty sure the water is freeze-your-ass-off cold." He laughed.

"It wouldn't matter; I can't feel the lower half of me anyway." I gave him a warm smile. "Onward ho!" I put out my arm and pretended to go into battle.

"Isn't that my line?" he teased as he clicked his tongue and Sunfire took off again.

"Wait, what? Did you just call me a ho?"

Midnight took off after him, and I was back to putting all my concentration on keeping my leg muscles tight so my vagina didn't get a beating. The distance was actually a lot further than it looked, and it took us about twenty minutes of solid riding to get to the lake. The horses galloped some, clearly enjoying the exercise, and walked at a lighter pace when they got tired. As soon as we came to the water's edge, the horses slowed. At the point where we stopped, there was an entire spread of food laid out and covered in little white canopies. A huge trough of water was filled, and there were large carrots on the table.

Andre jumped off Sunfire and led her to the trough to drink, which she did. He didn't tie her up, just let her have her freedom. He then turned toward me.

"You need some help down?" he asked and must have been teasing because yes, I did need help.

Not only did Midnight seem two stories tall. I seriously had very little feeling in my lower extremities.

"Please," was all I gave him as he offered me his hand.

As soon as I took his hand, I melted off the horse and almost slithered to the ground, but Andre caught me in his arms.

"Do you think I can put you down?" he asked, looking at me with adoration in his eyes.

"Let's give it a shot. Worst case scenario is I'll fall over."

With that, he set me on my feet, and I wobbled a little but didn't fall. However, taking a step was a whole different story. I thought for sure my legs were going to give out on me. They both were as heavy as tree trunks, and I lumbered them along like Frankenstein.

"Well, you didn't fall over." He slapped my ass, and I catapulted forward, catching myself on the table.

My ass was poked out, and my arms were bracing me. Suddenly he was upon me, his hard jeans-clad cock pressed against my ass.

"I haven't fallen over yet, but that was pretty damn close." I tried to move my legs to get some control over myself again, and Andre caught my hips. "If you do me out here under the Texas sky, Cowboy Grandpa, you're going to have to carry me all the way back to your place. I'm just giving you fair warning. I'm not taking your cock and a saddle in the same afternoon." I knew that would piss him off.

"Cowboy Grandpa is it now? Who's the one who can't walk? I'm feeling fine, ready to fuck you doggie style. I could probably carry you back." He moved in closer and put his arms around my waist to unbutton the fly on my jeans.

"You aren't really going to do it, are you?" I grabbed his hand.

"Unless you specifically tell me not to, I most certainly am." He slid down the zipper waiting for me to stop or protest.

"Andre, my crotch is on fire right now." It wasn't really a 'no' exactly.

"I'm sure it is." He slid my jeans down my legs, and I started to panic a little.

"I'm also pretty sure it's a complete and total mess … I mean, it has to be red, swollen, ugly, unsightly. I wouldn't go there if I were you."

He didn't listen, just kept pulling down my pants until they were off of me, leaving me naked from the waist down. He then came back and started unbuttoning my top.

I was starting to shake. "There aren't any folks running around out here right? Like people tending stuff on the ranch that might see me standing here buck-ass naked?" It was highly erotic and also just the slightest bit scary.

"Nope," was all he said as he slid my shirt off and started fondling my breasts.

It wasn't a cold day, but cool, and I felt the air on my skin. It was pretty invigorating if you ignored the fact that I was out in the middle of a farm without a stitch of clothes on. My legs were starting to feel better as the blood rushed back into them again. I heard Andre unzip his jeans, and I could already imagine what was about to happen. I did stand up, not wanting to be rutted from behind like one of his horses.

"If we're going to do this, I don't want to be mounted like a pony. Maybe I can sit in your lap or something." I was just thinking out loud when he picked me up into his arms again, like King Kong. "Didn't your momma teach you any manners? I mean, just because you came here by wagon train a hundred years ago doesn't mean you have to be a brute about things."

"You know I was going to be nice to you, but on second thought, you've called me old, just one too many times."

He marched us into the lake and, without warning, threw me as far as he could, which was actually pretty far. I landed in the icy cold water with a splash. My arms flailed, and I felt like I was drowning until I realized I could touch the bottom and stood up so that I was in the water waist-deep.

"What the hell, Andre?" I was almost seriously pissed off.

He walked into the water squinting his face at how cold it was. "Jesus, it's cold," he said when he reached me buck naked with his cock all stiff and happy.

"And why exactly did you throw me into the lake?" I beat his bare chest, kind of enjoying hitting him.

"How do your legs and lady bits feel now?" he asked, wrapping his cold, wet arms around me.

I hadn't really thought of my riding injuries, but the freezing, cold water pretty much helped everything feel better.

"I still hate you, but they actually feel a teensy, tiny bit better."

"Not gonna give me an inch, are you?"

"Oh, thank you, grand lord, of this estate for throwing me into the lake so that my vagina is more amenable to your invasion. I swoon!" I put my hand over my forehead and pretended to faint. He caught me, which I thought was funny. I liked that he was playing along.

"What are you doing?" I asked as he picked me up and walked with me through the water.

"I'm going to find a spot of land for my invasion. Never fear, fair maiden, I'll be slaying that dragon shortly."

"And by dragon, you are insinuating that my delicate flower is a fire breathing beast?" I scowled at him.

"Just as you assume that I should be in either a covered wagon or a stately Victorian manor."

"Well, at least I'm not as old as these here hills." I loved how we teased.

"Keep at it, Eliza - you're getting a stabbing whether you deserve one or not."

"Oh, no!" I pretended to be scared.

He carried me ashore and laid me down on a blanket set out on the beach. The sun felt good on my frozen skin. I hadn't seen the setup before, he must have had his staff make us a little beach hang out. The blanket felt soft on my cold body, and suddenly I was much more comfortable.

"Better?" he asked, looking amorous.

"Much. So, you own all of this?"

"I own much more than this," he said as his hand coursed over my body.

I stopped his hand. "It just all seems so … much."

"Wealth doesn't impress you?" he seemed surprised.

I shrugged my shoulders. "It's just money."

"But you had sex with me, knowing I had money."

"I had sex with you because you were hot. You have a thing about you; it's sexy. I fell hard for it." Why not confess? We weren't doing this for the long haul, so why not be honest? "I fell for you, not your money. I think fucking money is so overrated." I laughed.

He laughed. "You have a point. Now the first order of business," he slid down my legs and then opened them for his naughty mouth.

I really was still very sore down there, so I was hoping he'd go gently. He wasn't always that careful with my inventory, so I had the instinct to close my legs, just the slightest bit worried he'd be biting again. He caught me with his hands and pressed them open, not letting me move away from his invading mouth.

"Wow, ouch," he said when he saw me.

"Am I going to live?"

"Maybe not." He gave me a wicked smile before he dove in and started gently lapping my sore vagina.

"Oh, that feels so good." It was the perfect mix of softness and ache, which made my raw skin sensitive and alert to his attention.

Sucking on my clit and pressing his tongue inside me had me going absolutely nuts. He didn't use his fingers or anything else, just his tongue and lips, alternating between kissing and sucking, and I was a blathering mess by the time my body pitched into him. My vag was on fire, but he lapped at the flames in such a way I was just falling to pieces all around him. After he'd rocketed me to space I was a crumbling disaster. He laid down beside me and stared at the sky. I looked over to him and laughed a little. I was feeling fine, but his cock was just standing at attention like a good little soldier.

"I'm not sure I'm ready to take all this on." I got up on my elbows to take his cock into my hand. "But I could return some oral lovin' if you want some."

He shifted his body so that he was easier to reach. "I'll take whatever you're offering."

With that, I scrunched down on the blanket a little and kissed the top of his swollen head. It was already dribbling a little, and his pee slit looked like a smile. I loved his cock and it was actually quite pretty as far as penises were concerned. It was huge, but not scary, just very there. Not too girthy, but long and so smooth, and a very pretty color. He had a natural outcropping of hair, but because he wasn't a very hairy man, his pubes nicely framed his pretty cock. I really was excited about getting my mouth on it, so I dove right in. I couldn't take him all the way down my throat, but I tried. I think he appreciated the effort because when I started choking, he stroked my head gently and laughed, making his cock reverberate in my mouth. That had me laughing too, and I had to spit him out to catch my breath. I looked up at him adoringly; we were having fun.

"Don't bite off more than you can chew," he warned and then retracted. "On second thought, don't bite at all."

I gnashed my teeth to tease.

"Maybe hands are best …"

I went back down on his soft velvet steel and used both my hands and my mouth to bring him to orgasm. I could tell he was about to blow, so I pulled my mouth off him and pumped him hard and fast until he cried out and shot up to the sky. It was fun having him at my mercy. After he came, he wrapped his arms around me and held me close. He didn't say anything at first, and for just a moment, I felt a little awkward. It was all well and good when he was biting me, or hard fucking me, or throwing me in a lake, but laying there like we were, was loving. I wasn't sure I was ready for his tenderness.

I sort of wanted to hate him enough to leave him the next day. Surely, we couldn't make a work-thing work. This was just good ol' adult fun. It was more realistic than porno, but not so real as the white picket fence and two point five kids. It was just for the moment. But this embrace didn't feel like 'for now.' It felt like 'forever.'

I stiffened and pulled away. I couldn't do emotional intensity - not with him. By the look in his eye he understood. We didn't say anything, but we stared at one another for a beat.

"I can't fall in love with you," I blurted out.

"I'm not asking you to." His expression looked just a little hurt.

"I mean, you're the CEO of a company where I'm an intern. The power dynamic is off. I don't want to feel beneath you."

"Unless you are literally beneath me?" His eyebrow raised, and we were teasing again.

"I want to stand on equal ground."

"Do you have any more cliches up your sleeve? Oh wait," he picked up my arm. "You aren't wearing one."

"You know what I mean." I sat up with my hands on my hips.

"I do. Let's not make any decisions right now." He stepped into the water, waded out a few feet, and went for a swim. "Come on in; the water is freezing." His smile was hard to resist, but I knew the minute I followed him into that water, I'd follow him anywhere.

Chapter 10

Andre

The truth of the matter was, I had no idea what I was doing with her. I liked her more than I should have. The age thing didn't bother me really, except for as much as she didn't want to be discredited for her youth and inexperience, I didn't want to be disregarded in my old age. When I would be in my eighties, she'd be in her sixties. It's not like she'd be out running around the town, but I'd have to keep healthy and fit to keep up. Then it hit me - I was planning a future with her. I shook the thought out of my head. It couldn't happen, not with Eliza or anyone.

The water was freeze-your-nuts-off freezing, and I was ready to get out as soon as she got in. Good thing she didn't last long, and we soon found ourselves wrapped in blankets I'd had supplied for us and sitting at the table looking out to the lake. A cluster of long-legged birds, herons, gathered on the far side of the lake, and she found the sight of them amusing.

"Do you ever just come out here and chill?" she asked, sipping the cold wine I'd had set out.

"No, I never have the time."

"So, do you have someone here every weekend? Is this like the standard afternoon activity for people you like to fuck?" She didn't ask the question disrespectfully, but the question itself was a little rude.

"This is my home first and foremost, but yes, I do bring women out here when they come to stay. There's not much else to do out here unless you like energy storage or horses. Most women I date don't care much for either, so the lake is always my go-to." I probably shouldn't have told her that.

"Do you ever think about marriage?" It seemed like a question she posed just out of curiosity, but it did make me nervous.

"No, I don't want to be married." I truly didn't.

"Even if the perfect person came along?"

"Are you insinuating that's you?" I had to ask.

"No. I'm almost positive it isn't me. Just anyone?"

"If I married them, they wouldn't be just anyone. They'd have to be pretty spectacular to tame an old bear like me. My meter has almost run out on being pleasant. I'll kick you out tomorrow morning, so I can turn back into a pumpkin. I can't handle people in large doses. Whoever married me would have to be either very busy or just as anti-social."

"Why don't you like people?" she asked, nibbling at her food.

"Why do I hate them, you mean? I have no use for people. Most lie or cheat, everyone wants a piece of my money, and I just find people to be self-serving and dull. If they claim they aren't, they're lying."

"So, you're saying that in, I don't know, a coupla more years you're going to turn into Ebenezer Scrooge?"

"Never gets old with you, does it?"

"Not yet." Her smile was so infectious.

"Give or take a coupla years ... that's the plan."

"Fun." She rolled her eyes.

She really was too much.

"You be careful with that eye-rolling, or I'll have Midnight gallop you all the way back, and you won't be able to sit for a week."

"Maybe you can come to my cubicle and give me a tongue bath during my lunch break." Her side-eye was on point.

"Well, as fun as that sounds, as soon as you and I are back in the office, you can't say a word about what happened here this weekend. I'm actually going to have you sign a nondisclosure agreement to keep you quiet. This isn't really a good time to say it, but no time is. If you do say anything about me or what we've done this weekend, I'll not only have you fired, but I'll create a scandal that proves you're lying." Suddenly I was feeling mean again. "This doesn't go beyond this ranch or this weekend."

"Good," is all she said.

Funny how I set up to push her away, and she ended up breaking my heart anyway.

"You're not having fun?" I wasn't sure why I asked her that.

"What do you want me to say? Yes, I'm having fun. I get it. I don't make the cut, but the fucking, eating, and horse riding is awesome. This is just this weekend, and this is what you do every weekend with the women you fuck. I understand. Next weekend it's Bonnie in accounting. No hard feelings, I'll sign whatever you want. If you want me to leave tonight, no worries. You sound the call, Ebenezer, and I'll be on my way."

"I guess I deserved that. Stay the night, please. I'm certainly not done with you yet." I leaned over and kissed her lips. "Trust me. My leaving this relationship at 'hello' is going to benefit you more than me, I promise."

She gave me a determined smile I knew was fake. "Thanks." And we were over that hump ... barely.

We had our lunch, and the conversation was quiet. She watched the birds on the lake and asked about energy storage, which I believe was to avoid asking any more questions about me that would disappoint her. She was quite well educated and understood the higher science of renewable energy, which was encouraging. We actually had fun talking shop. She wanted to go into environmental ethics for businesses and I, by the nature of how much money was to be made, focused my attention on renewable energy and storage, an untapped market that was ripe to make billions. As soon as we could mass-produce the storage systems safely and at reasonable cost, every house, apartment building, and office would be outfitted with a solar and wind package to go with storage devices, making the use of renewable energy more feasible. It was so endearing to see her face light up talking about a clean energy future. She was a beautiful nerd, and it made me all the hotter for her.

When we were done with our lunch, we put our clothes on and walked to the horses. I left our picnic on the beach for my staff to clean up.

"Ugh, I'm not sure I can brave this again." She wasn't talking to me but the horse. "You are so beautiful and majestic, and I know you have fun running through the fields, but I'm not sure my lady parts will survive a full-on gallop." She offered Midnight a carrot and a big smile.

He whinnied as if he actually had heard and understood her. He was a remarkable horse and good-tempered, and he did have an interest in Eliza. Perhaps he could sense her sweet demeanor. She was very much like him, stately and majestic, a little wild and ultimately kind. I guess that's what I liked most about Eliza; she was kind. Anyone named Elizabeth Piquel, who grew up being called 'Pickle' her whole life, would either end up a saint or Satan. It was nice to see her choose the former over the latter.

"So, you promise to be nice?" she confirmed with the horse.

He dipped his head to her, and for a moment, their foreheads touched. It was an incredible sight, a horse and a woman communing, I was almost jealous. The walk back was long and peaceful. I took Eliza to see the hangar where we held the storage prototypes, and she was satisfactorily impressed with what we'd come up with so far.

"Look at these, wow, soon every residence and business in America will have the means to make and store clean energy, that is ... wow. I'm so excited for you, and one day, when I'm slapping a fine on any company who violates their energy agreement, I can say I knew you when."

Geek humor, I loved it. "One can only dream." I laughed as we made our way back to the house.

"I hate to put Midnight away; we've had so much fun together. He was so nice coming back; I barely hurt this time." There was her infectious smile. "I could stay out here with him forever." She stroked his mane, and he must have enjoyed it as he leaned into her touch. "Some crazy rich bastard is gonna love him." She turned to me, and her smile widened.

"Let's hope. So, do you want to shower with me or without me?" With the riding sweat and lake scum sticking to our bodies, we both needed to freshen up.

"I'll shower solo, big guy. You're too dangerous to be trusted." Her smile slid into a smirk.

"These are the last few hours we have together, remember? After this, I become a werewolf."

"Gee, I'm not sure which to choose, a perpetual werewolf who doesn't ravage my pussy or horn dog that does? Decisions, decisions. How about I take a breather, clean up the pits and bits, and meet you on the flipside? If I'm staying the night tonight, I doubt I'll be allowed to sleep in your bed without some kind of nocturnal gymnastics." She cocked her head, and her quirky, nerdy, cuteness exuded.

"Suit yourself. But you're showering in my wing. If I can't touch, at least I can look."

"You do know how creepy that sounds, right, Ebenezer?" She rolled her eyes.

"I plan on getting much creepier, trust me." I rolled my eyes too, and we both laughed. God, she was fun. "When you're done in the shower, wear the cocktail dress you bought; we have an evening planned."

She gave me a quirky look, and then her face crumpled. "You think I might be able to rustle up some underwear somewhere? I think it slipped your mind to buy some this morning."

"Nothing slips my mind," I winked at her, and she huffed as she entered the shower room and shut the door.

The shower room was adjacent to my bedroom and office. She wasn't aware that I could see her come out of the shower if I was sitting at my desk in the office. So, I sat at my desk and just anticipated her return. I thought about all the ways I'd be ravaging her later, and my excitement for her renewed. When she emerged, she wore a tiny, black dress that was perfect. It hugged her ass, dipped down to her breastbone, and gave me enough of a view of those perfectly toned legs that all I wanted to do was cinch up the dress to reveal her glorious pussy, which I knew had nothing to hold me back from it.

"You look divine," I said as I approached her and slipped my tongue in her mouth for a passionate kiss. "My turn for the shower, I said as I slapped her ass, feeling its firmness just under the fabric.

I stripped right in front of her and walked into the shower room without closing the door, just to see if she'd stay and watch. To my disappointment, she didn't, but it was also a test, how horny and malleable was she? If she had watched, I'd probably have to do more to extract her from me that evening as we were nearing the end of our soiree, and I couldn't have her latching on. Luckily for me, she moved to the living area where I could barely see her out of the corner of my eye and whipped out her phone. Admittedly, having her engaged with her phone and not me was a bit of a disappointment, so I showered fast and dressed in nothing but lounge pants, no underwear for me either. I wanted everything to be easy to access that night.

I walked into the living room with my hair slicked back.

"Wait, I'm wearing a cocktail dress, and you're in your jammies?" She seemed adorably irritated.

"My house, my rules." I plopped down next to her, smelling fresh and feeling good. "You hungry? My caretaker texted me and said our dinner is ready." I took her hand and kissed it, not even sure why I did.

"Sure." She catapulted herself off the couch and looked like she was ready for a fight, or a round of kickboxing, not sure what.

"You okay?" I asked, feeling a strange tension between us.

"For some reason, I want to kick your ass," she confessed.

"That's not unusual, but I don't think I've done anything to warrant an ass-kicking."

"Only, you dressed me up like a sex toy." She put her hands on her hips and glared at me.

"Oh, that. Yeah, I did. It's only for the weekend; you'll be virtually forgotten tomorrow." Um, not what I should have said.

"I don't get you, Andre. You give me this great fun picnic, weird, but fun. I get to ride a million-dollar horse, you buy me beautiful clothes, and yet you keep treating me like a slut."

"Nothing wrong with being a slut." I give her a devilish smile.

"Only, I'm not one. Do I enjoy having sex with you? Yes. Do I do this every weekend with all of my new bosses? Nope, you are the one and only one. But I keep falling into these traps, and it makes me feel like shit." Ooh, I loved her chutzpah.

"Okay, so you want it laid out for you. I'm going to fuck you after dinner, then again sometime mid-evening and also probably before you leave in the morning. You can be assured that I'll have that ass in my hands and my cock straight up your pussy at least three more times. Between that, we'll eat and sleep." I gave her a sly grin. "You good with that agenda? I bought you a pretty dress so that I could strip it off of you. The only reason."

"Okay, so what stops me from going home right now?"

"You like fucking me." I smiled and shrugged. "I don't want you to leave. You don't really want to leave. You, too, want my cock in your pussy." I was being very crass and having a lot of fun doing it.

"I want to get to know you."

"You can only know me so much, and that's as far as you will get. The less time we spend talking, the less I'll have to throw you off course."

"Why can't we be friends?"

"I'm not friendly, so you want dinner or not? Or I can just fuck you on the couch and starve?"

"I'll take dinner before I have to take you." She laughed. "At least you know what a big gaping asshole you are," she said, full of snark as she hooked her arm in mine, and I led her to the dining area outside, elegantly lit with mood lighting and candles. Just before we sat down, she pulled out her phone and dialed a number.

Chapter 11

Eliza

I wanted to call Andre out on his shit. He was this man living all alone on his huge ranch with expensive horses and a lake and dozens of women at the ready, perhaps more or less than he let on, but he wasn't really living. I wanted to know him. At least get a piece of him before I had to go to work and just fantasize about him from afar.

I called Peyton because I wanted to talk to a human before being subjected to more of Andre. I felt like Andre couldn't exactly classify as a human at that moment, and I just wanted to hear another person's voice.

"Hey, Peyton," I said when she answered the phone.

"Hey, girl, what's up?" She was her bubbly cool girl self.

"Ugh, I missed the work bus, a loser as I said in my text, but I can't get a ride home until tomorrow," I started.

"I can come to get you if you want." She was so sweet.

"Thank you, you are so amazing, but I'm gonna crash with a co-worker. I'm good, I just wanted to give you a heads-up. I won't be back until Sunday." I kept my voice calm and sweet.

"Okay. Well, have a good weekend, and we'll see you soon. Let me know if you need a ride; it's totally no problem." It was good to have an understanding person in my world.

"Thanks, Peyton, I really appreciate that. See you soon." I ended the call and looked at Andre.

"Crashing with a co-worker?" His eyebrows raised.

"Would you have rather I said, fucking my boss?" I raised my eyebrows right back at him. "So, Ebenezer," I sat in his lap as soon as he took his seat at the table.

With him only wearing lounge pants and me sans underwear, I straddled his lap and ground down on him, feeling him harden under me. "What's for dinner?" It was hard to keep a straight face.

"You if you're not careful." His naughty little finger slid right up my skirt to the million-dollar prize.

I loved the feeling of his finger inside of me as I ground down on him a little before I kissed his lips and whispered in his ear. "You're not getting another piece of me, not one tiny little morsel unless you talk to me tonight and not about energy storage, as sexy as it is." I then licked his ear, and he shoved a second finger into me.

"So, you're pretending to be the boss tonight?"

"Yes."

"We're having lobster, herbed risotto, and field greens. For dessert, homemade lavender ice cream with vanilla cream puffs. Compliments of Jane, my private chef." He then leaned over and bit my bottom lip. "Then I'll be having you."

"Sounds perfect." I raised my eyes at him. "I'll sit in your lap, and you can feed me. I won't go anywhere, and you can stay hard all through dinner, but you have to answer my questions. Or we can just leave us at energy storage and global warming, and I'll sleep in a guest room. Alone." I moved closer to him and licked his top lip. "What do you say?"

"I say you're playing a dangerous game." His mood darkened a little.

"Have you killed anyone?" I leaned back, reached onto his plate, grabbed a lettuce leaf, and put it into my mouth.

"Not yet." He laughed as he took a fork and knife from the table, stabbed at the lobster tail, cut a piece, dunked it in butter, and brought it to my lips, running the hot butter along them before commanding me, "Open your mouth."

I did, and he slid the lobster in. It was so good I almost orgasmed on his lap.

"Can I play along?" His eyes narrowed into a sinister glare.

"It's always more fun that way." I smiled.

"How many men have you slept with?" he asked as if I hadn't slept with anyone before.

"Before you? One. Wait, one and a half." I smiled triumphantly after I chewed my bite.

"You?"

He smiled. "No men."

"Too bad. It would make you more exotic."

"I'm not exotic enough for you?"

"You're every billionaire in every romance book that ever had a horse and an open field on the cover," I dismissed.

"That pedestrian, am I?"

"Just your run-of-the-mill, mean ol' boss in a ten-gallon hat." Which he probably didn't even own.

"Did you want to marry the one and only other man you fucked?" He reached over and cut a piece of lobster for himself.

"Nope."

"Then why did you fuck him?" He put the lobster in his mouth as if it were the sexiest thing he'd ever eaten.

"He was there, I was there, I needed to rip off the V-tag, and it was college - what can I say. We did it, it was, um ... done. And we went our separate ways." I opened my mouth for more food.

"So, you're looking to get married, tie a man down, squirt out a couple of DNA projects, and move somewhere obscure?" Wow, he hated families.

"Hmm, well. Feed me, and I'll tell you." He cut me off another bite, dipped it in the risotto, and fed me a very precariously balanced bite. I talked while I chewed. "I want kids, yes, absolutely. I also want a partner to raise those kids with. I don't care if I'm married; I just want the guy to be my friend. And I hope we always have a fun sex life, so I'm taking notes; I might save a few of these ideas for the real deal. This lap dinner is high on the list."

For some reason, that hurt him a little. "You'd just recreate something we've shared?"

"If I had a real guy? You bet." I flashed him a careless smile. "Okay, my turn to ask a question. You like to throw your seed around a lot. Like you're flinging cum here, there, and everywhere. What if, and I know it's hard to think a dinosaur can, but what if you made a little munchkin? What would you do?" I knew I had him by the balls there.

He immediately threw me off his lap. "You are on birth control, aren't you? You're not trying to corner me into having a baby I don't want and would be legally forced to pay for?"

"Nope. I have an IUD; I can show you my 'Your Health Portal' that has all the info on it if you're worried. I don't dick around with people. If you knew me, you'd know that." I glared at him, took the plate we'd been eating from, sat across from him, and cut myself a big bite of lobster. I was starving.

"Okay. Sorry. I'd make her get an abortion." He grabbed the plate next to him and started on it.

"That's pretty monstrous."

"You get what you pay for. I don't dick around, either."

"What if she objected to it because of moral reasons?"

"I'm sure her morality could be bought."

"Wow, you know some crap women." I continued to eat.

"Why? Because they'd do as I asked and end the life of an unborn child?"

"It's their body; they'd have to decide what they would and wouldn't do with it. It's pretty awful that you think you would make that choice for them."

"I told you, you wouldn't like me very much if you really knew me." He shrugged his shoulders. "And I might add this little tête-à-tête was your idea. Bet you don't feel much like talking anymore or fucking for that matter."

"No, I do. I just don't feel like staying past tomorrow, so mission accomplished there. If we lived in an alternate universe, and you weren't an abortion-demanding sex-crazed Ebenezer, what kind of woman would you want? And I'm not implying that the woman is me or even remotely ever going to be me, just for clarification. But what would a woman have to do to win your heart?"

"Well, she'd only have to do one thing, find it. You ready to fuck now?"

"Sure, after the lavender ice cream. I've never eaten ice cream made of something I wanted to put in a vase or my bathtub before."

With that, I changed the subject resolving myself to the fact that Andre was a vacuous lost soul with a massive cock he used well enough to entice me to stay a few rounds before I said goodbye to it forever. He opened a freezer chest that was on the table and all of this vapor like you see in a Halloween yard display came billowing out. He pulled out two very cold, silver bowls and set one in front of me and he took the other. Next, he opened up a silver dome, and there were two huge puff pastries under it. He stabbed one and put it in my bowl, and he left the other one.

"I'm not a fan of the pastry, but the ice cream is probably something you'll want to slather all over your body."

I took one bite, and he was right; it was like sex on a spoon. "Geeze, how does your chef make everything taste so amazing?"

"Years of practice and five Michelin stars."

"Just to cook food for your ol' grouchy ass?"

"It's fun to have money. Only you'll never know."

"Nope." I popped another spoonful of heaven into my mouth. "I'm happy to just pretend."

"It can be more trouble than it's worth."

We finished the ice cream, and as I was still sore and getting a little sleepy from such a big day, I suggested we retreat to the bedroom. It never ceased to amaze me that his house had nothing but priceless pieces of art and very little else. The living room had one camel-colored leather couch, a massive television, a few odd-looking floor lamps, and a marble coffee table. Outside of that, there were massive paintings of women in various stages of undress, a landscape of his property, both at dawn and sunset. The art was glorious, but the rest of his place lacked personality. When we reached his room, he unceremoniously started to undress. I figured since we'd be naked anyway, I did the same.

"So, do you think I can say goodbye to Midnight before I leave tomorrow? I'm really going to miss him. I just want to touch his nose one more time."

"I don't see why not," was Andre's less than enthusiastic reply.

"Great." I looked at him, and his semi-hard cock wasn't as impressive as it was the first night. Perhaps he was tired of me already.

I had a few choices, ask for a quickie and a guest room, start to spar with him again as he was more fun when we were fighting, or take the opportunity to just show the poor rich, lonely, old man some love. The next week I'd just be a lowly intern with a helluva school workload. So, without ceremony or warning, I dipped to my knees and smoothed my hand over his tight stomach, and started to caress his body as a means of waking up the one-eyed monster.

"What's this?" he asked of my suddenly odd behavior.

"I'm going to pretend that you're a mild-mannered man with a regular well-paying job, who doesn't have any evil emotional baggage. I'm going to act like we bridged the whole age thing years ago with elegance and grace. We decided I'd raise the kids and have a work-from-home environmental ethics job, and you'd be the Lord of all things energy storage until you were too old to think anymore, and I'd dutifully change your diapers and made sure you drank your Ensure with vodka, and we'd live out our days as goofy old grandparents on a billion acres of land. You can play along if you like or not. Your mean-ass pussy pounding is actually quite delightful and makes me cum. Every. Single. Time. You animal."

With that, I popped his cock in my mouth so that neither of us would say any more. I loved the taste and feel of him, and so I concentrated on that. He raked his fingers through my hair and melted into the bed where he spread his legs for me, and I repositioned myself so that I was more comfortable giving him head on his stone floor. I worked my mouth up and down on him, though I wasn't so great at getting him down my throat, porn-style. I guess my fantasy wife didn't have a cavernous throat, so instead, I pumped him with my hands, intermittently fondled his balls, and sucked and played with his sensuous mushroom head, outlining the ridges and valleys with my tongue.

Whatever I was doing, he must have liked it because he hoisted me up to the bed and rolled me onto my back. "Someone is eager tonight."

"Lobster and indignant women make me horny." I loved the dark seduction in his tone.

He dove down and licked my lips too; that was weird but fun. Everything he did was weird and fun. To freak him out, or to take my fantasy to the next level, I wrapped my arms around his big broad shoulders, dove my tongue into his mouth, clamped my legs around his waist, and French kissed him like a teenager, all deep and passionate, like the world was ending. He actually laughed into my mouth.

"What are you doing?" he broke our kiss to ask.

"This is our last night together. I told you, I'm pretending we're in love. Come on - it's fun." I kissed his chin. "Make love to me. Make tons and oodles of babies inside of me." I humped his stomach with my legs spread to tease.

"Well, this is definitely your fantasy, not mine."

"Suit yourself. I'll play your fantasy if you play mine." I wasn't exactly sure what I was getting into, but the fantasy angle made sure that we weren't being ourselves. I had realized, as the weekend progressed, that I was pretty sure he was right about me not wanting to have anything to do with the real him.

"Fine." He held me at arms distance. "Call me Master."

I rolled my eyes. "Oh my God, seriously? Ugh. Master."

Chapter 12

Andre

I wasn't sure what game she was playing, but Eliza didn't seem the type to disrespect someone's wishes. The poor woman was just trying to have some fun with me before I sent her packing. I was feeling pangs of regret telling her that I didn't want to see more of her after the weekend, but I knew myself too well not to renege on my promise to myself. She'd hate me anyway, so I might as well just let her go. We'd fuck and play, and tomorrow, I'd say goodbye.

At that moment, she was licking the inside of my ear, making me crazy. My cock was harder than I had ever remembered it being, and so I ground down on her as she bit my earlobe. I knew when she wrapped her legs around my stomach that she was dripping wet for me already and I could get the first round out of the way just to ease my pain. Seeing her on the horse all day, swimming in the lake, lying on the beach together, it was lovely and intimate. Now I wanted her.

"On your hands and knees," I ordered, hoping she'd still play along with me.

She kissed my ear and wiggled underneath me, pulling herself out from under my body. "Yes, Master." She winked as she got on all fours and shook her ass in my face.

Not exactly the submission I was fantasizing about, but fun, nonetheless. I spread her ass cheeks open and used my fingers to check and see if she was as ready as I assumed she was, and sure enough, the basement was flooding.

"Now you're gonna take my cock!"

"Oh, yes, Master." The ridiculous way she said that made me laugh.

Wanting to dominate her so that I didn't have to want more than I could have of her, I grabbed my erection and slammed it into her, and to my surprise, she rose up from all fours and arched her body into my chest. My cock stayed lodged in her as her arms coursed upward and caressed my face as she slowly fucked herself on me in a sensual dance.

"Like this, Master?" she asked, withdrawing and impaling herself on me over and over again.

I used her position to wrap my arms around her and play with her breasts. As she was making this sensuous, I wanted rough unbridled passion, so I pinched her nipples so hard she screamed out, and her eyes watered. She then slammed herself back on me, knocking my balls backward as she grabbed my invading hands and tickled them off of her breasts.

"Master, you forget I'm your lover, not a two-penny whore you dragged out of the alley." She kissed one of my hands and placed it back on her breasts. "Be nice to your beautiful princess, Master …" she drew out the name with such mocking seduction, I became unglued and threw her forward.

"I'm going to fuck you!" I grunted as I literally mounted her, pounding and pressing in so deep I thought my own head would explode.

"Oh, God yes, Master, harder! Fuck me harder!" she yelled out as her teeth latched on to my arm and she bit me, hard.

"What the hell?" I stopped and pulled myself out of her to see the ring of teeth marks on my skin. "Eliza?" I looked at her in complete disbelief.

"You know. I was wondering, should I have a bath since my Vajayjay is still so sore from riding, or should I just ask for a room of my own so that my aching body might take a much-needed break. But as of tomorrow, I'll be gone, so I thought, I'll brave you, Andre Michelson. I'll go one more night with you as I love our sex, it's fun. I thought maybe I'll make love to you since it seems no one does. But what just happened here won't ever happen again." She grabbed the sheets off the bed. "We're done."

"And what exactly happened here?" I was confused, but in the back of my mind, I knew.

"You were hate fucking me. I don't know who broke you. I seriously don't, but I'm not here to pick up the pieces. I'm not your punching bag, your fuck toy, your slave, or even YOUR intern. And as of this moment, I'm no one to you. I need a place to sleep with a lock on the door." She stood there wearing nothing but a sheet, and for a moment, I was speechless.

I was too arrogant, too angry, and too horny to be a better man. "Fine," I yelled at her and walked naked to the doorway. I gestured down the hall. "Take your pick. Sleep in one of the guest rooms." I wanted to push her out into the hall but restrained myself.

I wasn't a monster. I just … she made me crazy. She went into the second room down, and like an obsessed maniac, I stood at the door and listened to her sob. She was right; I was definitely broken. After waiting until her anguished cries faded, I went back into my room. My cock had gone flat and there was no bringing life back to it. I ended up watching the international news in my living room until three in the morning when I finally felt tired enough to go to bed. At dawn three hours later, I woke up, answered emails, and made a pot of coffee. I had resolved myself to apologize to Eliza and give her the undergarments I had secretly bought for her as a truce. My plan was to fuck her silly so that she'd refuse the underclothes, but now they were sort of a peace offering.

At eight, when I thought it a decent time to approach, I knocked on her door. After not getting an answer for several minutes, I panicked and threw the door open only to find her gone and the bed made. She left. I just had to find a note or something to confirm it. I checked my phone to see if she'd texted me, and she hadn't. I ran to the kitchen and found my caretaker there.

"The woman who is staying here, have you seen her?" I tried not to sound desperate.

"She's in the barn," he said with a quiet curiosity. "What would you like me to fix you both something for breakfast?"

"Something light. Yogurt, granola ... bran muffins. I don't know." At the moment food was the last thing on earth I wanted.

I walked to the barn to find her in front of Midnight's stall. She was talking, so I hung back. Knowing exactly how creepy I was being didn't stop me from eavesdropping one bit.

"I hope your new home is a happy one. I can't imagine you get enough exercise and love here. I hope whoever buys you doesn't just use you to make money." The horse whinnied in response. "I love you." She kissed his nose. "And if you get the chance, please show Andre some love. He's so," she sighed. "He's so ... I don't know, deprived, I guess. Maybe someone can love him or be his friend? Who knows, the man is pretty hard to love. He gets close, then throws you off a cliff. Anyway, you deserve better. And I deserve better, I know."

The horse threw his head toward her in aggressive agreement. "And, Midnight," she added, "when you get the chance, tell him how rude it is to stalk someone and listen in on their private conversations with horses they can't afford." She put her head on Midnight's muzzle, and I knew I'd been caught. She turned to look at me.

"I'm sorry." There was so much more I wanted to say, but that was a good start.

"Can your driver take me home now?" She didn't look at me.

"You don't want to give me a chance to explain?" I tried.

"No." She still just connected with the horse.

"Okay. I'll have him take you home." With that, I turned and left her with my award-winning horse.

An hour later, she was gone. She didn't say anything when the driver came to take her away. I had a bag on the counter for her when she came back from the stables with some undergarments and a note.

I'm sorry things got out of hand - A

When I came out of my shower, the bag was gone, and so was she. The house felt big and empty. Jane was washing up the dishes, and I didn't even acknowledge she was there. I went to my home office and did as much work as I could stand, and then turned to internet-stalking Eliza. She had an impressively absent online footprint. She was listed as a former employee at her accounting firm, and she was also listed several times as a guest at Legende. She volunteered at the SPCA, she won an essay competition about environmental ethics in communities, and she liked to post cute quippy sayings with inspirational photos on Facebook. The rest of her life was private and would need a hacker to dig into it.

I considered texting her but figured the move would be too desperate. I looked at my watch, and it was only seventeen more hours until Monday, and I'd see her at work. I went over what I'd done wrong and couldn't find anything too over-the-top offensive except for I was a little rough and demeaning, and yet she was digging for a connection, and I was fighting tigers. In the end, that's what killed the weekend. What was my damage? Well, nothing really earth-shattering. I was just ignored most of my life. I was given way too much money too young, and I never knew if women were after my money or me. In truth, I liked being able to fuck who I pleased, and it was surprisingly cheap, considering I was able to extract women from the bowels of nightclubs, internship programs, and temporary assistant pools.

All I had to pay for was a night out, a bouquet of flowers, and perhaps a dress or two. Cheap compared to the alimony or child support I'd inevitably have to pay if I got into anything more long-lasting. I was happy being me and content with the people I fucked and tossed away. I fully expected Eliza to be just exactly that, a throwaway. I should have been thrilled it ended so cleanly. I did sort of hope for a few more rounds, but we fornicated a lot. My cock was actually pretty sore, so all a win, right? Except I missed her, and that pissed me off and made me hate her more.

    I watched a stupid movie, drank my expensive Scotch, got drunk actually, and went to bed. I didn't even make it to nine that night. I literally passed out drunk on the couch. It was a banner weekend.

Chapter 13

Eliza

I probably shouldn't have left the way I did. Perhaps I should have explained myself, but I was so pissed. I knew he was pushing me away, but I also knew it was just a weekend. We were playing house, having fun, then I realized I couldn't do it. I just couldn't pretend. When he wanted me to submit to him, it wasn't a game. He was grasping for control, and I hated it. Fine, if we were playing for the weekend, but what he was doing felt too real. There was a power dynamic involved, and he pulled the boss card. I had never had anyone hurt me. He didn't physically hurt me, but he sure was aiming for emotional annihilation.

When the car dropped me off at my new house, which I had hardly even seen, I smiled at him and waved a thank you. He didn't even open the door for me, so clearly, I was just one of Andre's women. I walked into the house and was immediately bombarded by my way too energetic roommates.

"Oh, my God, you're home," Peyton started. "I was just about to worry about you. But you did say you were with a coworker and you'd be home Sunday, and here you are. I can't believe they only have one bus for interns, like that sucks hard. And they lock the parking lot? What kind of monsters do you work for?" She was just chattering, but she had no idea how much of what she was saying was actually the truth.

"Pretty freaking monstrous, and it's too far away. I thought I was doing the right thing going with this company, but I think I've made a mistake. The university is too far in the wrong direction from the company, and it's going to be hard enough getting to school from here, so I'm gonna hit the old intern streets again looking for something else." I tried to keep it light.

"Wow, that really sucks. There aren't that many clean energy businesses around; I mean, it's mostly just wide open spaces, oil and cattle ranches, but good luck." Peyton's ignorant cheeriness was making me the slightest bit nauseous. "So, you didn't meet Genevieve when you were here last, so here she is!" Peyton said with a flourish of her arms in the air.

"Hi," I said awkwardly.

Genevieve was another incredibly beautiful young woman with flaming red hair, a killer body, and was like three stories taller than me. I didn't need to feel like shit, but just being near these two beauty queens had me feeling ugly and short. They sort of reminded me of Harper and Ophelia. Harper was foul-mouthed, gorgeous, and fun, and Ophelia was model beautiful with brains to match. I was always their sweet roommate. I was doe-eyed and sort of a girl-next-door type. Not ugly by any stretch, and I had a rocking hot body, but just a little plain. I could wear makeup and make my face into something amazing, but I was sort of against that.

Peyton and Genevieve were effortlessly beautiful and cool. Of course, I'd end up with two flawless roommates; it was like fate or God or whoever was in charge just hated me.

"Hey," Genevieve said. "Peyton told me that you were here. Sorry about getting stuck in Houston; what a drag. Hope you and your new intern buddy made the best of it."

"We sort of just binge-watched Netflix and ate too much pizza. It's nice to meet you. Are you guys busy tonight? Maybe we can all hang out. I've just barely unpacked, and I feel gross from the drive, so I might hit the shower, but we can all chill later?" I figured since I'd be living there, I should at least befriend the natives.

"Totally," Peyton jumped in all bounce and hyperactivity.

"Yeah, def. I have a gig tonight and you should come," Genevieve threw out there, and I was confronted with the idea of meeting a gaggle of her cool friends and feeling like a complete zero.

Who cares if I'd just fucked the richest man in Texas, it wasn't like he'd ever admit to it. I was just a weekend distraction.

"Sure, that sounds great. Listen. I know this is weird and stuff, but do either of you know a place where I can get my hair cut?"

I had shoulder-length, mousy brown hair, and suddenly I had the urge to shave it all off. Well, shaving would be a little drastic, especially in corporate America, but a little spiky haircut with some highlights would definitely up my confidence game.

"Oh, my God, you should go to my friend Josh. He's so fabulous, and he's literally within walking distance. He's just in beauty school right now, but seriously he can hook you up for nothing," Genevieve flung out like a person dealing crack behind a dumpster.

"Do you think he can take me today?" I needed a change, pronto.

"Sure, let me call him." And that was that.

I went to my room, took a shower, then lay down on my bed, and fell asleep, much to my surprise. I had wanted to get my room in order and settle in, but a nice nap escape from everything was more important. After I left Andre's bed, I went to his guest room and tossed and turned all night, waking up every hour. I was so stressed when the sun rose that I made my way to the stable to talk to Midnight. Believe it or not, the only male I fell in love with that weekend was the horse. By the time I left Andre's house, I didn't even like Andre anymore. Since I'd had such a weird weekend, I fell asleep pretty quickly after laying down. I almost had a heart attack when Genevieve knocked on my open bedroom door.

"I didn't want to wake you up, sorry," she started. "Josh has an opening in an hour, and I thought I should tell you. He doesn't usually work on Sundays, but since you're new in town and I told him you were looking for a change, he got excited and decided to take you today. You still up for a little makeover?"

After I wiped the sleep from my eyes, I was ready to go. I'd be a new me on Monday. I only hoped Andre would barely recognize me so that he'd leave me alone. No, it's not what I really wanted. I wanted him to regret treating me badly, and I hoped he'd ache for what he was missing. Either way, I was going to be a different Eliza. There was no going back.

And different was exactly what I got.

Josh was cute, super flamboyant and gay, friendly, with this fun southern drawl. "Okay, darlin', so are you gonna let me just play?" he asked, teasing his hands through my hair. "'Cause girl, you have such gorg hair, but it's long and heavy. We can lighten this up, go with a Tinkerbell vibe. Maybe get my boyfriend Crispin to give you a cute nose piercing? What do you say?"

Nose piercing? Oh, holy hell, if I was gonna go wild, then I wanted to go wild all the way.

"I'm all yours." I threw my arms up in the air, and that was it.

The sound of scissors slicing and nipping was most terrifying. I could hardly bear it, but Josh wouldn't let me look at myself until he was all through. He snipped and diced, colored and foiled, and blew dry and fluffed and primped, and then came Crispin the man with piercings in places that shouldn't have been pierced, and I almost passed out, but I made it past the nose piercing with just a little light-headedness and a quarter of a trash can of vomit. Not too bad, considering.

"Oh Jesus, Josh, she's gonna blow, get me the can!" Crispin screamed as he pulled the needle out of my nose. I was able to hold in the puke just long enough for him to finish putting in the piecing before I was blowing chunks.

It was a very intense experience. After a nice refreshing swill of mouthwash and a deep breath, I was turned around in my chair to reveal the most beautiful woman I'd ever seen. Granted she was really edgy and just a little too much for the office, but damn she was beautiful.

"You look like a completely new person. Not that you needed to look like a new person," Josh backtracked.

"No, I did. Wow, this is amazing. I look amazing." I got up and hugged both of them hard. "I can't believe this is me!" I was so happy my face hurt from smiling too much.

"Okay, now that you're a goddess, let's go out with the girls for drinks," Josh suggested, and I was down.

My roommates, Josh, Crispin, and I all went out to a local bar, which couldn't have been a bigger dive. There were dart games on the wall, stale whiskey, beer, and cigarette smell in the air, a jukebox like you'd see on TV, several patrons without teeth, and some very hairy looking women. Some of the women looked tougher than the men in some cases, and I guessed it wouldn't matter if they shaved or didn't; their pussies would probably rip a man's dick clean off. The other hairy women were the ones with hair piled high on their heads, plastered there with copious amounts of Aqua Net or another flammable shellac that kept their hair pumped up.

The place looked like it got stuck in the seventies and never made it out. We drank, we danced, we played darts, and it was crazy fun. Way more fun than I'd had in a while. I did think of Andre a few hundred times and thought perhaps I'd bring him to a dive like that just to tame his ego, but again, I'd never really 'see' him again, so who cared? When I got home, I was tired, drunk, and still looking fabulous. I said goodnight to my roomies and thanked them for an amazing time, and I probably kissed Josh and his boyfriend a million times, telling them they changed my life. It was undoubtedly all too much, but we were in Texas; it was go big or go home. Since I had no desire to go back to DC, I did Texas big.

The next morning when the alarm went off, I was hating life, but I managed to drag myself out of bed, dress appropriately for work, restyle my hair, and put alcohol on my nose piercing before catching an Uber to the intern headquarters. I visited my shitty car to make sure everything was there and hopped on the intern shuttle bus on time. It was nothing short of a miracle. When I paraded with the rest of the interns into the office, Andre didn't even notice me. Score one point for me.

I found my way to my bare little cubicle and started in on my first boring intern task, data entry for Bill. Carl and I were assigned to imputing addresses in the new office database software system, be still my beating heart. I had to get three coffees by noon just to stay awake, and also to sort of sober up. The place was deathly silent as no one dared talk since Andre's door had been open all morning. Once he came out and looked around, and I ducked my head down, hoping not to be detected. An hour before lunch, he charged out and made a beeline straight for my cube.

"Where's the girl who sat here last week?" he asked in the voice of Satan as I kept my head tucked down.

"I'm the girl who sat here last week." I looked up at him and made eye contact for the first time all day, and did all I could not to glare.

He finally recognized me as soon as we were face to face. The look of shock that registered was fun.

"You're moving cubes," he announced like a complete and total dickwad. "You're Bill's intern, so you need to be on his floor."

"Great!" I flashed a big smile and gathered up my meager belongings.

Bill's office was down one level, and I was actually thrilled to be out of Andre's line of sight. Being away from him would help me shake this stupid chemical attraction that was searing my nerves. Even with him standing there ten feet from me, my blood raced. I wanted to kiss his lips again, I wanted him inside of me. Even though ninety-nine point ninety-nine percent of him was a heinous asshole, that tiny fraction left was someone I could actually care about. As crazy as it seemed, there was something good buried deep down inside of him. Getting the hell out of dodge or at least on to the fifteenth floor was the best course of action.

"Check in with me at lunch," he added as I was walking away.

"Why?" I said as I left him.

Chapter 14

Andre

Fuck fuck fuck fuck fuck. That woman drove me wild. What the hell did she do to her hair? And a nose piercing. I so wanted to toss her over the desk in that cubical and fuck her silly for having the audacity to be even sexier than when I'd left her. The damn woman plagued me all of Sunday after having left early in the morning completely decimated by me. I had plans to leave her with a sweet memory of raw unbridled sex, and instead, I got a sleepless night alone on the couch grappling with the fact that my need to dominate her had actually driven her away.

When I met her, she was a fresh-faced girl wearing too much makeup for her night out where she had drunk enough to make her tipsy and fun. When she showed up in Texas, I thought here was my chance to explore more of that sweet angelic woman; instead, I found a tough gal who could go toe to toe with me, and it not only vexed me but also set me on fire. I thought I could eat her alive, and what was I doing? Picking up the pieces she left in the wake of her hurried departure. Then I come into the office expecting to see her be all sweetness, licking her wounds and avoiding eye contact, and instead, I'm confronted with a vixen with her mind set on revenge sitting where Eliza should have been.

Who gave her permission to cut and dye her hair? And that nose ring? Ugh, If I hadn't already decided to give her to Bill, I would have had her working exclusively for me, in my office, away from anyone who could touch her. I had to reel in my thoughts and get a solid game plan going. I needed her to spy on Bill for me and tempt him sexually, so that I could get intel on what he was really doing with my company.

I'd heard reports that the oil drilling operation he was running was actually a fracking operation in one or more of our oil drilling locations. Fracking, the hydraulic fracturing of soil to extract fossil fuels was not illegal in Texas, however, our company promised our investors and those who did business with us that we would not use fracking as a means of oil extraction. Since the increase in earthquakes in Texas could be attributed to fracking, I mandated that we wouldn't be using any production method that put lives, businesses, and communities at risk.

Bill promised me he had switched over all of our operations. Though it was a huge and costly move, it was one I felt necessary to take. Also, it made our oil operations that much more difficult to secure and thus the push to our move toward clean energy. I may have been a complete shit to people, but I believed in the future and preserving our environment. We had a scare in a small town near the Mexican border where we had started a series of new wells. They experienced a devastating earthquake that brought homes and businesses to the ground. Luckily, there were no fatal injuries. However, we were just starting our oil operation in the town, and with the land already vulnerable, I made sure that Bill used a different method of oil extraction in that and the surrounding towns. He gave me his word that he had made sure there was no fracking in the small town. The paperwork he submitted to me on the surface looked like he complied, but there were a few sketchy details.

Eliza was the kind of woman that Bill would drool over, even more so with that sexy new hairstyle. I was setting her up as bait, but I fully planned to make it up to her financially. I instantly regretted my decision as I looked over and saw her little cubicle was empty. I wasn't making the best choices. I had to admit to myself I had feelings for Eliza, or they were going to eat me alive. I could hardly focus on work. Since there was a big intern luncheon scheduled for that afternoon, I decided to text her to 'remind' her because I was still technically her boss.

Today is the intern luncheon @ 1:30 large conference room.

I waited for her reply and got nothing. I tried to focus on other work and started to really kick myself for sending her downstairs. It was going to be torture not being able to see her during the day. It would also have been torture if I had to look at her all day, so it was a no-win either way for me. At noon, I still hadn't gotten a response. So, I emailed her on our work email, reminding her again.

Intern Luncheon @ 1:30 large conference room — attendance is mandatory.

The little troll still didn't respond. At one o'clock, I was on edge.

Please confirm attendance for the Intern Luncheon! - A.

I waited another fifteen minutes, and I was about to go downstairs when I got a text.

Confirmed

When I saw her walk in with the other interns, my blood was molten lava in my veins. She was smiling and talking with several of the interns, which infuriated me. She could go home with any one of them, and that made me even crazier. I didn't want her to be a free agent, I realized. I wanted to control her. Perhaps I didn't want to keep her or start anything serious, but I certainly didn't want her to start anything serious with someone else.

Why did you cut your hair? - A

I texted, unable to stop myself.

It needed a trim. - E

That is NOT a trim! - A

She was texting me back from inside the conference room where the interns were gathered around a spread of sandwiches and soda. It was pretty abysmal, but of course, I was the one paying for it; I never wanted to spend too much. It would be strange if I approached her right away; we were supposed to welcome them, spend about three minutes with each one, and go back to our offices.

The head of HR announced as the executives entered the room, "On behalf of Michelson Energy Corp, I'd like to welcome you all to our fall internship program. We have an exciting three months ahead of us, and I am thrilled that you are all here. You were hand-selected by me, and so I know that you are the best of the best. Maybe some of you will come back to us after graduating from your programs or will stay on with us part-time. Whatever your journey, we are excited about spending the next few months with you. Enjoy some refreshments and mingle. Everyone is wearing a tag with their name and department on it, so feel free to ask questions and let that curiosity fly."

I actually forgot to put on my name tag, so I went to the table as the interns awkwardly dispersed and put it on, dreading having to speak to anyone but Eliza. However, she had flitted her ass over to Hillary in accounting with another of the nameless, faceless drones. I grabbed a soda so that my hands had something to do and drifted over in their direction.

"Yes, so the accounting for such a large corporation is pretty intense, considering we have project budgets, marketing budgets, and production and sales to consider, however, I've been in the department so long I could recite the codes in my sleep." Hillary laughed, and Eliza joined right in with her like some kind of solidarity sister.

"Ah, the ever so exciting world of balancing the books," I chimed in to find Eliza wiping a glare from her face.

That was a fun moment.

"Oh," Hillary sounded disappointed, but she mostly hated me, so why would she not?

"This is Andre Michelson, the CEO of Michelson Energy Corp. If anyone knows about how costly it is to run a company, it would be this man here."

"Oh, I'm sure a bean counter would have a pretty good guess." I laughed, pretending it was a joke.

The man that Eliza was with was fumble-mouthed. "It's so nice to meet you, Mr. Michelson; what a wonderful company you have here. I'm hoping to get into energy engineering in the future …" Blah, blah, blah, I blocked him out to stare at Eliza, who wasn't looking at me, but rather through me.

"And you?" I asked as soon as the man was done droning. "What's your expertise?" I loved watching her squirm.

"Bean counting," she said with a devilish smile.

I needed to toss her over my lap and spank the hell out of her.

"I didn't think we hired any accounting interns."

"Yes, we hired three," Hillary said with her usual pained expression.

"And are you one of them?" My gaze drilled into Eliza.

"Nope. Oh wait, is that Bill Blascoe? You'll have to excuse me. I'm his intern, and I haven't even had the chance to say 'hi.' Enjoy lunch."

"Hi, Bill," I heard her say as she walked away from me. "I'm Eliza. I'm your personal intern as of just a few hours ago. I thought I'd introduce myself." She confidently thrust her hand out to him, and he took it as he oozed over her good looks. It didn't help that she was wearing a skirt that was nearly inappropriate for work, which made her legs look like works of art. Her breasts weren't half bad in her blouse, either.

"Well, hello." Bill was all smarm. "I didn't realize I was getting a personal intern, how wonderful." His face oozed insincerity.

"I guess I'll be at your beck and call," she said. "So nice to meet you. I'm actually going to go back and hit the desk to work on this database project and get it out of the way before you set me on something else." I could have kissed that plastic smile right off her face.

"Well, fine. I'll see you later then." They shook hands again, and she parted.

I was tempted to follow her but decided to let her stew for a little while. Make her think that she'd successfully escaped me. I breezed past a few more interns and made sure I talked to enough of them not to get in trouble with HR and then returned to my office. I waited until the end of the day to text Eliza, but I knew better than to wait until closing. I didn't want to leave her stranded again. Though I would have taken her home gladly, I was pretty sure she wouldn't want to go with me, not at that point.

I need to see you in my office. - A.
I'm going home. Whatever it is, it will have to wait until tomorrow. - E.
We don't close the office until 5:30. - A.
It's 5:24.

Damn, my conference call had lasted longer than I expected it to. I would just have to wait until the next day. I let her leave without incident, but when I got home, all I could do was stew and think of her.

We need to talk. - A.

I finally texted her around ten o'clock that night and got no response back. I waited until midnight, and then I was pissed. I couldn't wait until the next day to grab her and make her sit and listen to me. The only problem was, I didn't exactly know what I wanted to say.

Chapter 15

Eliza

We have to talk - A.
I stared at that text for an hour, then replied.
No, we don't - E. and I erased it.
I have nothing to say to you. - E. Erased.
Fuck off! Deleted.
Why can't you be normal? Ugh ... delete, delete, delete.

I just decided to go to bed and turn my phone off. I didn't have the strength to resist him, so I just made myself ignore him, though I dreaded what he'd say to me in the morning. At least it would be in his office, in a public place, where he couldn't do anything awful. The next morning, I commuted to work on the intern transport. The following week I'd have to drive without taking the intern bus, which was kind of a relief and a curse as I wouldn't have an excuse to go home. Also, the following week, I'd only be in the office for three days as I started my classes at grad school and would need two full days on campus. I was really looking forward to that. In fact, those two days were going to be my lifesavers, as I could tell Andre was going to be a serious challenge to my mental health.

When I walked into the office with the rest of the interns, I expected Andre to be in his office, not caring about us, but to my great shock, he was at the coffee maker making coffee I wasn't even really sure he drank.

"Ah, Eliza," he said casually, turning around as I put my lunch in the fridge. "May I have a word with you in my office?"

Fuck, fuck, fuck, fuck.

"Sure." I smiled and waited for him to swirl sugar into his coffee.

When he was done, I followed behind him wordlessly as we walked toward his office. He shut the door, and I stood there, not sure if I should sit down or just stand.

"Do you think you're cute not responding to my texts?" he started.

"What do you want me to say? Are you bullying me? Torturing me? Trying to make me feel like shit? I don't know why you would be texting me. Aren't we done? I thought this was just a weekend, right? I mean nothing to you. I'm just a fun pussy." I glared at him. "I mean if you didn't get enough, I'm so sorry, but after this weekend, I realized I have to be something more than a casual fuck. It's not my style, and my intern salary isn't enough to include cock sucking, so—"

I didn't even see him coming, but just as I was about to take a breath to say more, his mouth was on mine, and his tongue was spearing my face with such passion I was seriously confused. I wanted to melt into him, but I couldn't, my fight was too strong.

"What the hell?" I asked, pushing him away.

"You make me crazy," he said breathlessly.

"Well, tough titties for you!" I stood my ground. "You don't own me."

"Clearly, or you would have never cut your hair," he scoffed.

"So, you don't like my hair. I don't care. I like it." I took a deep breath, ready to throw anything within reach at him.

"I didn't say I didn't like it. I said you would never have cut it without my permission."

"Since when do I need your permission? And here's a news flash: even if I were your wife, which would never happen even if you were the last man on earth, I still wouldn't need your permission to cut my own hair. Now, if you don't mind, I need to get to my desk. I have a project due in an hour." I was so ready to be done with him.

"I have something I need to discuss with you." He suddenly was somber.

"Well, it will have to wait until lunch. I don't want to look like a slacker my first week on the job." I turned to leave his office, hoping he'd let me go.

"Fine, meet me here for lunch. Indian food fine with you?" He was serious.

"I brought a sandwich." I was just being contrary; Indian food was fine.

"Fine," he conceded, what a surprise.

"Fine." With that, I left his office feeling tingles of need, pricks of anger, and the overwhelming desire to cry, which I didn't do, thank God.

When I arrived at my desk, I was met with three emails reminding me that the datasheet I'd been working on was due. I banged it out as quickly as I could and turned it in with forty-two seconds to spare. At that moment, Bill, probably the slimiest man I'd ever met, oozed up to my desk.

"So, you're my new intern?" he asked as if he'd just paid me two hundred dollars for a blow job.

"That's me, new meat." Whoops, that was the wrong thing to say.

"I'll say."

What? Yuck.

"So, I just finished your data project for HR; now, I'm all yours. What do you have for me, boss?" I kept my voice light and airy so as not to bring on any unwanted smarm.

"I want you to come into my office and rearrange the files."

Oh great, he was one of those.

"Sure, any particular order you want them rearranged into?" I asked, trying to sound like I didn't know exactly what he was doing. At least it would be mindless work; I wouldn't have to focus on much.

"I just want you to pull all the files that are older than 2001. Anything that is before that box up and label."

Seemed easy and mindless and would take a few days. Since I was wearing a short skirt I hoped to tempt Andre by wearing, I chose the upper files first, so I didn't have to bend over. It didn't stop Bill from staring at my ass, and at one point, he even stopped me.

"Why don't you start at the bottom?" he casually suggested.

"With Z?" I gave him a look like he was insane. "Um, that's funny." I laughed like an idiot and went back to work.

I think he was trying to figure out a way to make me bend over, but luckily, he wasn't smart enough to make anything up on the spot. I even took my rebellion one step further, pulled the file drawer out, and took it to my cube.

"What are you doing?" he asked.

"Oh, taking this to my desk so I can sit down and really dive in. There are a lot of files here." I gave him an exasperated face.

"I'd rather not have sensitive information out in your cubicle," he said, sounding very nervous.

"Wow, okay. Sorry. Where would you like me to go?" I was feeling cornered.

"Bring your chair into my office."

Great.

So, I pulled my chair into his office and set the box down on the table. I figured he'd just have me move so he could look at me if I sat with my back to him, so I sat catty-corner, not exactly with my whole back to him, but most of it. I spread out the files to look like I was hard at work, and he took a breath as if he would say something but didn't in the end, which suited me fine. We were sitting there in awkward silence, so I just started mindlessly looking through dates, happy to have mind-numbing work that didn't put me in too much jeopardy. I was actually so lost in the endless monotony I didn't realize that it was lunchtime until Bill interrupted me.

"Well, I'm headed out for a lunch meeting." He stood up. "So, we can reconvene later. I have plans today, but perhaps we can have a working lunch tomorrow." He leered at me.

Ugh.

"Um, sure, I mean if you're willing to pay overtime." No way was I going to get in the habit of 'working lunches.' Not for a creep like him.

"Hmm. We'll see, but I don't think interns get overtime."

"Oh. Well, okay, then I'm not sure interns do working lunches." I gave him a big toothy grin and giggled to throw him off.

"We'll see," was all he said as he shut the door.

Just as soon as I heard the click, my phone blew up.

Where are you?

Andre had texted me.

Coming.

I replied.

Be here now.

Great, he was in that kind of mood. I just ignored it as I rode the elevator up with Bill.

"What was that?" he had the audacity to ask.

"Um, a friend." I gave him another ambiguous smile.

"You can't take personal calls at work."

"Well, it happens to be work-related, so I'm golden. And are you sure I can't take calls during my lunch hour? I'm gonna have to check with HR on that. I mean, you would know, you're a big wig around here. But just in case, I'll get to the bottom of the whole overtime, lunchtime, phone time debacle. I mean, I am brand spanking new, what do I know?" I was so mind fucking him.

"No, bother, just don't let it interfere with your work."

The elevator dinged on Andre's floor, and Bill watched me get out of the car and head straight for Andre's office. I could feel Bill's beady eyes on me as the doors closed. I knocked on Andre's door, which he opened for me, looking ... expectant? Not sure what the look was exactly.

"Ugh, Bill's a scumbag." I plopped down on his couch.

"I thought I told you that," he blew out.

"Why don't you fire him?" I was seriously curious.

"We started the company together; it's not that easy. But you can help me get enough information to have him removed from the company."

"If you started the company together, why isn't his name in the title?" Why would a monster like him pass up the chance to have his ego stroked with a name on the header?

"I used my inheritance and invested my own money into this company, so I got the name. He got a lot of other perks that skirt the line of legality. So, you're not impressed with him?" He seemed almost giddy about that.

"Yuck, why would I be? You can see his kind of sleaze coming from a mile away. You must really hate me saddling me with that jerk." I shook my head. "And speaking of jerks, why am I here?"

He flourished his hand over several pristine white bags with the name Mahal Indian Cuisine scrolled on them.

"Peace offering." He faked a smile.

"Hmm, the way to a girl's heart is a good chicken Tikka Masala, but why?"

"Because I have a favor to ask you."

"Oh." I know my face fell, but he was so unpredictable, I was getting whiplash. I had to stick to my mantra: I don't care. I don't care. I don't care. I needed to stop wanting him. He was bad for every single cell in my body.

He smiled to himself as if he was having a good chuckle at my disappointment.

"I need you to do a bit of spying for me. I think Bill is engaging in activities that we don't condone here. About two years ago, I banned fracking, which is the hydraulic drilling of oil using pressurized water under the earth's surface."

"Thanks, I know what fracking is," I said with a smirk.

"Well, we banned it at the company going for a next-level approach to the energy business. We told our customers we were going green and that our old school oil operations would continue until the wells dried up, then we'd be going one hundred percent green. Well, two years ago, some dying oil wells near the Mexican border suddenly started producing a ton of oil on Bill's watch. The upside, we brought in a lot of money. The downside?

There have been and continue to be earthquakes in the economically depressed town that are ruining the infrastructure and have caused a lot of damage to homes of people who can barely afford their mortgages let alone damage done by earthquakes. Yes, they are getting assistance, but not enough. If these earthquakes can be linked to fracking, our business can be rightfully sued.

"Now, Bill promised me that we weren't using these techniques and the earthquakes couldn't be linked to us, but I recently found files on a shared drive with his business associate that indicate he's set up a secret operation using our funding and our contacts, to open new sites using fracking near old ones that are no longer producing. I've been out to the sites, and the wells are not ours. They belong to a company called Fasco and yet, I believe Fasco is only a facade for a part of the business Bill has been not only siphoning funds into but building a business on, making money, and going against our mandate. He put money into this company and has been paid back four times over, yet he's not allowed to go rogue.

"If he did, he'd have to set up an entirely unrelated company that wasn't our direct competitor per our contract. So, in short, I think he's using Michelson Energy Corp money to run fracking operations in poor border towns where he can get cheap labor and make minimal payouts so that he pockets the surplus. He's violating an agreement we made with the state to be a clean energy company. If we are found, we could be sued. We promised we would not use fracking technology or any energy collection method that would compromise the environment. Our entire draw is that we're cutting edge green. So, I assigned you to work with him so that you can suss out this illegal operation. He may not have the files in his office. Most likely, he doesn't, so you're going to have to get really close to him, personally …"

"No! Oh no, hell no. No way. Uh-uh. NO!" I stood up and was just about to walk out.

"In return, we'll explore our relationship." I stopped only for a moment.

"We don't have a relationship," I countered.

"Yes, but we do, we just aren't admitting it."

"No, you either like me, or you don't. You can't hold my spying on your friend as collateral."

"It might show me how willing you are to elevate us to the next level."

"No. Again, we are not in a relationship because of you, not me. I'd be down to 'explore' what we have if it were real. If you were with me the way you were at your lake. Not the dominant Christian Grey wannabe you were in bed. Yes, a little dominance is fun, you're surely the alpha type, but I'm not less than you. Money is nothing. It comes and goes. Humanity, love, compassion, caring, communication, those are the riches you lack, my friend. Getting into a relationship with you is a death wish. It's no prize, trust me."

Chapter 16

Andre

Ouch.

"Then why do it?"

"I'm not doing it. I'm outta here." She turned to leave.

"Wait." I took a deep breath. "We both know why you'd stay."

"Do we?" She stood there and challenged me.

I could have just said it, and I probably wouldn't have gotten any protest, but what fun was words alone? My office had windows that I could easily blackout with the press of a button. I reached behind me to the desk, picked up my phone, and pressed the app that controlled the windows. In one press of a button, they went from smokey gray to black, and the door locked. No one would be disturbing us. We had just one hour for me to convince her I was worth spying on my partner for.

"You know exactly why." I stepped toward her, and she reared her head back while still sitting on the couch.

I didn't care, I leaned in and kissed her. I knew as soon as I started making love to her, she wouldn't fight me. I loved the taste of her as I dove my tongue into her mouth. I sat next to her and gathered her up into my arms. I never broke our kiss, just swung her legs into my lap. Convenient for both of us that she was wearing a skirt just shorter than company regulations would have allowed. It was very easy to access her pussy with my greedy finger after nudging it under her silk panties' elastic. I dipped my tongue in deeper to mirror the dive of my finger as it became saturated with her wetness.

"So eager for me," I breathed into her mouth.

I pulled my finger away to show her the evidence of her arousal, and she rolled her eyes.

"You could probably sex up a nun if you tried; it doesn't prove anything." Oh, I loved her defiant obstinate attitude.

"Really," I said as I massaged her breast over her blouse, pinching her tit as soon as it peaked. "You could just walk out of here right now." I made sure to press my erection into her ass.

She struggled to get up from my lap, but I held her tightly. "If you let me go, I could." She wiggled and writhed.

"Try to get away then," I clamped my arms around her.

"What game are you playing?" she asked after unsuccessfully trying to extract herself from me.

"The only way out of my arms is to have sex with me," I kissed her damp forehead, perspiring from the effort to leave my lap.

She relaxed her body. "If I asked you to let me go, would you?" She was very serious, and it worried me a little.

"Of course." I let her go. "I thought you liked a little bit of struggle. You are free to leave if that's what you truly want."

"What do *you* truly want?" She righted her clothes and looked deep into my eyes.

"Trouble is, before you, I thought I knew. I don't want anything long term, but you challenge me in a way. I want to be provoked. I want more than a weekend." That was all the confession I planned to give.

"And so, you're willing to risk your reputation and mine by having a nooner in your office?"

"It's been almost three days, I think a nooner is very reasonable at this point. You aren't coming home with me tonight, and I sure as hell am not waiting for the weekend to get a piece of you, so lay back on this couch, and let's get this done before we run out of time. I had the couch custom made for this very thing." I gave her a wide smarmy grin.

"You know that's disgusting right?" She was teasing, thank God.

"Let's fuck and then gorge ourselves on Tikka Masala. We can debate my need for an extra deep couch after I've had you on it." I stroked my cock feeling its uncomfortable hardness.

"I really should walk out of here …" I think she was saying that more to herself than to me.

"Name one redeemable quality I have and convince yourself to stay." I unbuttoned my trousers, hoping the sight of what she was doing to me would entice her.

"You're broken." She looked right at me.

"You can't fix me. Name something else." I slid my zipper down and pulled my aching cock out.

"You're a mystery?" She was grasping.

"Come on, it's okay to say it. Just say what is really on your mind." I stoked myself as I approached her again.

"The sex is phenomenal." She sighed in exasperation.

"Fuck, yes, it is. Now lay back and spread your legs. We haven't got much time." As much as she hated me for being right, she knew she was with me for the sex, and so she laid back on my extra deep couch and spread those incredible legs. I put my hand back on her pussy, and she was already dripping. I kissed her lips as I spoke. "You like me more than you want to admit."

She grabbed my face and brought me into her for a kiss. Her mouth passionately entrapped mine as she lapped at my tongue. Her legs lifted in the air and coiled around my body and then cinched around my waist hard, toppling me down to her. I wasn't expecting that and she caught me off guard. There I was with my stiff cock out, tumbling over her body. She wanted power; that was clear.

"What are your terms?" I finally broke from her to ask as I spread her legs under me and moved her panties aside, ready to fuck.

"Treat me like an equal!" she demanded. "You might be older than Egyptian relics, but we are still both consenting adults. I'm not under you - I am beside you." I loved the fierce look of conviction on her face.

"Well, at the moment …" I had to tease.

"I mean it, Andre! I won't make love to you until you acknowledge my worth. I'm not asking you for forever; I'm telling you to respect me." She propped herself up on her elbows just as I'd slid into her wonderful pussy.

I was so far gone at that point I would have clucked like a chicken.

"Yes, okay. You are my equal." That was hard to say, but did I mean it? Truly, I did, and I even surprised myself acknowledging that. "You can stand toe to toe with me, but don't think you can run me over."

"It's love, not a demolition derby," she said softly as she spread her legs wider for my cock and laid back down.

I wanted to come back and debate the word 'love,' but love had many dimensions. It didn't have to be an all-consuming love of my life. I could still love her and not lose myself to her. So, in the interest of a good office nooner, I gave in.

"Yes, you're right." I stilled my slow slide in and out of her only for a moment as I unbuttoned her blouse and popped her tits out of her bra.

I had to have a taste of them as I'd been thinking of them all morning. I didn't want to talk anymore, I just wanted to savor her. I sucked hard on each nipple, loving the taste of soap and skin cream. God, she was so delicious in more ways than I could think. She had me twisted. I hated how much I wanted her as I hooked my arms around her shoulders, and encumbered by my suit coat but too riled to take it off, I started drilling her hard and deep. This got me a little moan that escaped her involuntarily, which fired me up more as I laid all my weight on her and pistoned into her heaven. To make more room for me, she lifted her legs up as her skirt shimmied to her hips. With her vagina's clench and her first orgasm that afternoon, my balls tightened. I wasn't going to last long.

"Oh, my God," she gritted out as she rode the tide of her ecstasy. "We shouldn't be doing this at work."

"Fuck that; I'm the boss. I can have you anywhere I want you." I'm sure she wouldn't mind that bit of dominance because at that moment, all I wanted to do was own her, especially her smart little mouth.

I pumped her harder, chasing my own release as I slid my hand between us and poked my finger at her rock hard clit. I pummeled that while I fucked her deep and fast, and she bit the lapel of my jacket, squeezing around me again, and this time she jerked and shuddered so hard she shook. That was all I needed. I came in her so ferociously I was seeing stars. I actually had to close my eyes and breathe before I dared to move. I collapsed on top of her as her body heaved to suck in air.

"You weigh as much as a mac truck." She wiggled under me, and I came to my senses.

"God, that was good," I praised as I slowly pulled out of her warm tight heaven. "You are so damn strong and tight." I slapped her thigh.

"Well, I don't get railroaded by Thomas the Train that often, so my lady parts are nice and fit." She cupped her sex feeling my cum. "Do you have a towel or something? I'm a mess, and I'm sure I smell like your cologne. How exactly am I going to explain this to Bill?" She suddenly seemed pretty worried.

"I've got it all under control." I kissed her as I sat up and continued just to enjoy the swirl of euphoria around me.

She sat up as well and brought her skirt back down, trying to make herself presentable again. "Geez, Andre, you'd think you'd hadn't had sex in years." She leaned her head back and looked up at the ceiling. "That was intense."

"Good intense, right?" I asked as I came over with a box of Chicken Tikka Masala. I scooped a spoonful and held it to her mouth. "Open up."

"You aren't going to …" before she said more, I scooped the bite into her mouth. She chewed then finished her sentence. "… feed me, are you?"

I kissed her again. "I might." I laughed before I scooped another bite for her.

"You might want to put droopy away first."

My cock was still out, and while not exactly droopy, it was sagging. With minimal effort, I could go another round with her, which was exactly what I had planned to do.

"Just letting him get some air." I took the spoon and slid the greasy, delicious curry over her bottom lip, not letting her take a bite before I licked it off.

She nipped at the spoon, and I slipped it into my mouth before she could get to it.

"Can we just eat like people?" The earnest way she looked at me was sweet. "And he needs to go back home." She leaned forward, tucked my cock back into my trousers, and zipped me back up. It was actually really sexy. "In case someone comes in. Also, I need a napkin or something, please. I don't want to be that intern who's fucking the boss."

She stood up, grabbed a napkin to pat herself with, then took a spoon from the bag, and brought it over with two slices of Naan. "This is fun, though," She dipped the bread into the Masala and spread it on my lips, then licked it off just as sensuously as I had, but bit my bottom lip upon her retreat. "I'm actually pretty hungry, though, so if we're going to use each other as plates and utensils, we need to focus." She dipped her bread in the curry and took a big bite. "Indian food was a good call."

Chapter 17

Eliza

He had me all twisted. I wanted to hold my own and not get seduced into office sex, but it was hard to resist him.

"What are we doing?" I asked, eating the delicious Indian food. I only had an hour to eat, and I was actually starving, so I wanted to eat. I set everything from the takeout bag on the table and tried to act like a civilized human being.

"We're having lunch," was Andre's quippy comeback. He still hadn't moved from his place on the couch he claimed was custom made for office sex.

"Yes, obviously. But us. It's dangerous having sex in your office." I chided him like a mother might.

"But fun." He threw a flirty smile back at me.

"You need to leave me alone."

His flirty smile slid into a smirk. "Says the woman who couldn't get her legs open fast enough."

"Yes, I like having sex with you, but as I said, I don't really do this. I don't just sleep with the boss and certainly not in his office, so I'm going to ask you to make a commitment here. If you want me at your beck and call, especially where office sex is concerned, I need to know that I'm something more than just a fun time. If I'm just a way for you to get off, I'll buy you some toys you can play with at lunch. If I'm a human being you'd actually like to get to know as a person, mind you, I didn't say marry, just perhaps befriend, then I'll consider a sexual relationship. But it will have to include dates and romantic things, not just knocking uglies on your office 'fuck couch'." I was trembling a little inside, standing up for myself against a powerful man, but he wasn't going away, so I wanted him on my terms.

"Friends? Hmm, that's a tall order, Ms. Pickle. You've asked me to be your friend before, and that didn't go so well." He pretended to be pondering the thought.

"Or enemies and I walk out of here right now. I'm good either way." I glared.

"Are you, though?" He reached out and touched my hand. "I don't think either of us is that 'good' without each other right now. So, okay. A few dinners, some conversation, and a lot of sex, that I can commit to." His smile was finally genuine.

I leaned over and kissed his cheek. "Thank you." I then began eating as I watched my lunch hour diminish.

"So, Bill has me 'filing'." I rolled my eyes. "I'm going to wear something super ugly tomorrow, be warned." I just started talking with him casually as if we were already in a relationship.

"I'm not so sure that's the approach I want you to take."

"What?"

"Bill's hiding things from me, and the only way I'm going to get to them is if I have an insider who has an intimate knowledge of what he's doing. I want you to go in the opposite direction. Instead of wearing something unflattering, I want you to pour on the sex. Your new spiky hairstyle and that nose ring are enough to set any man's cock on fire; pair that with a micro mini, and he'll be tenting his trousers by noon. I want you to flirt with him and make him think that there's a chance for him. If he invites you out to dinner, go. If he wants you to stay late, stay. Get as close to him as you can, but don't have sex with him. Absolutely don't, you're mine, and I won't let him get his grubby …"

"Hold your fire there, Grandpa, there is no way in hell I'm playing this game. First of all, I'm not yours; you don't own me. If Carl, the intern, looks like a tasty snack, I'm gonna take a bite, and you aren't allowed to say anything about it. Same as if you want to bone Yolanda in accounts receivable, I'll just have to go in the corner and lick my wounds. What I asked you for was friendship. I didn't sign over a deed to my body, mind, or soul. Second of all, what you're asking me to do is dangerous. I am not about to get raped. Men don't like cock teases and don't usually brave them for too long. If I 'pour on the sex' as you asked and go out to dinner with the man, there's gonna be some expectation…"

Andre then jumped in and interrupted me.

"No, you're right, so play the 'waiting till marriage' card. Be sexy as hell, rile him up, but tell him right off you're waiting for Mr. Right. He'll try to throw you off your course, and that will buy us time. You have to get to his personal files; you are going to have to buddy up with him to the point that he thinks you'll let your guard down. I know for a fact he isn't going to want to ruin his reputation for you, especially if you call HR on him. He might try to make you capitulate but don't. Just be innocent and coy. Get as close as you can. I need to know what he's doing. If you care about environmental ethics, this big takedown should be your motivation. Forget me. Clearly, I'm not enough to entice you, but bringing down a big environmental perpetrator might be just exciting enough to make you want to do this all on your own." His eyebrows raised, and he knew he'd caught me.

He was right; the idea of nailing the bastard was appealing.

"You know me pretty well." I smiled and dug into my food.

"I know you better than you think." He then dragged my chair over to him and started kissing my neck.

"You're not hungry?" I was still pretty starving.

"I'm eating," he whispered in my ear as he fanned hot kisses across my neck.

"Well, if you don't mind, I'm eating here." I made sure to chomp very loudly. I didn't want to have any more office sex before having to return to my cubicle.

I enjoyed my food while Andre lazily played with my breasts. "So, with this new arrangement? How do you want to work it to work out timing-wise?"

I loved how we were talking about the calendar and schedule as he felt me up.

"Well, starting next week, I have to go to school two days a week, so I'll be here, Monday, Wednesday, and Friday doing dastardly things with Bill, the Bad Guy. That leaves Friday night and the weekends for fornicating with my new friend." I flashed him a big grin.

"Fine, so this Friday, I'll take you out to dinner, then we can spend the night at my place. I'll need Sunday to regroup." He stopped fondling for a moment to consult his calendar. "That should work. I'll make sure to block out the time so that my assistant doesn't schedule anything."

"Works for me, but I'm taking you to dinner." I took the last bite of food as I was finally getting painfully full, and I grabbed his hand, which had already snaked its way into my blouse.

"I'm not sure I'm up for you taking me out just yet," he tried to protest. "You just got here; we'll end up in some trashy college dive."

"Exactly." I extracted his hand and kissed it.

"I've done my fair share of trashy dives, Eliza," he dared to warn me.

"Not with me, you haven't." I wasn't going to budge.

"Eh, whatever. As long as we get to fuck." He was being playful, which I loved.

"What time is it?"

He looked at his phone. "One-thirty. What time do you have to get back to your desk?"

"Two." I started unbuttoning my blouse. "We have to make this fast, though, because I'm going to have to clean up after. Don't want to look like I've been worked over when I get to my desk. And now," I unzipped his pants, seeing the bulge forming there, "he can come out and play again."

"Goody," Andre teased as he lifted my blouse off of my body, peeled away my bra, and went to town, sucking hard on my nipples. He pinched one with his fingers, and the other he sucked until they were both raw and sensitive. "I'm gonna fuck you over my desk." He hoisted me out of the chair and shuffled me over to his desk, where he pressed me down on the cold, sleek wood. "I've been fantasizing about doing this with you," he confessed as he hiked up my skirt and pulled my panties down. It was so raunchy it was actually fun. He slid his fingers into me and pumped them in and out with deliberate slowness.

"You're so incredibly ready for me, Ms. Pickle." His voice took on a sinister edge.

"I love your cock, Mr. Michelson," I said with my head on his desk and an odd angled view of the papers and things he had there.

They all seemed huge and distorted as my anticipation of his entry was making everything so intense. Finally, after his fingers were tired of plucking, pumping, and pinching my pussy, I felt the swollen and warm tip of his cock pop into me. I braced myself for him, and he slammed into me so hard I jutted forward. Luckily, he had his hands on my hips, or I would have been pushed into all the crap he had on his desk.

"Oh, God," he groaned as he slid himself in to the hilt.

All I could feel was him. His cock was my entire world at that moment. I didn't care about one single thing. At that point, if he didn't even know my name, I'd be fine. I loved the way he felt in me so much I just let myself let go and enjoyed his fantasy. He used his hands to hold me steady as he pressed his cock into my g-spot when he laid over me, taking me hard from behind. A ripple of lightning shot up from my toes and shivered my insides as I came. At his mercy, he didn't stop for me, just let me shatter under him as he continued his constant pounding until I heard the familiar grunts and pinched moans of his own release coming, and he slowed himself down, not wanting to end too soon.

"Fuck, Eliza," he cried out.

I wiggled out from under him and stood up. Turning around, I put my arm out and marched him to a chair where he plopped down in exhaustion, with his cock still standing at attention.

"Yes, Mr. Michelson, fuck Eliza is exactly what you'll do." I kicked off what was left of my panties, which had been stretched to the point where they were going to be obscene to wear in the office, but again at that moment, I didn't care.

I straddled his lap and grabbed his cock, then positioned it at my slick entrance and sat down on him, grinding away until he was fully lodged in me. I sat facing him so he could see the looks of ecstasy I would give him. I then bounced up and down on him as he smiled, grabbing my hips as he had done before, and I surprised him by leaning forward and claiming his mouth. I passionately kissed him as I brought myself to a second orgasm in his lap. As I threw my head back to enjoy the waves of pleasure, he held me tight in his arms and jackhammered into me until he was groaning and grunting his own release. As if possessed, he grabbed me to him and held me hard as my spasming vagina milked every last drop. We may not have been lovers in the traditional sense of the word, but our bodies sure loved each other. We were like a drug to one another.

I collapsed on him, completely exhausted, and we simply breathed each other's air until the moment became too intense.

"I have to get cleaned up to go back to my desk," I said, weakly parting from him. I was seriously spent. I wasn't sure how I was going to muster the energy to go back to my desk and work. And I had the issue of a stretched-out pair of panties and a pretty rumpled skirt and blouse to deal with, not to mention all of him that was in me. "I don't know how I'm gonna make all this look right again."

I was seriously worried.

"Don't stress; there's something in the bathroom for you to change into." His smile was warm and genuine.

"Really?" I could hardly believe he had a change of clothes in my size, but he did tend to keep a lot of things around for the women he fucked.

If he had a custom-made couch for sex, he probably had a bunch of women's clothes lying around too.

"Just go in there and see."

I walked into the ensuite bathroom to see a beautiful dress hanging on a peg on the wall. With it was a Victoria's Secret bag, which I could only assume held lingerie. My heart began to beat. I didn't care if he was an asshole; this was the nicest thing he'd ever done for me. I was seriously worried about going back into work smelling and looking like I'd just had sex with the CEO; now I'd look fresh. Strange that I'd have a new dress on, but that would be easier to excuse away than looking like a two-bit hooker coming in from work. My body tingled all over as I slipped into the beautiful floral print dress that hugged my body in all the right places. In the bag was a pair of silky high cut briefs in a pale shade of pink and a matching bra. The outfit was sweet and defied the image my new nose piercing and spiky hairdo presented, but strangely complemented the look. When I walked out of the bathroom, I felt fresh and alive.

"I love it- thank you. I'm sure you have a bunch of stuff lying around for your afternoon delights, but this is pretty, and I feel much better not having to wear um … these." I held up my rumpled clothes. "Still not sure how I'm going to explain the wardrobe change, but I'll figure it out in the elevator on the way back downstairs."

"I think I can help you with that. Here …" He reached out his hand for me to give him the clothes.

I thought it was strange that he'd want my dirty clothes, but I handed them to him, and he dumped them in the Indian food bag. I guess he thought I'd just ignore the issue by hiding the clothes.

"Thanks." I put my hand out to take the bag with my clothes in it back, and then he opened one of the containers and dumped the sauce into the bag. "What the hell?" I was seriously pissed he'd just dumped food on my very expensive clothes, and then it hit me.

He'd given me an alibi. I dumped food on my dress, and the rest people could make up for themselves.

"Voila! The reason why you have on new clothes. Next time, I'll just get you naked first. I have a shower in my office for that very reason."

"Geeze, you must have a ton of sex in your office."

"I don't get to leave it that often, so …"

"Well, thanks for having an inventory of cool dresses on hand. I feel so much better."

"I bought that dress for you this morning from the same place we bought your other clothes. They have your size; all I had to do was pick out the style. I knew I'd be having you for lunch, so I was prepared."

"And you chose a floral print?" I twirled a little in the dress.

"I like thinking of you as an innocent since, in essence, that's what you are. I know you're going out on a limb to do this with me. The haircut, the nose piercing, both ways you're trying to level yourself up so that you aren't so sweet and innocent anymore, and it's admirable. I get it. I'm corrupting you, but I like seeing a little bit of the old you from time to time." He stood up and smoothed his hands along the side of my hip. "You're beautiful," he said and seemed like he really meant it.

"Thank you." He was right, he was corrupting me, and I had been innocent, but not in the way he imagined. I just trusted the world. I trusted it a little less after arriving in Texas, so it was nice to embrace the naive woman I once was. I looked up at him, kissed him, and then gathered my bag to leave. "It's the perfect dress- thanks for thinking of me."

"Don't forget Friday," he said, stepping back to his desk as if we'd just had a meeting.

"How could I?" I said with a loving smile as I walked out of the office and back to my cubical one floor down.

Suddenly I was dreading having to seduce Bill when all I wanted to do was spend time getting to know Andre. However, if I could find corruption in the company it would be good for both of us, so I marched down to my doom.

Chapter 18

Andre

I knew how dangerous it was to have sex with her in the office and worse to commit to more than just having sex with her, but something compelled me. I had wavered a little, influenced by the magnetic attraction I had to her, but I needed to get myself back in check. I couldn't have her thinking she'd wrapped me around her little finger, so I planned a countermeasure just in case. First, I took stock of what I'd agreed to. I promised to be her friend and to invest in more than just a sexual relationship. At the time, it sounded like a great idea, yet it also made me very nervous. I wasn't sure how to make such a relationship work, especially if I wanted to keep up my grisly reputation.

I waited until three to go down to Bill's floor and check on Eliza. I had a legitimate reason to be there; we were both supposed to go and see a production site about an hour off-campus, and so I'd be spending the rest of the afternoon out of the office and away from Eliza. I approached her cubicle, and Bill's assistant, Axel, was standing over Eliza 'instructing' her, but I had my suspicions that Axel was just as big a prick as his boss.

"So, yeah, I tend to be really clumsy. Sorry for the smell. Do you want me to take the bag to my car?" Eliza batted her great big eyes.

"No, that's fine. I'm used to it now; I have just been sitting there for the last couple of hours wondering why I was suddenly craving Indian food." He burst out into fake laughter that made my stomach sick.

"Sorry. I'm glad I had this dress in the car. I only bought it last night and … well, as luck would have it, I had a change of clothes. I'm so clumsy," she grumbled to herself.

"Well, you don't look like a clumsy person." He leaned in a little more, getting comfortable.

"Floral prints don't really suit you," I said as I traipsed across the threshold of Eliza's cubicle.

Her eyes widened. I'd just caught her flirting outside of the playing field. She was to flirt with Bill and only Bill, not every man who passed her desk.

"Tell Bill I'm here." I stood over her, glaring.

"Oh, hey, Andre. I'm just about to go in there; I'll let him know." Axel casually stood up.

"I suggest you get back to work. I was supposed to have the Calhoun audit at two, and here it is three o'clock …" I said.

"Right, I've got it all loaded up, just waiting for the bossman to sign off. So, Eliza, the next time you go out for Indian food by yourself, let me know. I'm always down for Chicken Vindaloo, and maybe I can help you from landing your lunch in your lap." He laughed at his own alliteration. "Get it?"

"Yep, got it." She forced a smile and gritted her teeth as he walked away.

"And so, this dress doesn't look good on me?" Her stare was pure molten lava. "Is that something a boss would say to an intern he doesn't know?" she said under her breath.

"It's what I would say." I glared back. "Be careful who you play with, Eliza darling. You don't want to get me mad. We just decided we'd make a real go at being friends, so don't make me your enemy," I warned her, feeling angered and jealous.

"Well, since when did friendship come with exclusive rights? I'm going to have to consult the Constitution of Friendship Rights for clarification on that. Let me go tell Bill you're here." She got up and purposefully brushed her hip across mine, and I so wanted to grab her and throw her over the cube's beige temporary wall and just pluck those panties down and give her what she deserved again. Instead, I waited for her to knock on the door and enter Bill's office.

The dress I'd bought for Eliza definitely sparked Bill's interest; I could tell by the way his eyes drifted over her body.

"Keep working on that filing project, Eliza, and update me before you leave as to where you've left it. I hope we're done tomorrow because I have some other more important stuff I want you to do." He leaned into her much the way Axel had and put his hand on her shoulder.

I wanted to swipe it off her shoulder. More, I wanted to rip it out of its socket, which surprised me.

"Sure thing, Bill." She stood up and batted her eyes. "I'm almost done." Bill let his hand drop from her shoulder, but not before it took a swipe down the side of her breast.

Since it was only the three of us in her cube, which was stationed just outside of Bill's office, no one noticed but us. Her face lit up into a flirty smile.

"Great. You're going to be such a great asset to me. Thanks for tossing this one my way," Bill spoke over Eliza's head as if she wasn't even there.

"Sure, what's one more intern? Come on. I just got a text. The site manager is already there." I turned and left, knowing I'd burned Eliza pretty good.

***

"You are a complete and total dick!" she said, sliding the hot dog into her mouth, and I had a hard time thinking of anything other than dick.

I hadn't seen her much that week. We had the double whammy in my office the day of the floral dress and Indian food incident, and then the next day, she didn't show up to work, which I remembered was her school day. The following Wednesday, she was kept in Bill's office, then Thursday she was back at school, and Bill snagged her for the entire day Friday, so there I was in a dive bar with loud music eating hoagies and hot dogs with, admittedly, the best French fries I'd ever tasted.

"Yes, I've always been a complete and total dick, this isn't news." I also took a bite of my hoagie, and truthfully, the rich, thick slabs of meat, coleslaw, and sauce were better than I'd ever admit.

"But you make me feel like crap at work. People have started to notice." She took another bite of her hot dog.

"Notice in what way?" The idea that people might suspect we were having an affair bothered me some.

"Well, first they see me going in to eat lunch with you, but when we're out in the office, you say shitty things under your breath. Axel was like, 'What's up with him?' I just told him you were an old family friend, and you promised my mom you'd be nice to me. I guess he bought it, but seriously, you could lay off on the underhanded remarks. They don't really build a person's character."

"I'm sorry, was it my job to build your character?" I knew I shouldn't have said it the moment I did.

"I'm starting to think this isn't just an act with you. Like you really are exactly as crappy as you pretend to be, and if that's the case, I'll probably need to renege on our whole 'friends with benefits' arrangement for the simple fact that the 'friends' part is woefully lacking."

Perhaps I'd gone too far. I put my hands up. "I surrender."

"Don't patronize me, just apologize. Be a grown-up," she scolded.

"This from a woman who calls me old?"

"You can be old and still a dumb ass." She drank her beer and threw me a look.

"I like this place. The ambiance can use some work, but the food is amazing. How did a girl from DC know that a dive like this was going to be epic?" I thought I'd throw her a bone.

"My roommate Genevieve is in a band that plays here, in fact, she's on in ten minutes. She's the one who recommended it." Her frown melted quickly.

"Is this an ambush?" I worried a little because we weren't at the meeting friends stage of our relationship.

"No, you're a friend of the family. Like an uncle. They already know I have a friend here, so it won't be any surprise." The woman was evil.

"Uncle, you say?" I made sure to darken my tone. "Let's just leave it at friend; we don't need to go into any specifics."

"Sure." She took another bite, and I was truly happy I was going to be taking her home; it was going to be a fun couple of nights.

Because of the bar's noise, we made small talk until her friend's band started setting up. Since she mentioned that her friend was a woman, the only woman in the band was a gorgeous leggy woman with fiery red hair. She was model beautiful and would have been someone I'd have considered before Eliza, but the quirky, fun woman I chose was slowly stealing my heart. I couldn't let her know, but daring to bring a man like me to a dive bar where her friend was in a band was a risk others wouldn't have taken.

And the big surprise of the evening was her friend had an incredible voice. The music was a haunting mix of alternative and country - as if Billie Eilish and Blake Shelton had a baby. It was fun, exciting, and I was getting hard as a rock. So, the question was, did I out myself to people she knew, no one in my world would ever meet her, or stay at a distance and pretend she was just a pal? Since I was thinking only with my dick, I decided to throw caution to the wind. I scooted my chair up beside her and brought her in closer.

"I decided I don't care if your roommate knows about us." I licked her ear and kissed her neck.

"Good," she squealed, changing the tone of my discreet seduction. "Let's dance."

She grabbed my arm, and before I knew it, we were out on the dance floor. I am not a dancer, not by any definition of the word, and I was about to drag her back to our table when I realized that the people throwing their limbs around with reckless abandon weren't dancers either. So, I moved my hips a bit, trying not to stand out too much, but the real fun was watching Eliza; she could move with such unwitting seduction. It took a lot for me not to grab her and grind on her just to feel her body. Her smile was infectious, too. She was having fun. I eventually did nab her and hold her to me as we moved together to the music. The warmth of her body excited me, and she knew I couldn't last much longer without her.

Luckily, it was the last song of her roommate's set. Genevieve joined us at the table, and we engaged in some light chatter. It was evident that the women didn't know each other well, but there was a lot of mutual admiration. Eliza and I finished our drinks, and I called for my driver to take us back to the ranch. She'd been in charge most of the evening; it was time for me to have my fun.

"I have to admit that was better than I was expecting," I said.

Her happiness oozed around her. "I was surprised by two things tonight. Genevieve's band is amazing, and you're a much better dancer than I ever thought you would be."

"Well, I guess I'll take that as a compliment. So, are you good now with your moment of being in charge; have you had enough? I'm ready to take the reins any time." I rubbed her knee and tickled my fingers up her thigh.

"I like having the upper hand." She grabbed my hand and held it between her legs where she'd halted its journey. "It's fun to be the boss."

She slid her hand over to my raging hard-on and instantly catapulted herself into my lap to straddle my cock. I clamored for the button to raise the partition between us and the driver, something I was about to do anyway, but Eliza made it a frantic necessity as she immediately started grinding her panty-clad pussy on my erection, driving me insane.

"What you're doing there is dangerous," I warned. "We still have quite a long drive; are you sure you want to be doing this in the car?" I made sure to use enough command in my tone to scare her just a little- I couldn't have her getting the upper hand.

"Shut up and kiss me." She moved in and claimed my mouth.

Chapter 19

Eliza

I loved calling the shots with him. We had fun at the bar, and on the car ride to his ranch, I thought I'd rile him up a little to keep control. I liked him better when I had some power over him. I loved the feeling of his hard cock on my panties; it was almost as good as having him inside of me. I pulled his mouth to mine and kissed him as I undulated my hips back and forth on him until he was panting for breath when I finally released his mouth and got off him.

"There is no way you can leave me like this." He threw his head back and looked up at the roof of the car. "We still have another half hour until we're back at the ranch." He placed his hand over his aching cock.

"I'll make you feel better in a moment, but I have some ground rules. Are you ready to hear them?" If he wasn't going to be real with me on his own, I was going to force his honesty.

"You're setting conditions?" He laughed.

"Yep. Tonight is my date night. You can set your conditions tomorrow." I stood my ground.

"And you'll take care of this?" He looked down at his jutting erection.

"You know, I will." I flashed him a smile.

"Ugh, fine, what are your conditions?"

"You have to be real with me all night. Lose this alpha CEO exterior and just be real with me. It's my night. I want us to pretend to be lovers who actually love each other." I slid my hand over his slacks and the bulge that was pressing outward to make my point.

"Okay, for tonight, you and I are lovers." He looked at me and wasn't being angry or snarky, just soft and kind.

"Well, then this is all yours." I leaned down and unzipped his pants, then dug out his hard cock. The soft velvet skin over his slick mushroom head was so sensitive to my touch. Just one graze of my finger over the tiny little slit, and he shivered with desire. I bent over and kissed it and licked it softly, teasing.

"Oh, God, woman, put it in your mouth!" He grabbed the back of my head, and I reared back.

"You mean to say, 'Please Eliza, please. Your mouth feels so good.'"

"Right, yes, what lovers would say. Please, my dearest, please. I need your mouth."

I shrugged my shoulders. "Better." I then placed my mouth around him and slowly worked my way down.

Finally, when his cock tickled the back of my throat, I relaxed and swallowed a little of him down, then pulled up, caught my breath, and repeated the process until his hips were humping into my mouth. He was going to shoot his release right down my throat if I wasn't careful. The act of taking him into my mouth and submitting to his needs the way I had made me so hot. I got up from my hard labor and straddled him again. I was dripping with need after anticipating having him inside me, so I slid over my panties and rocked my way onto him.

"Fuck, this is good," he said under his breath.

"It sure is, pardner!" I faked a Texas accent as I continued to rock him into me until I had his entire length seated inside me.

God, it felt good to be so full of him. I then moved forward, wrapped my arms around his chest, and rode to town ... so to speak. Being on top made sure I was in complete control of his pleasure and mine. I ground down on him so hard he let out a whimper, just a tiny one, and that was it. He clamped onto me and started fucking me hard, holding me in place while he thrust inside of me, hitting my G-spot over and over again. I wasn't going to be able to hold on much longer. I bit my lip as my insides twisted. All the control I had was out the window, and I went into a white-hot blur of need. I ached for him so hard as he pounded me that I just let go. My vagina muscles clenched into place, and the rest was explosions and a lance of excitement that speared up from my toes, through my pussy right to my heart. I came so hard I thought I might pass out, and within moments, he grunted and yelled, loud enough for the driver to hear, and I felt his hot cum fill me.

We stayed frozen in place as the car drove through the security gates and onto Andre's property. I was breathing so hard, I couldn't speak. We were both hot and sweaty despite the cool evening.

"We've got to get out of the car," he said with little enthusiasm as he gently lifted me off him.

He had wilted a little but hadn't gone soft. We'd be at it again in no time. I was still spinning as he placed me in the seat beside him. I tried to fix my skirt, but there was no point. At least this time, I planned ahead and brought plenty of clothes for our weekend. The car stopped in front of the ranch as Andre tucked his cock back into his pants, but it was pretty obvious what we'd been up to with the big wet spot where I'd been sitting. He tried to cover it by buttoning his coat, which worked, sort of.

His driver opened my door, and I smiled at him, feeling weird and naughty. Andre let himself out of his side of the door.

"Thanks," he said to the driver. "We won't be needing the car anymore tonight."

I walked over to him and took his hand, something I'd never done. It was my night, and we were lovers for the night, so I figured I had the right.

"So, sweetheart, what do you want to do?" He was sort of mocking, but I didn't care.

"I want to see Midnight, first, then I want dessert and a dip in the hot tub, then sex and bed."

"Sounds fun. I'll order us some peach cobbler and vanilla ice cream. Midnight has not been sold yet, so I'll take you out to the stables now." He set his keys on the ring near the door and took another set.

His home was still pretentiously sparse. I forgot what it was like being at his ranch with just the semi-nude paintings and the few bits of minimalistic furniture.

"And I want to see a movie!" I blurted out. "Naked, but not a naked movie."

"Demanding, aren't we, darling? I can't wait until tomorrow, sweetheart, when you have to do all the things I want you to do." He shrugged his shoulders, mocking me with his lilting, giddy voice.

"Oh, boy. Just don't drag out any whips and chains."

I took his hand, and we walked out to the stables. By the time we reached the horses, he was truly holding my hand.

"They're in for the night, but they always love a treat."

He went to a small office at the front of the stable. Inside was a cupboard where he brought out a stack of fresh carrots.

"We'll give some carrots to all of the horses so as not to show favorites." He winked at me.

He had about ten horses, so we went to each stall and he introduced me to each one. My favorite beside Midnight was his little foal, who was only a few months old. As we went down the line, I could tell Andre was very fond of his horses; perhaps they were his only true companions. When we got to Midnight, he opened his stall and let me in. At the sight of me, Midnight bowed his head so I could pet him. I looked into that majestic horse's eyes and just saw deep into his soul. I loved him so much. I didn't know how I could love an animal as much as I did him; I barely knew him. I barely knew Andre, and yet at that moment, I was completely at peace. I was tired from the car sex and the long day at work and then the dive bar, but in the quiet night under the moon in the stable, I felt calm.

We stayed there for about twenty minutes with me just talking to Midnight. We then fed the rest of the carrots to the rest of the horses as Andre finished his introductions of each one. On our way back he got a text.

"The peach cobbler is hot and in the dining room. I have a few entertainment areas in the house. In the basement, we have a theater; there is a media room next to my office on the main floor, and we can turn on the projector outside, though I would advise against being outside naked."

"The theater sounds fun."

"And you really want to be naked?" he asked with more excitement than I had expected.

"Sort of, maybe clothed for the movie and naked for the hot tub?" I didn't really want to sit in a big theater without my clothes on.

"Sounds like a plan."

So, we ate warm peach cobbler with vanilla ice cream, which was the best I'd ever tasted and watched a light romantic comedy. He hadn't seen the movie, but it was one of my favorites, and I still laughed at all of the funniest places. I didn't know if he was laughing at the movie, but he did laugh several times, genuinely. When we were done with our desserts and the movie, he led me to the hot tub. It was no surprise to me that the pool and hot tub looked like Roman baths. His ranch really wasn't very ranchy in any way. The only place that even looked like one might expect a ranch to look was the horse stables. His house was more like the Louvre Museum.

I didn't want to get swept up in the grandeur of his life, so I just took off my clothes and stood there naked.

"Someone is very eager," he teased.

"I like having sex with you, but I want to cuddle in the hot tub first." I stepped my foot in, and to my great relief, it wasn't too hot.

"I like having sex with you too and cuddling sounds ... interesting." He walked into the tub and fully immersed himself.

He moved over to me, grabbed me, and brought me into his lap. As soon as he sat me down, I could feel him hardening under me.

"What did you want to be when you were young?" I asked him, letting my hands play in the water as I tried to avoid his cock.

I wanted time with *him*, I'd already had plenty of time with his dick.

"A superhero. I wanted to save the world." His hands caught mine. "You?"

"A princess. Strangely enough, I also wanted to save the world, but instead of wearing tights and a cape, I would do it in a tiara and a gown. Also, I wanted to be a doctor for a while and figure out how to help my brother learn to talk." I flourished my arms into the air.

"Guess we're both saving the world, just in a different way. How old is your brother?"

"He's two years older than me, but he still acts like a child. I haven't seen my family for a long time. My mom and dad don't really want me home. They keep telling me to see the world and not to let their life bog me down. I talk to my mom on Sunday nights. They are quiet people, and that's sort of what my brother needs. He's been their focus for a long time, so I just sort of stay out of their way. I know they love me, but they don't have the bandwidth for me and a non-verbal autistic son." I didn't really want to confess that much, but that was the truth.

"No wonder you want friends so badly; they sort of need to be your family." It was a very astute observation on his part.

"Yeah, when you're alone in the world, friends make it brighter. I always felt bad being the healthy kid, and I think they always felt bad having to focus on him, so friends did become my family. You're right. I guess we are kind of alike in that way."

"We are sort of. Do you miss them?" He was being sincere, and I loved it.

"I don't really. I know that's kind of callous to say, but I haven't been back home since I left for undergraduate school."

"Then you are a lot like me. I don't miss my family much either." He started caressing my shoulders and arms and changed the subject. "Were you able to get anything from Bill this week?" His arms slid around my waist, and it felt amazing.

"Just that he's a lechy scumbag. You really want me to give in to him?"

"I don't want you to give in completely. Hold him off for a couple more days, then give him a little at a time. I want you to get enough information so that I might have evidence that he's misusing the company funds for his own gain and going against our directives. In short, I want him fired, but I need a lot of ammo to do it." He raked the fingers of his other hand through my hair. "So, I'm dying to know, why did you cut it?"

"I've always been a good girl. I played by the rules. I wanted to be more rebellious. I'm evolving, and so I wanted my appearance to reflect that."

"What are you evolving into is the question?" He leaned in and kissed my neck.

"A woman who knows what is right for her. Someone who is learning to take control of her life."

I turned and ran my fingers through his hair. "If you were to evolve, who would you become?"

He stared at me a moment and didn't answer.

Chapter 20

Andre

I didn't have an answer for her. Evolve into what? Wasn't I already who I wanted to become? She had mentioned many times how old I was. Was I not old enough to have already evolved? The truth was, I was no more advanced emotionally, socially, or spiritually than I had been in high school. Driven to a fault, I put business and money before anything else in my life. I had acquired enormous equity, art, investments, and property, but I lacked what Eliza truly valued; a relationship worth losing everything for. This gave me pause; was there more I could do? I looked at Eliza sitting in my lap with warm streams of steam framing her beautiful face and her cute new pixie haircut. Could she be something that would push me further along in my evolutionary journey? Time would only tell.

"I'd become better in business. I'd win these energy contracts and grants. After that, I guess I'd retire to this ranch and its art and horses. Perhaps I'd breed them full-time; I'm not sure. I never give any thought to anything too far in the future."

"Some say that's the best way to plan a life. Just live in the moment."

"Well, at this moment, I'm ready to take you to bed. We've had a long night, and I think I've been quite a gentleman. I deserve a reward." I couldn't just sit there with an erection anymore. I had to have her.

The cuddling was cute, and if she wanted it to create feelings of warmth and tenderness, she would be happy to know her mission was accomplished.

"But it's still my night," she pretended to pout. "And I'm not a shriveled old prune yet. I thought I might stay until I have skin that looks more like yours." Her teasing was going to get her into so much trouble.

"Actually," I looked at my waterproof watch. "It's twelve fifty-one; we are fifty-one minutes into my day. Off to fuck we go!" With that, I lifted her into my arms and hoisted her out of the water.

"Wait, can't we negotiate this?" She was wiggling and squirming so much I almost dropped her.

"Nope, I danced at a dive bar, now you're going to cum on twenty-four hundred dollar Charlotte Thomas sheets. My day has begun." I wasn't going to take any push back from her. I'd been fair; it was my turn to be in control again.

"Wait. So, I only get Friday night, and you get ALL of Saturday? How is that fair?" She continued to squirm.

"My house, my rules." I looked down and smirked at her.

"Fine, next weekend is at my house." She jutted out her chin and knew she had me there.

"Maybe we can negotiate next weekend, but this weekend is mine, and your time is up."

I continued the conversation until I flopped her onto my bed, dripping wet and naked. I really could give a fuck about the expensive sheets; they could be washed, the bed would dry, but my cock couldn't wait, not one second more. Even though I had dryers in my bathroom, I couldn't be bothered to use them. I had to have her at that moment.

"First, I'm going to start with the appetizer. Spread your legs for me, Eliza. I'll be right back," I demanded as I grabbed a towel from my bathroom and patted myself dry.

"And if I don't!" she yelled out to me.

Damn defiant little vixen.

"I'll spread them for you, your choice." I pumped myself to get ready for her after I tossed the towel onto the bathroom counter.

"So, this is about how much fight I'm willing to have?" She was a stubborn one.

"Or how much pleasure, your choice. I'm getting what I want whether you like it or not!" I knew it was harsh, but that was me; she wanted to tempt me, well, here I was.

"And what is it you want?" Interesting question.

"I want you writhing under me in ecstasy." I get my kicks no matter what, but I wanted to see her enjoy it. That damn defiant hairstyle and her nose ring were to find herself, yes, and also to set me off. Well, bravo, Eliza, you've done both.

"That's easy." She spread her legs as I approached.

"And I want you devoted to me."

She snapped her legs closed. "That's gonna take work."

She glared at me and was so damn cute I just kissed the glare right off of her mouth.

"I bet it won't," I whispered in a low tone as I breathed hot on her neck and trailed kisses down to her clavicle, her sternum, each of her pert delicious breasts, her diaphragm, her belly button, the neatly trimmed tuft of hair above her pussy, and into heaven.

I spread her labia to reveal the treasure inside and went to town lapping at her taut little bud before diving my tongue into her beautiful vagina. She literally had the prettiest pussy I'd ever seen, and I'd seen a ton. Her breathing escalated, and I felt a moment of triumph.

"Don't think that just because you can get me off, you win." She was still protesting.

"Are we competing?" I lifted my head up to ask. "If so, I won the moment you agreed to come here; game over." I returned to my feasting, and for whatever reason, that kept her quiet.

I lapped at her and returned the favor she'd done for me in the car when she serviced my cock. I could feel her body tensing up with desire, and that was my call to action. I stopped my feasting and gently turned her over so that her ass was in the air.

"Um," she protested just a little but allowed me to position her.

"I want to own your heart," I whispered in her ear as I laid over her back.

"Just make sure you make it in the right hole. I'm all for you owning my heart tonight, but the backdoor is an exit only. You don't own my ass." She craned her head back and smiled at me.

"Noted." I kissed her cheek and neck and then used my hand to position myself at her entrance.

I thought about how I might savor the first stroke. Would I be gentle? Would I be eager, passionate, wild? I chose sensual as I gently rocked myself into her, enjoying the little sounds she made as I worked my way in deeper until I was there at the hilt, fully surrounded by her. Her sex, her body, her smell, her fire. That was all I needed to get things moving. I was able to go so much deeper and enjoy so much more of her in that position that I found myself completely overwhelmed. She, on the other hand, couldn't move. She just had to take me. I loved having her under my complete control, and more, I adored that being at my mercy had given her so much pleasure. I snaked my hand around her body and fingered her clit from the front as I took her from the back. Without too much effort on my part, she began a glorious orgasm that locked my dick in a vice of pleasure and, before I could pull myself out and calm the hell down, I was rocketed to a climax so hard and mind-blowing, the world blurred for a moment.

I had hoped to do much more with her on that round, but the truth was, as much as I tried to dominate her, I was putty in her hands. She could mold me into anything. When I finished and pulled out of her, I didn't want to go far. She curled her body into mine and pulled the comforter up over us.

"I loved that," she said in a sleepy haze. "I loved how you held me down with your entire body weight and made me feel safe. She lifted her head and looked over to the statue on the other side of the room. "Good night, Fred and Ethel." She then turned her head to me. "Good night, strange, unpredictable, friend."

I leaned in and kissed her lips. "Good night, sweetheart." My body was warm, and affection heated my blood. What the hell was she doing to me?

She settled into the pillow, completely spent, and fell fast asleep. I tossed and turned for a moment, unable to clear my head. I thought about working for a while to ease my mind, but I just ended up staring at her beautiful face until sleep stole me away.

***

The next morning, I woke up, and she wasn't in bed with me. I immediately panicked. I knew there was little chance of her leaving; it was just that I'd expected to wake up with her by my side. I was looking forward to it. I threw on a pair of pajama pants and started roaming the halls on the prowl, and I found her in my kitchen working away at something.

"I thought you'd still be in bed." I took the seat across from her so I could watch whatever magic was happening.

"My dearest," her smile was brilliant. "For some reason, you snored last night, and when I wake up, I'm up. So, I decided I'd make us some blueberry pancakes. I always screw up pancakes, so I'm a little unsure why I took this on, but viola!" She pushed a plate of half-burned, half undercooked monstrosities in front of me.

"They smell good." I had to give her something. "There's some syrup in the cupboard. I'll grab us some plates, and let's dig into these bad boys."

"Are you serious?" She laughed. "We are really gonna eat them?" She seemed halfway relieved that I didn't tease her about them.

"Sure, how bad can they be?" I got up and grabbed some plates from the shelves over her head, and kissed her as I brought them down. "I love that you just got up in here and did this."

"Well, at first, I didn't think there was anything in the kitchen, but I started pushing doors, and they opened. You must have had an engineer create the kitchen." She retrieved the syrup, some extra blueberries, and powdered sugar.

"I had an engineer create the whole house. Sorry about the snoring; when I'm really tired, I tend to saw logs."

"No worries; it was cute. I just got stressed. I don't always do great in other people's beds." She sat down, took a few pancakes, and put them on her plate.

"Why is that?" I took a couple of pancakes, slathered them with syrup, and popped a few blueberries on them.

"Oh wait, there are bananas too." She brought out a plate of sliced bananas. "And I was just about to make coffee."

"Well, throw some banana on my plate, and I'll make the coffee, and if you don't mind, I'll cook up a few strips of bacon. I like my meat." I dipped my voice to be playful.

"Sure." Her smile was so sweet.

I wasn't much of a cook myself, so I understood the stress she might have been feeling, cooking in the most user-unfriendly kitchen in Texas with the CEO she was screwing.

"So?" I still wanted to understand why she wasn't comfortable waking up with me that morning. "Why didn't you stay in bed and cuddle me." I played with her own words.

"Today is your day. I wanted to respect your need to be you, you know, cold and aloof."

"Hmm, right. I do tend to be that way. I appreciate it. Sorry it caused you to worry, though. You know, I'll let you in on a secret. After losing my parents, I decided just to close up shop and stop feeling. It's a normal human reaction to grief, but I've held on to it for a while. I decided that I'd make money and build up my company and find love that way. And I did that, and it's worked, but it's hard to hug your money. I like the idea of you and I being friends. I must confess I don't really think I have any. This is new for me too, but thanks for being honest about your feelings. When you wake up tomorrow, just do what you do, I won't be mad."

"Thanks. If we keep seeing each other, I promise to be less weird."

I cooked up some bacon and put coffee in the espresso machine. I was probably the world's worst cook, but how could I fuck up bacon and coffee? Well, I burned the bacon, but the coffee came out okay. By the time breakfast was served, it was all just a little awful, but the wonderful realness we shared with each other made up for it.

"Perhaps cooking classes might be fun." I laughed after braving as much of the over-syruped pancakes and the too-greasy bacon as I could stomach.

"Yeah, that would be fun." She had eaten just about as much as I did as we both surrendered to breakfast.

"Wanna go for a horseback ride?"

"As long as there will be no galloping, I would love to go on a ride with you." I just loved her sweetness, and it was at that moment, I realized how much I was missing sweet things in my life.

Chapter 21

Eliza

The weekend was fun. We spent a lot of time with the horses riding around his property. I saw the hangar where he was working on the energy storage units, we went back to the lake again, and later that night, we ordered food, watched another movie, and made love all night long until we passed out in each other's arms. The last time we had sex was the most loving. He actually held me after finishing. I loved our rough sex when he dominated my body and mind, but to just love him and share a physical experience that was caring and intimate made me feel things for him I was reluctant to experience. I was slowly falling in love with him despite how complicated and emotionally unavailable he really was.

I went home on Sunday, completely exhausted. He still had his driver take me home, which made me a little bit sad, as I wanted to spend more time with him, but I understood that it was almost a three-hour drive round trip, and he was a busy man. I'd already taken up most of his weekend. When I walked into the house, my roommates were puttering around doing their thing.

"So," Genevieve started right in as soon as I walked into the kitchen to make myself some tea. "Who was that distinguished gentleman you came to the bar with last night? He was so sexy." Her eyes glazed over with a distant wanting.

God, how would I answer that question?

"He's a friend I met in DC. He's actually close friends with my best friend's husband if that makes any sense. It was my night to pick a place to eat, and I promised I'd come to see you play. You are so good, by the way, your singing is amazing, and the songs are so cool, very eclectic."

"Thanks, we're working on getting a recording contract. Who knows? Maybe we'll be the next big thing. So, you two were really roasting the dance floor. Sure he's just a friend?" She sat down at the tiny table that was in the breakfast nook and sipped her coffee.

"For now." I brought my tea and joined her.

I really had to start doing my homework. I had my first paper and a test due the following week but talking to someone who wasn't as confusing as Andre was refreshing.

"I've had a few of those. They are pretty challenging because you never know what is going on with them."

"We've left it at friends with benefits, but I agree it gets really weird at times. Are you seeing anyone right now?" I needed to redirect the conversation away from me.

"Not at the moment; I'm taking a break. My last boyfriend was another musician, and that didn't go so well. So, I'm focusing on me right now." She smiled, and her face lit up.

Both of my roommates were exceptionally beautiful. I felt more so with my new haircut and attitude, but sometimes, I had to admit they intimidated me. How Andre the asshole CEO didn't intimidate me, but they did, was weird. However, with Andre there was an ease; even though he had a dangerous side, it was very obvious that he had a physical reaction to me each time we were close. That gave me a lot of confidence and power. I sat with Genevieve for a little while, just talking over life and relationships, then poured myself more tea and hit the books. The rest of Sunday flew by.

I woke up for work on Monday, dressed in a new and adorable outfit that I bought for cheap online, and walked into work feeling refreshed and ready to tackle not only Bill but the office version of Andre. Immediately Bill was on me.

"Eliza, can I see you in my office?" He was stern and condescending.

"Yes?" I walked in, not having had my morning coffee and certainly not ready to deal with Bill's bad behavior.

"Did you finish the files? You were supposed to be done with them last week." He huffed and paced the room.

"Yep, they were done last week."

"Fine, I want you to dictate notes from my phone call in case I need to involve my lawyers. Sit down," he said as he tossed a yellow legal pad with a pen clipped to it at me.

"I'm going to be on the phone with my soon to be ex-girlfriend, so I want you to take notes on what is being said." He picked up his phone and opened the line so that I could pick up the landline next to me and listen in.

"Isn't this illegal?" I asked, knowing damn well it was.

"It's illegal to record her without her knowing," he answered.

"And shouldn't I let her know that I'm on the line?"

"No, you are my assistant. It is assumed that you will be on the line.

Just take notes; you don't have to worry about what is right or wrong." He was so irritated I just shut up.

I was pretty sure that if a boss ordered me to listen to a conversation if something heated up legally, he'd be going down with me.

He made the call, and a woman answered the phone.

"Jeanne," he started.

"Hey, Bill," her voice heated up.

"I'm calling to let you know something I'm sure you felt coming for some time now. I am ending my relationship with you. It's been over for months, but this call makes it official. I will need the car, the keys to my condo, and the diamond ring I gave you all boxed up and ready to give the messenger I'm sending over in an hour. I'll have movers move your things out. Just make sure you take anything you will accuse me of stealing from you. The movers will inventory your things and have them sent to you. I just need your new address." He was so cold and ruthless; I felt horrible for the woman who was obviously crying on the phone.

"You can't do this; we've been together for over a year, Bill. What's going on?"

It was hard to take notes and make mental assessments simultaneously, but I was managing.

"Just box up what I've requested and give me an address." He was stone cold.

"I can't give you an address in an hour; I have no place to live. You just kicked me out of my home." She seemed to be shaking with rage.

"My home, I paid the bills and the mortgage, it's my home. So, you need to leave now, or I'll have the police come and evict you. If you have no address for me to send your things, I'll have them sent to a storage unit, and you can pay the bill and settle up when you find something. Be out at five o'clock today, or I'll send someone to get you out. As you don't pay rent, you are a guest. I can have the police remove you." She was sobbing when Bill hung up the phone and looked at me. "Did you get that?" I wanted to roll my eyes so badly.

"Yes," I said quietly.

"Good. I want it on record the day I called her, and the time I gave her so that if the police ask, I have a witness. Now, Andre tells me that you live a forty-five-minute commute from here. You'll stay in the apartment; it's just down the street. I don't want you coming in late to work."

"Um, thanks, but I'm a grown-up. I'll get here on time," I countered; there was no way I was going to live in the apartment he just kicked that poor woman out of.

"I'm going to insist. We will have some very late nights, and I don't want you driving late. Also, you have a shit 2000 Hyundai Elantra, so it can't be relied on."

"I'm fine with my own place; thank you." I just dismissed him.

I couldn't be bothered with a fight, but there was no way I was going to stay at his place, not after he just kicked a woman out of it. I could tell where he was heading ... like 'oops' opening the door when I was in there at night. I'd stay at my own place and make it on time to work. If he ever showed up at the apartment and wondered why I wasn't there, I'd make an excuse.

For the rest of the week, I barely saw Andre. He was in a meeting here, rushing off to another meeting there. Once he was in the break room when I was there with a few other interns, just hanging out having lunch. He came in and completely ignored me. It was appropriate but for some reason, made me angry, especially because Bill was all hands and innuendos. I was booking his calendar which included a lot of in-office massages, which I thought was very strange. I didn't worry about them until he wanted me in there to make sure nothing funny happened, which was horribly awkward. I used the time to thin out the files I'd just reorganized, and I tried to be as quiet as possible, but he always wanted to talk to me while he had nothing more than a towel on his body. It was the strangest, most horrible thing. I really wanted to go to Andre and complain, but instead, I just kept a list of dates and times and thought perhaps they'd help Andre make a case against him. It went on like this for weeks. I would spend my office days just doing grunt work for Bill while he made inappropriate comments and accidentally touched me whenever he could. I was supposed to spend the weekends with Andre, but he had to go out of town on two of the weekends to off-site locations where they were experimenting with the storage devices on a large scale.

"I'm going to go crazy without fucking you," Andre said in one of our very few office rendezvous.

I didn't like having sex in his office, but since I couldn't see him on the weekends for a while, I had to be with him any way we could.

"You'll survive," is all I said, since I hoped we were beyond just fucking, but we hadn't quite gotten back to the level of emotional intensity we found on our last blissful weekend together.

"I promise this won't last, and soon I'll have you back home with me." He kissed me as he finished up and rinsed off.

"You mean back to your ranch," I corrected him.

"Yeah, that." He just stared at me strangely. "I'm going to miss you, but it's only for the next few weekends."

It was the next five weekends, to be exact, that we weren't able to be together. I would have assumed he was seeing someone else, but he'd text me every night, and the things he'd say made me think he wasn't really dating anyone other than his left hand. Poor guy, I actually felt sorry for him. I enjoyed having the weekends to work on schoolwork and hang out with my roommates—we were really becoming close. We loved going to the bar where Genevieve sang, and sometimes I'd just watch Peyton paint and was mesmerized by her talent. I wasn't creative like that, but I was fine with what a big fat science nerd I was, and I blew my roommates away with my knowledge of environmental fixes for some of our most polluting problems.

I called Harper and Ophelia on occasion and chit chatted, and we made plans to meet after the holidays as they were quickly approaching. Halloween had just passed, and to fuck around with Bill, I wore a French maid's outfit to work. While it was meant to send Bill into a tizzy so that I could get an invite to his house to go through his drawers, it actually riled up Andre so much we had another session in his office where he just bent me over the desk. It made me laugh how predictable men were. I loved those afternooners, though, because I'd seen so little of Andre. Each time we had a quickie in his office, we were becoming more loving and amorous. And his nightly texting was almost at an obsessive teen crush level, which I also thought was sweet.

I was running into a problem finding any dirt on Bill. His files were all in order, and the accounts I saw were fully legal with both Andre and Bill's signatures on them. If there was anything shady happening on Bill's end, it was hidden somewhere else. I finally told Bill there was no way I'd take the keys to the apartment, and he backed down when I came in early to the office just to prove that I didn't need his apartment. He relented but would often bring it up, saying if I'd only taken his offer of a place ... bla, bla, bla. It was Wednesday, my in-office day, and I was running around doing bullshit errands like getting Bill coffee, lunch, a donut from the breakroom when he called me into his office.

"I think you should come with me to this thing on Friday," he announced, and my heart sank.

It was supposed to be my first weekend with Andre in over a month.

"I kind of have a thing on Friday." I tried to remain vague.

"We have to go to a fundraising event where there will be prominent politicians and investors who are giving us money for our next phase of production. I have to go with a plus one, and you're it. Clear whatever you have or find a new job." Fuck, I really hated that guy.

"Fine," is all I said as I lumbered back to my cube and whipped out my phone to text Andre.

I have to go to a thing with Bill on Friday :(Sorry. We can hang out on Saturday. - E

I have the same thing. I'll be there. I'll take you home with me afterward. - A

I'll insist I drive. I can just follow you in my car. - E

NO, you will not be driving your car. We've gone over this before your car sucks. I'll drive you, we'll work it out. Going to a meeting. - A

I wished he'd say something nice like I love you, or big hugs or anything, but that wasn't Andre's style. He wasn't affectionate at work or in texts. I knew that should have been a red flag, but our relationship was evolving slowly.

Friday came, and I brought a cocktail dress to wear to the fundraiser, which was at a members-only club in Houston. Bill had become overtly handsy after inviting me to the event, and my anxiety spiked. What would an evening with Bill look like? Well, I was soon to find out.

"Are you ready to go?" he asked Friday late afternoon several hours before the cocktail party was about to begin.

My driving routine with Andre was to leave my car in the garage on Friday and Saturday, and his driver would bring me to the office so I could pick it up. That way, Andre was sure that I wouldn't be driving my shitty car that far. Now I had to worry about being at Bill's mercy.

"What time does the event start?" I asked, trying to sound as innocent as possible.

"Not till seven, but I thought we'd get a bite first, my treat." Just as I had suspected.

"What are you thinking?" Again, I did my best to be nonchalant.

"Well, my house is close by …" he threw out offhandedly.

"Um," There was no way I was going to his house.

"I need to change out of my work clothes, and you'll probably want to freshen up. You can do that at my house and then I can take you to this sweet little restaurant I know about thirty minutes out of town. If we leave now, we'll have plenty of time." His smile turned instantly lecherous.

"For you to get dressed and stuff?" I involuntarily took a step back.

"Sure." He took a step forward, and I knew that was the dance we'd be doing all night long.

When we went to his house, I stayed in the car after having already put on my cocktail dress in the office bathroom.

"This is ridiculous," he complained.

"Seriously, I can just stay here. I have to read a book for class, and I have it on my phone." I waved the phone in the air. "I'll just wait here; you take your time."

"You don't want to freshen up?" he asked in an accusatory manner.

"I'm as fresh as I'm gonna get." I gave him a big cheesy grin.

"Fine." He left defeated, and my heart started to beat again.

Keeping myself in a public place was the only goal for the night. Dinner was as cringy as one would expect. He kept trying to pry information about my sex life out of me without being blatant enough to get his ass sued.

"So, when was the last time you were on a date?" he started.

"A while ago. I just got here."

"But you're friends with Andre? That confuses me."

"He's friends with Reid, who is married to my best friend Harper, so I'm sort of three degrees separated from his friendship. We're pleasant." At that moment, I was actually craving Andre's version of cold office etiquette; I would have much preferred it to the veiled sexual aggression I was getting.

"Are you pleasant with any of the other men in the office?" What the hell was that supposed to mean?

"I've just met a few of the other interns, so I guess pleasant is a pretty good descriptor. How about you? Are you in a relationship? Did you pick up anyone new after you gave your girlfriend the boot?" I knew it wasn't the smartest move, but I had to get off the hot seat.

"After I got rid of my monster wife, I'm just into casual stuff. Jeanne stopped texting me finally, but she wasn't my girlfriend, just someone convenient."

"So now you're only into casual stuff like reading and nice hikes?" I knew I shouldn't have gone there, but it did make him laugh.

"More like long nights with lots of nocturnal aerobics." His eyes narrowed.

"Fun," I shrugged my shoulders and pretended to be as ditzy and dumb as he must have thought I was.

"Are you into that?"

"Nocturnal aerobics? No, I mean I might pull an all-nighter or two if I have to finish a paper, but I save the heavy lifting for the gym." I shoved a huge bite of salad into my mouth and didn't even care if I looked like a blind man operating a forklift; I didn't want to keep talking. I had salad dressing all over my face, so I wiped the cloth napkin across it, totally messing up my lipstick, but who cared? The more hideous I looked, the better off I was. He didn't seem to mind.

"If you're that hungry, you should have ordered something a little more substantial than salad," he scolded.

"I like salad," I said with my mouth full. I was even grossing myself out a little.

"I can see," again with the smarmy grin.

Chapter 22

Andre

I walked into Luque's for the Fight Climate Change Fundraising Party, where I'd be unveiling the first of the storage prototypes, and I immediately saw Eliza with Bill. I knew I was the one to set her up and make her work with him to find his illegal projects but seeing her with him made my blood boil. She was wearing a pretty little black cocktail dress that showed off her well-toned thighs, thighs I'd had wrapped around my body so many times I could hardly keep count. There she was, walking with him, smiling casually, with a drink in her hand. Bill was too close for comfort, but Eliza seemed to be holding her own pretty well.

"Dating the intern already?" I asked as I walked up to them.

"Just letting this one out for some air." Bill's smile was positively disgusting.

"Um, I'm right here, fellas." Eliza played along.

"Well, let's get you some more to drink, shall we?" he said in a seductive tone to Eliza before he turned to address me. "Are you ready for your big speech?"

I hated the mocking sound of his voice.

"I am," is all I said.

"Well, I'll see you for that." He put his arm around Eliza, and I almost punched him in the face, but I was the one who put her there, so I just breathed through my anger.

She gave me a glance that told me she was okay, and I just counted the hours until she was mine again. Just at that moment, Dylan, an old friend, and colleague, walked by. I'd have to leave Eliza on her own with Bill, but at least I was in the room if he tried something funny. Dylan was a hard man to get a hold of, even though I'd texted and called several times, so being able to physically apprehend him was a necessity at that point.

"Dylan." I stepped in his path as he turned his head from one conversation and headed into the next.

"I owe you a call," he said, pointing his finger straight at me.

"Weeks ago, you owed me a call, now you owe me an explanation." I did my best to look legitimately pissed off.

"What can I say? I'm swamped." He shrugged his shoulders.

"So why are you avoiding me?" I put him to it.

"I don't want to get involved here. Fracking is so political and messy. I don't want my name on anything; just manage your business." Well, it was obvious he'd gotten my calls.

"No, it is dangerous. A community near the border was almost leveled last month from an unnatural earthquake. That is where our wells are. Ninety percent of the town is ours, and I have never once signed off on a fracking operation, so someone is doing something on the company dime behind my back. I want you to find out who. You can be discreet; send in someone he doesn't know. We have a batch of new interns at the moment." My eyes shifted to Eliza to check in on her. "He'd never suspect if we had a late addition."

"As I said, we're busy, and I don't want to get involved. You're an asshole, but you have a big heart. Not sure how that juxtaposition works, except I don't want to be a part of it. Bill has been my friend since we've all been in college. I'm not interested in burning that bridge." He was about to walk away from me when I grabbed him.

"He's paying you, isn't he? I've been your friend for just as long; in fact, I had to endure your snoring for three years when we roomed together in college. I'd say you owed me this; only if you weren't on his payroll and signed a contract, you couldn't legally audit my company, could you?"

Everything was starting to fall into place. Bill had covered his tracks very neatly.

"I'm not admitting to anything but the fact that I have too much on my plate already. Find another auditing firm. I'm sure your books are squeaky clean; get someone else to do the audit." He flat out refused me.

"No one else would know his tells. No one could see the codes and ways he hides his shit. Only you know when he's bluffing; that's why he has you on retainer, so now I can't hire the one man who could sniff out his lies?" At that point, I was boiling with anger. "Well, fuck you, Dylan, you're no friend of mine."

I turned and walked away from him, so enraged I almost started throwing things.

"Well, that's no great loss," I heard him say behind me, and it took all my power to stay calm.

I needed Eliza; she had a settling effect on me. Also, if I could have torn her away for a quickie, that would have even been more helpful, but as I looked over to where she and Bill were standing, I saw that he was caressing her back. I was about to intercede again when a perky woman wearing a 'Hello my name is Barbara" sticker approached me.

"Mr. Michelson, hi, I'm Barbara," she nodded to the tag and flashed an awkward smile. "Do you mind coming with me so we can go over your speech and the logistics for this evening?"

Ugh, sabotaging Bill's evening would have to wait. I was shuffled off to an empty event room where my speech's specifics and the donation to my company were laid out. It was pretty standard, but for people who stressed about these things, they were really keyed up.

"We are excited about this investment into our new storage technology, and I know you won't be disappointed in the slightest. I have a video of our receptors and a demonstration of how they work. Also, I have you on the calendar to visit next week and see them for yourself. This is all legit, and we will be changing the face of clean energy. In three years, renewable energy will be a whole different ball game."

I was rattling off my spiel, which excited people as it always did. I had given hundreds of speeches; giving a speech wasn't anything, but keeping Bill's grubby paws off Eliza was. I was sequestered until speech time, which left Eliza to her own devices. As I took the stage, I saw her with him sitting at a tall table nibbling on appetizers. He had his hand on her thigh, and I almost went completely apeshit, but I held it together long enough to give my speech.

"And so, thank you for the generous investment into our future and the future of the future, as clean energy becomes how we energize," I concluded my speech, happy the ordeal was over when Bill stood up from the table and approached the podium.

"Mind if I say a few words?" he asked, looking calm and approachable, but that was usually when he was most dangerous.

"If you have to," is all I said as I stepped aside.

"Hi, all. I'm Bill Blascoe, and I'm the co-founder of the Michelson Energy Corporation. I didn't want my name on the company as an idealistic kid, but I do want to tell you that this brand new method of energy storage was my brainchild, and I just want to say that, after ten years of dreaming, it feels so go to see reality taking shape. I want to take only a moment of your time to thank you for funding a large portion of our rollout. We are going to be grateful to you big-ticket patrons forever but be excited because you're gonna soon be seeing some crazy returns on those investments. Enjoy the cocktails, dancing, and snacks, and thanks again for making a contribution, as Andre said to the future." He handed the mic back to me and traipsed back over to the table where Eliza sat, looking confused.

"Yes, none of this would have been possible without two dreamers teaming up in college. Thanks, Bill, for reminding us." I had to get that dig in.

The truth was the energy storage was Bill's brainchild, but like all things, he dropped the ball after fantasizing an impossible plan. It was my pragmatism, drive, and research that got the company to where we were finally seeing a legitimate profit and had a product that would make us all billions of dollars richer. He'd be a part of that payout, contractually. Bill was the guy who had great ideas on paper but zero execution skills. On the other hand, I knew when I heard a good thing, and I went for it with logic, reason, and tireless hours of work. No wonder Bill started a side gig doing exactly what we were trying to eradicate. It was easy money, and there was a high demand for hydraulic drilling. The problem was, now there were earthquakes, and the lives of people in depressed communities where the oil wells were being set up were at stake.

"Had to throw your two cents in?" I asked Bill with a scowl on my face as I got a tall whiskey on the rocks from the bar where he'd dragged Eliza for more drinks. She wasn't looking as resilient as she had and perhaps was getting a little drunk. I knew what a lightweight she was, and that made me even more worried about her. "This wasn't about clamoring for credits; we got a nice stack of cash from The Rodenmeyer Foundation. This event is about thanking them, but let's not ever forget whose brainchild the storage devices were, though I wonder do you even know what modifications had to be made to actually get them to function?" My voice was civil, yet my words spelled war.

"No, but that's what we paid people to do. I don't mind the oversight. I just thought I'd throw in my gratitude." He was equally sarcastic and biting. "I think Eliza and I are going to head out. It's getting late, and we've made the rounds already."

"Are you heading back to the office?" I asked, trying not to look at Eliza in a panic.

"Ah, don't you worry. I'll take good care of her, and I'll keep everything on the down- low. No need to stress human resources out," he said, pulling Eliza to him.

"Actually, my car is at work, so we should probably go back there." She gave me a worried glance mixed with fierce determination.

I pulled out my phone as my eyes glanced toward it, telling her to call me.

"Ah, we'll make it back to the office at some point." He winked at her and passed her a tall drink, probably loaded with stuff that would knock her out. My blood pressure spiked, and for the first time in a long time, I wasn't exactly sure what to do.

"Great," she gave a flirty smile and flashed me a look that said, 'I got this,' which I was clearly not happy about, but since Dylan blew me off, she was my only hope at that moment.

Dylan ran corporate audits for the state of Texas; he was a legitimate guy and took his job way too seriously. If he found anything other than Bill's bad behavior, I'd want that swept under the rug until I could deal with it appropriately. Dylan knew that getting into business with me meant possibly breaking a few minor rules, rules that he didn't want to ignore because his pregnant wife was about to have a baby, and he was vying for the head of the workforce commission for the state of Texas. If he were on Bill's payroll, it would be detrimental to Dylan's career. As much as I hated to admit it, Eliza getting into Bill's house was my best shot at finding anything he was hiding. So, I bit back my anger and smiled.

"Well, you two have a wonderful evening," I said as I left them, which was much harder than I ever expected it would be.

"You know we will," Bill said as he squeezed Eliza, and my heart constricted.

Chapter 23

Eliza

I could do this, I told myself. I had to find what Bill was hiding. After spending a short amount of time with him privately, I realized he was shady and scary. The people he met and the things he said all seemed veiled in secrecy. I decided my best course of action was pretend to get drunk, act ditzy, and see if I could catch him slippin'. I was nervous and uncomfortable, but the look of jealousy on Andre's face was worth every minute. When he left us, he was so hot under the collar that it warmed my heart a little. He wasn't one to show his emotions, especially at work, so to see him try to keep a lid on his envy was so fun. Despite the horrible task ahead, I was actually enjoying myself. I'd never thought of being an actor, but the exercise was proving to be a ton of fun. The boring speeches were over, and the crowd was starting to thin out, so I waited to see what Bill's next move might be.

"Do you want another vodka cranberry?" Bill turned to me to ask.

I raised my glass to him. "You just got me one!" Definitely getting me drunk was on his bucket list.

I was going to pretend I was drunk, but every time he was engaged in conversation, I found my way to a discarded glass and unloaded some of my drink. Since he spent most of the night talking to people, I didn't have to worry too much about engaging him in conversation, and I got the chance to dump my drink a lot, but after the speeches, most people were starting to leave. I could still see Andre out of the corner of my eye, which made me feel more confident about what I was going to do.

"You ready to get out of here then?" Bill seemed completely bored.

"Sure, this was a fun night," I said, amping up my acting skills. "Thanks for bringing me."

"I hope you learned a thing or two."

The fact that Andre had an asshole best friend in college who he went so far as to create a business with was probably another big fat red flag I was ignoring. The truth of the matter was, I was fully prepared to give Andre the benefit of the doubt since day one. I saw him as a lost, lonely man, who I had the audacity to think I could fix. People don't fix people, though. I had to keep reminding myself that I was in this for the experience, the adventure, and the sex. I was little Elizabeth Piquel, who had cut her hair, got a nose piercing, and was on her way to being the woman she dreamed she'd become. So, I had to woman up and be her.

"I did, thanks. I learned a lot. You know I do a lot of reading in grad school, and I read a helluva lot of papers, but the truth is, life gives you the best lessons." I was waxing academic when he took a step in closer, and my palms began to sweat.

"So, are you ready for a few more life lessons?" he asked with dark seduction.

"Um," I wasn't sure how to answer that.

"Why don't we go back to my place and have a nightcap?"

"Sure, that sounds fun." I did my best to keep my drink down as I was starting to feel sick.

"It will be fun. You'll get to see where all the magic is made." He put his arm around me.

"Like solar energy systems and wind turbines?" I put on my happy face.

"You are somethin' else." He laughed. "You know I heard that nerdy girls are the best in bed. You wanna test that theory?"

"Let's see how nerdy I can get. Do you have a home office? Blueprints for a clean energy power grid, that stuff really gets me off." *Keep breathing,* I told myself.

"Of course, my home office is literally where all the magic happens." He sided up to me and ushered me out the door.

I craned my head back to see Andre. His face had gone red, and it looked like he wasn't breathing anymore. I just smiled at him and followed Bill out to the valet stand where he ordered his car. Now was the time for conversation, so I asked Bill how he and Andre met, which kept him engaged in conversation until we reached his house, which was an old school mansion in the middle of acres of land. It wasn't as impressive in size or style as Andre's ranch house but looked pricey and showy in a gaudy, overdone kind of fashion.

"Wow, you have a lot of house for one person," I commented as he pulled into the garage, and my heart beat with a fearful kind of nervousness.

"Yeah, probably too big, but I've got a lot of personality. I make it work. Also, I don't want my mistresses bumping into my wives." He laughed, thinking himself hilarious, I assumed.

"That makes sense." I had no good comebacks because I didn't find the joke funny at all.

The night went downhill from there.

"Let's get us something to drink." He slapped my ass after he opened my car door, and I stepped out of the vehicle.

I let out a nervous giggle and was really questioning everything when he opened the garage entrance to the mansion as I followed him down a corridor.

"If you're really interested, this is where most of the science and innovation for the company happens. At the office, I keep our account records, and I'm there when you are, but usually, I work from home since most of my research and prototype work is done here." He geeked out on me just long enough to give me what I needed.

"Wow, that is so cool. You wanna give me a tour of what you're working on?" I did my best to sound nerdy and enthused.

"Not on your life, little girl. That is my most prized and confidential work. You can't get in there unless you marry me." He winked, and I knew he was joking again. We reached his lounge, and he motioned to an overstuffed brown leather couch. "Why don't you have a seat, and I'll fix us something special."

I knew by the way he said it I'd have to be on my toes. The night would be a total bust if he roofied me.

"Not too strong; I've already had a lot to drink." I batted my eyes and pretended I was an idiot.

"Ah, I'm sure you'll love this," he said as he started to mix up different kinds of alcohol in expensive bottles. "What do you say we take these out to the jacuzzi?"

"Isn't it too cold?"

"Not for a jacuzzi. I also have heaters out there; it's nice at any time of year." He brought the drinks over.

"And I'm guessing you don't care that I don't have a swimsuit unless you've got a bunch of them laying around for all those wives and girlfriends you juggle."

This got a little huffing laugh. "Aw, natural is fine with me. I plan to go in with just my birthday suit." He took a sip of his drink.

"Doesn't this take the whole boss and intern thing to a weird level?"

"Only 'weird' if we make it weird." The way he stared at me totally gave me the creeps.

I had to strategize. I could probably keep him off me in the hot tub if I just played around with him, be coy, shy, etc. Then I'd act like I'm tired, demand to go to bed ... and then play too drunk. If I could wait until he's asleep, I could get into his office and start digging. It was so risky, dangerous, and not very well thought out, but I was going for it. I could always blame everything on being drunk.

I took a deep breath and a gulp of the very intoxicating drink and dove face-first into stupid town because I knew what I was attempting was completely idiotic. But I wasn't always known to make the most informed choices, so I threw off my dress and stood up.

"Lead the way." I threw my arm in the air and splashed a little of the drink on his couch, intentionally.

"Yes, ma'am."

He got up and started unbuttoning his shirt. When it was open to his navel, he picked up his drink, and I followed him outside to where there was a bungalow with a jacuzzi housed within.

He set his drink down, took his shirt off, and then the undershirt, and I finally saw his pasty white flesh revealed. That man must have spent a lot of time in his office because he had the daddiest of dad bods. And he was intermittently hairy with a thin dusting of wiry hairs in the oddest places. I did my best not to laugh, I really did, but damn he was a strikingly unattractive man and much more unappealing naked as I discovered when he dropped his pants. His face was handsome, but his body was a fright.

"Well, here goes nothin," I commented as I took off my bra and panties, suddenly feeling more naked than I'd ever been. "Okay, in we go." I immediately got into the hot water even though it was scalding, and I had to grit my teeth closed to get over the initial shock of heat.

"You're a dive-right-in kind of girl I can see." I hoped he'd sit across from me, but no, he chose to slip in right beside me. "How about giving me a little taste?"

With that said, he turned my head to him and started kissing me. His nasty sloppy tongue was licking at my lips and pushing hard to get into my mouth. If he had succeeded, I surely would have barfed the moment his tongue touched mine.

"Slow your roll, turbo. I said yes to the jacuzzi, not a make-out session." I reared my head back and gave him an incensed look.

"Why do you think I invited you to this event?" His eyes were wide and incredulous.

"To teach me about the business. I mean, it was a fundraiser, and I'm an intern; the assumption wasn't too far off base. But my boss inviting me to a fundraiser only to get me naked in his jacuzzi and stick his tongue down my throat, that seems a little rapey to me." I glared at him.

"So, what are we going to do, just splash around?" He laughed it off and went back to his drink.

I decided then would be the perfect time to splash him in the face. "Maybe," is all I said and took one more fortifying sip of my drink, the last I would have as I dumped some of it into the jacuzzi when he had his head turned.

"This is dangerous," he leered seductively. "You have a fucking sexy body." You don't, I thought. "How do you expect me to resist it?"

"I don't expect you to resist me; I just didn't want you charging at me like a bull." I gave him a wink. "We can be a little more playful about this, right? Or are you just gonna hang with me here for a few and then fuck my brains out?" I started slurring my words and acting like a college freshman at a frat party.

"Yep, that was the plan." He oozed on in for round two of the kissing game.

"Well, fine. But I don't want to fuck in the jacuzzi; I'm an old-fashioned kinda girl." My fingers twirled in his matted scraggly chest hair. "I wanna fuck in a bed." The closer I could get to his office, the better.

I knew I wasn't going to be able to get him to go right to sleep, so I revised my plan; get him close, pretend to barf, come back all apologies and bad breath, and wank him hard until he came as many times as it would take to make him pass out.

"I like that kind of old-fashioned," he said as he moved in for the kill.

His medium-sized cock didn't do much to impress, but why would it? Nothing on him was remarkable, and if he was a decent human being, perhaps his whole package could have been tolerated, but he wasn't a decent man, not even a little.

This revelation made me think of Andre. Was he a decent man? I wasn't sure, but at least his package was so worth enjoying, and inside I knew there was a good man afraid to come out. With Bill, I think all the digging in the world wouldn't find much. He was zeroing in for a kiss again, and I knew there was no way I could stomach it, so I pecked him on the lips and smoothed my hand over his floppy tummy. It was sort of like a Buddha belly, and it was the least terrifying part of him.

"I love this," I said playfully. "I wanna make a wish."

"Ha, some men work out, others are too busy. Our friend Andre is obsessed with the gym, but he doesn't usually date girls from the intern stack, too bad for you."

"He seems like a very aloof man. I mean from what I know of him and what my friends say about him."

"He's a dick." Bill dove his hands to my breasts and started kneading them like they were bread dough.

The night could not end fast enough. His little willy was spiking up in the water, and I did my best to avoid it as he dragged me into him, but his little poker did get a poke in or two. I decided to give up on the idea of even touching it; my altruism wasn't worth being molested or exchanging in unwanted sexual behavior. Instead, I would just go for the drama.

"I'm ready for bed now," I said, slurring my words more. "Just let me finish this first." I turned my head away from him and pretended to finish off my drink by letting it dribble down my chin into the water.

Luckily he didn't notice because he turned to finish his own glass. "Alright, let's get this show on the road." He hopped out of the jacuzzi with his chubby cock flying and offered his hand for me. "My room is just down this way. We can enter from the outside. I'll get us some towels from the bathroom when we get there."

"Sounds good to me." I smiled drunkenly and made sure to waver a little on my feet.

"Woah, there …" He grabbed me around the waist. "Don't fall over before I get you on your back." He pinched my side, and I almost legitimately vomited.

The walk to the bedroom was terrifying, but I just kept breathing and bucking myself up. I had left my clothes in the living room, so my plan to pillage Bill's home office also had to include clothes retrieval. I needed to get my mind in the game.

"So, what's contraception look like? I don't like condoms, but I'll make an exception for tonight if you don't have anything else," he said as he stroked himself harder. "I gotta few laying around here."

"We're good, I've got contrac ... contrass ... crontran ..." I pretended to fumble with the words.

"You on the pill?" he finally blurted out, frustrated.

"Yeah, that." I pretended to fall over on my feet and land on the bed. "But wear a rubber 'cause just in case I forgot it."

I noted going down the digital clock by his bed said it was almost one in the morning. I only had to bluff for a few hours before, hopefully, his natural circadian rhythm would kick in.

As soon as I was on the bed, he pounced. Again, I almost legitimately barfed the moment I felt his raw penis on my body. Yuck. It wasn't really that hard to act for him. He got a few kisses in, and then when his mouth went to my breast, it was Oscar time.

"Oh, shit!" I made a gurgling sound. "Oh, fuck." I make sure to lurch my belly a little since he was smashed on top of me.

"I know, baby, just take it." He wiggled his nasty ass cock on the top of my pussy, luckily I was dry as a bone, and he hadn't tried to penetrate me.

"No, no ... arghhah. I'm gonna be sick." With all of my strength, I bucked him off me and ran to the bathroom and locked the door, catching my breath and sort of laughing at the same time ... to myself, so that he wouldn't hear.

Next came a lot of gacking sounds, splashing of water into the toilet, and me pretending to wretch my eyes out. I made sure to make it long, drawn-out, and dramatic.

"Are you okay in there?" He didn't sound worried but pissed off.

"Yeah, sure fine ... just that shit sneaks up on you. What did you put in my drink?" I pretended to wretch again with more splashing.

"Nothing," he groaned.

When I came waddling back in, I pretended like the world was still spinning. "Maybe I should just sleep." I crawled into bed, and he tried it with me again.

"Just lay there, and I'll do the rest."

Was he serious? As soon as I felt his cock poke my ass, I was back to my shenanigans. I saw the remnants of my drink on the table, and so when he moved to his side of the bed to fish around in his drawer for the one fucking random ass condom he had floating around in there, I poured the last of my drink on my side of the bed and pretended to retch again. He turned around and looked at me as he pulled a condom package out of the drawer.

"Oh, God, I am so sorry! Jeeze, I barfed in your bed. At least it's only liquid this time. You should have seen the toilet ... oi what a mess." I turned over and pretended to fall asleep.

I heard him rip open the condom wrapper and was ready to run when I heard him start cursing.

"God damn, fuck it all! Fuckin' dick-killing bitch!" He must have been trying to pump himself back up as I heard skin slapping behind me, but my best guess was he must have lost his erection.

I made another gurgling sound, trying not to giggle, and he turned out the lights. "Goddamit, Eliza!" he said under his breath. "Next time, no drinks. I'll fuck you in the morning when you're sober," he mumbled as he turned over on his side and fell asleep.

Why he'd fall asleep with a pile of puke in his bed was beyond me? Perhaps he was legitimately drunk. He did seem to be throwing caution to the wind; maybe he held himself together when he was drinking but let his inhibitions down. I didn't care, I just waited for him to start heavy breathing, and when I heard the telltale signs of a sleeping man, I quietly got out of bed.

My heart raced as I made my way out of his room. I opened the door so slowly I thought I might have a heart attack, but luckily, I could get out without him even stirring. I stood in the hallway naked, having no idea where I was, but time was not on my side, so I raced around looking for the living room, and with a few missteps, I found it at the end of the hall to the left. I was happy to be reunited with my clothes, though my panties and bra were by the jacuzzi. I didn't have time to get those, so I just had to make do going commando. I was able to find Bill's office easily and closed the door as I quickly rummaged through his files, which were thankfully unlocked. I found gold about fifteen minutes into my search when the last filing cabinet drawer I opened had the name Fasco on it. Inside, with a quick glance, I saw clear evidence of hydraulic drilling recent enough to be connected to the earthquake they had just had, as well a fresh invoice for three new wells that had been drilled that week. Bingo! My heart nearly exploded; I had what I needed. There was also a laptop tucked behind the file, so without opening it, I nabbed that as well, knowing I would be in big trouble for stealing. I found a canvas bag with some random crap in it, put all the files and the laptop in the bag, and slowly closed the file cabinet.

I tiptoed out of the room, found my shoes and purse at the front door, and carefully snuck out. I worried that there might be an alarm, and there was, but Bill was so hot to get into my panties he hadn't set it. I knew there had to be surveillance, so before I left the mansion, I tucked the bag under my dress and pretended to be holding my stomach like I was still sick. I quickly called an Uber as soon as I was on the deserted street in front of Bill's house. I couldn't afford a trip all the way back to my house, so I keyed in Andre's address, hoping that a three in the morning surprise visit wouldn't bother him.

I had no other choice. The moment I sat in the backseat of the pristine Toyota Ultima, I breathed easy for the first time all night. I then laughed at myself; I should have been a spy.

Chapter 24

Andre

When the alarm on my front door went off, I didn't pay it too much attention. I glanced at the time, three-fifteen. I then got a text from Eliza.

Sorry, I'm outside. - E.

I was so relieved she was at my front door; I could hardly sleep thinking of her with Bill.

"Come on in," I said, opening the door. "Are you okay? Did he hurt you? I should have never let you do this." I was rambling, but I didn't care.

"No, I'm fine. Here. I think I got something, and I'm probably going to jail for it." She looked down at her feet.

"You aren't going to jail for anything," I assured her as I opened the bag she handed me to find exactly what I was hoping she'd get.

That damn rotten bastard. I had to put Eliza's life on the line to find that his cheating ass was running a fracking venture outside of the company. I knew it; he was Fasco. Damn it. I was ready to call in the police that night, but really, it wasn't a matter for the police. I wasn't sure exactly who I should tell, but possibly Dylan. We had to stop operations immediately, that was for sure, so in the morning, my first order of business would be to contact all the contractors that Bill had hired and tell them to halt their work until I could assess the situation. Eliza also pilfered a laptop, which I hoped would be full of exactly everything I needed to nail Bill's ass to the wall.

"I can't believe you got all this. You are a genius!" I kissed her cheek, and just the feel of her soft skin on my lips and the lingering scent of her had my cock stirring. I wasn't wearing underwear, and so the evidence of my arousal would soon be unmistakable. At that moment, Eliza Piquel was the most miraculous human on the planet.

"It was an ordeal; let me tell you." She rolled her eyes.

"He didn't force himself on you, did he? Or did you have to? Please tell me you didn't." I was genuinely worried that Eliza may have had to sleep with the bastard.

"No, but keeping him off me was a real test of my acting skills; also, now that I've stolen his stuff, I don't think he's going to want me to work in his office anymore or yours." She bowed her head down and looked defeated.

"How much are we paying you?" I didn't want her ever to step foot into that office again.

"Twenty-eight dollars an hour." She looked up with a glimmer of hope in her eyes.

"Three days a week, right? That's nothing. I'm going to double that to have you stay home. I'll write a letter of recommendation for your university regarding the internship, and I'll square it all away with HR. I'll say you were in an accident, hurt your back, and need to work remotely. It's no problem; we've done it before. I don't want you anywhere near Bill. If we have to, we'll launch a sexual harassment suit against him. He's not going to make a complaint to the company about the files he shouldn't have on a project he's forbidden to be doing. You're fine; I just don't want you near him. You'll spend your weekends here. I'm not going away again. This way you'll have more time for your schoolwork. I know you spend a lot of late nights trying to catch up," I accidentally confessed to her.

"And how would you know that?" She playfully glared at me.

"Perhaps I stalk when you're on Facebook." I threw it off as if it were nothing. "Now, let's get to bed." At that point, my cock was running the show, and I couldn't wait for her any longer. "I can look over what you got in the morning."

"Yeah, you're right. It's really late. We can talk everything out in the morning." She yawned and followed me down the hallway to my bedroom. "Fred, Ethel." She nodded to the statue before taking off her dress and neatly placing it on the end of the bed.

Every single time I saw her naked, I loved her body even more, and then I realized it wasn't just her body that I cared about. There she was sticking her neck out for me, risking it all for this belief in something good. I knew it wasn't just to impress me, or even to impress me at all because she didn't once seek my thanks or admiration for the act she'd committed. She simply showed me what she'd accomplished. As she slid into bed, she stretched out and curled onto the side where she usually slept.

"That's it?" I playfully complained as I edged over to her. "No good night kiss, no tongues, tickles, or that sweet vagina?" I brought my hand around to the front of her and pinched one of her nipples. "Don't you wanna play with me?" I whispered hotly in her ear.

"I do." I loved the smile that crossed her face. "I'm just a little tired."

"But we don't have to be anywhere but here tomorrow. I'll let you sleep in." I poked her backside with my cock. "I've been worried about you all night."

"You haven't." She turned around and started gently tugging on me.

"I'll have you know I have." I truly did worry about her. "I kicked myself for letting you go off with that douchebag." With her facing me, I pinched and played with both of her beautiful nipples.

"Yeah, he's a real creep. I'm just so glad I got out of there unscathed. I had to do a lot of faux barfing, but it was actually fun, sort of. I can say that now I'm safe." Her thumb rubbed across the soft skin on my shining cockhead that glistened with my desire for her.

I stopped pinching her and brought her in for a legitimate hug. "I am so glad you're safe, and you're never doing that again. You are the craziest, bravest, sexiest woman I have ever met." I kissed her soft lips and just felt nothing but an overwhelming warmth and care for her.

I rolled on top of her and kissed her more deeply.

When we broke our kiss, she looked at me. "You asked me to do it," she said, smirking.

"I'm an asshole. Why did you listen to me?" I was playing; it felt good to play. "Well, now I'm not letting you out of my sight; except to go to school, and on non-school days, you're staying with me. I'll hire you a driver. I don't want you alone ever!" I kissed her again and spread her legs wide under me.

My fingers found her pussy dripping wet, and so I sunk into my favorite place and pounded my frustrations away. Good thing she loved hard thrusting because I could never take it easy with her. She came every single time, multiple times. I relentlessly pumped her until my own orgasm squeezed my balls like a vice and had me shooting ribbon and after ribbon of hot sperm inside of her. God bless her birth control because we'd be having a whole football team of children with as hard as I consistently inseminated her womb. I loved our rough sex just about as much as I was starting to love her.

"Damn, girl. You sure can take it." I slapped the side of her ass as I pulled my abused cock out of her well-ridden pussy.

"Good thing too, because there is no middle ground with you." She clamored for breath as her eyes drooped closed, and within seconds, she was curled up beside me in a deep sleep.

Usually, I just rolled over to my side and let her have her rest, but that night I wrapped my arms around her and brought her warm body close to mine and covered us both with the duvet as we'd be chilled soon, and I wanted to preserve the warm and glorious feelings she gave me. I was seriously starting to love that woman.

We both woke up to the sound of her phone pinging. I set mine on silent on Saturday mornings, and I usually reminded her to do the same, but we were pretty busy, so it slipped both of our minds.

"Make it stop," she protested, still nestled against my chest.

She was not a morning person at all. I gently lifted my head up and retrieved her phone. The text was from Bill, and so I was shocked awake to read it.

You fucking better be dead by the side of the road, bitch where are you? How dare you tease my cock like that and disappear. I saw you sneak out of here on the surveillance video this am. You are so fucked on Monday. And I mean it, you are fucked as in your cunt is gonna be aching when I'm done with you! You owe me that pussy. I put up with your puking all night long; you will be paying me, bitch!"

I was so angry; I could hardly breathe.

"Who is it?" Eliza looked up as concern washed over her expression. "It's Bill, isn't it? He's threatening to kill me because I took his files?" She looked so nervous, the poor thing.

"No, I don't think he knows about the files yet; he's just mad you left without putting out. Don't answer it. We'll just let him boil. Do you have anything at the office you want me to get for you?" I brought her into me again.

"No, just standard-issue pens and stuff, the next intern can have them. I didn't leave anything personal there." She seemed a little far off and sad.

"Good, you won't be going back. Does he know where you live?" Suddenly, I was starting to worry.

'It's on my HR paperwork, but I think all of that is confidential, so no, and I'm not really at my house that much. I mean, I will be now, I guess."

"Maybe you should move in here with me?" I was thinking out loud. "He'll get your info the minute he finds the files are missing."

"I'm not sure I could handle you twenty-four seven." She was being serious, and I loved her for that.

"I handle me twenty-four seven, and I'm doing okay." I gave her a playful grin.

"Okay, is such a relative term." She kissed my neck and sent lightning bolts of fire through my body. "But I know I couldn't."

"I'd be at work most of the time," I encouraged her.

"It's hard to live with someone and just be a casual fuck. I mean, what would it be like? We are walking the halls, and then suddenly you'd say, 'Hey, you wanna throw down?' And I'd be like, 'I can't, I have a paper, maybe in an hour?' And then we'd have to ignore each other until we ran into each other again, and I'd finally say, 'I'm ready to fuck', and you'd be like, 'Sure, where do you want to go? Your room or mine?' Seems like it would be a very hard thing to maintain." She had difficulty keeping a straight face as she went over our possible casually fornicating roommates scenario.

"Well, we're friends with privileges, so it would be more like, 'Do you wanna hang out, get pizza, or fuck?'" I kissed her.

"Let's just do weekends for now. I'm not ready to move in, and we don't know if Bill is going to do anything at all." She kissed me back, and my determination spiked.

I suddenly needed her to know I wanted more.

Chapter 25

Eliza

Andre was coming on really strong, and I wasn't quite ready for it. I had told myself just to get used to our relationship being casual, and I was fine with that because he was ninety-five percent jerk, but his actions were a little less horrible these days, and that was scary because then I might have actually to like him.

"You up for a quickie in the shower and then go see Midnight? I have two offers I'm seriously considering; this might be your last weekend with him." His voice dipped a little as if he almost regretted selling the horse.

I knew I certainly regretted it.

"Yes, I would love to spend as much time with him as I can." I kissed Andre on the lips and popped out of bed naked.

I knew where his shower was and didn't want to waste time, not only because I wanted to see the horse, but I was incredibly horny, and I needed to have sex with him in the worst way. All the stress of the night before made me even more ravenous for Andre. He stepped up behind me, gave my backside a swat, and turned on the hot water. It didn't take more than a minute to heat up, and we were both in the shower, ready to go. His fingers were between my legs faster than I could say, 'pass me the soap.' I laughed.

"I thought I was eager." I grabbed his hard cock and started pumping my hand on him, just loving the feel of his thickness in my grasp.

"Oh, baby, I've been dreaming of you all night," he said as he turned me around to face the white tiled wall.

"You just had sex with me a few hours ago," I teased.

How many times had he taken me in the shower? Too many to count, but every time, it was like bolts of electricity searing my insides. He thrust himself in hard and fast, just as he always did, and I wondered if we'd ever just have lazy sex one day?

"Ah," I screamed out involuntarily as he grabbed my hips and impaled me on him harder.

"God, I always want to be in you," he growled in my ear as he wrapped his arms around me and brought me up to his chest, holding me tightly as I adjusted to keep him inside of me while standing.

It was a bit of an effort as he didn't stop thrusting deeper and deeper as he kissed my neck, and the warm water pelted us like rain. When his lust overwhelmed us, he lifted my leg and draped it over his arm so that I was in a very uncomfortable hold. He angled around closer and just started pummeling me, and it all felt much better. Painful, vulnerable, exposed, and at his mercy, he hard-thrust until my world spiraled into a pin of pleasure and pain then blasted out around us. I came so hard and was happy. Not too long after he pushed his entire body weight on me and his cock stiffened inside of me, his body went rigid, and he grunted in three short blasts as I felt him fill me with cum.

After all the stress I'd been under, it felt so good just to stay there with him inside me. We both caught our breath for a moment before he pulled his cock out, which, despite deflating, was always an effort. I let the water trickle down my back as his release escaped my body.

He fingered what was left of my pussy and kissed my cheek. "You are amazing," he whispered in my ear, and I was too sated to move as he began to wash my body.

I let him care for me as he always did when we were together. I forgot about the outside world when we were at the ranch, even though the outside world hadn't forgotten about us. When we were done with our shower, I was starving, having barely eaten the night before.

"What do you have to rustle up for breakfast?" I asked, still wearing only my towel. I didn't have my bag of clothes with me, which was stupid. I should have sent them home with Andre.

I did remember leaving my dirty outfit there the weekend before, and I hoped that perhaps someone had cleaned it. If not, I was going to be doing some laundry. I remembered how bad a cook he was; we were.

"Let's see." We walked over to the kitchen, wearing only our towels. I guess he wasn't worried about the caretakers walking in on us. "I have cereal and milk." He gave me a sheepish grin.

"That works for me," I smiled back and went to grab the milk from the fridge as he got the cereal out of the cupboard. "I'll order in for lunch and dinner. I was hoping to go out, but not with Bill on the prowl. Speaking of, have you heard any more from him?" He looked over at me with a concerned expression.

"No, I've been with you, silly." I put the milk on the table and sat there, trying to hold up my towel.

It was weird to be walking around almost naked, but when in Rome or a house that looked like a museum in Rome ... "Are we just gonna sit here and eat breakfast in our towels?" I asked, not sure what he was okay with.

"Well, I thought you wanted to go out and see Midnight, so ..." He brought over the cereal and a big bowl and took the seat I was about to sit in.

As I took a step to move to the other seat, he grabbed me and planted me in his lap. I could already feel him hardening again.

"We are never gonna get out to see that horse if you sit there and I sit here, that is for damn sure," I playfully scolded.

"I just want to feel you. We'll save the fun for later." He poured the cereal into the bowl, then added milk.

He then fed me a bite, scooped one for himself, and we continued that way as one hand played with my breast under the towel and the other fed me cereal. It was sexy as hell, and I almost wanted to give up on the idea of horse riding, but Midnight would soon be gone, and I wanted to spend time with him before he went. When we finished the cereal, we got dressed. Luckily, I did find my dirty clothes from the last time I was at his house, and they were clean. I was ready to ride.

"I should at least get you some clothes to have over here," Andre complained, still trying to get me to temporarily move in, but I was adamantly against it.

I wasn't going to do it. I assured him I'd be fine. He wasn't happy with my decision, but he didn't fight me. We both decided for my peace of mind and his, we'd not look at my phone until after lunch. Whatever threats Bill was making could wait, and we didn't need the extra stress, so we walked out to the stables, and my heart instantly felt lighter as soon as I saw the horses.

I never figured that I was a horse person, but Midnight changed me. He bowed his head as soon as I entered the stable and huffed through his nose.

"He sure likes you." Andre laughed as his arm slid around my waist.

"I love him. Just look at his eyes; you can see there is a deep thinker in there, an old soul." I just gazed at him with so much love for the majestic animal.

"I'd say you even like him more than you do me." Was Andre being insecure? No, not my assholey alpha? No way.

"On occasion," I said. It was the truth.

"I hope to change that."

"Um, I don't think you can change who you are, Andre," I threw off casually as he opened the horse pen.

"Perhaps, you don't know." He brought Midnight out, and my heart raced.

"Why the sudden change?" I didn't like playing games. "You're caring and attentive; what has happened to you?" I jutted out my hip and acted like a brat.

"Maybe I just don't want to die alone," he said as he gave me the reins. "I'll have you put on his tack. You should get used to doing it."

"Why? Aren't you just about to sell him?" I didn't mean to be so argumentative, but I was feeling very feisty.

"I am, but if you're going to be spending more time here, you should learn how to tend to the horses." Right, that was why.

We saddled our horses, and I tried not to think about the shift in Andre's personality, but it wasn't easy to do, especially when we got to the lake.

"What do you say we take a dip?" He looked at me and smiled.

"The lake is freezing. I'm not going in there in the middle of November. You can; I'll watch. I like seeing you naked." I sat back on the sand as Midnight munched on some grass and watched as Andre started to take off his clothes.

"Do you dare me?" He was being playful.

"I do." I was being smug.

And just like that, he jumped in, and within seconds, bounded back out.

"Cold, cold, cold." He shook his cold, wet hair on me, and I screamed.

"Why the hell did you do that?" I laughed at him.

"Why not?" He was still naked and shivering.

"I don't think I've ever seen him so small." I used a tiny little voice as I touched his shriveled cock, which had retreated with the cold.

"Leave him alone," Andre found his command again. "The poor guy is freezing." God, that sweet look he gave me, I couldn't resist.

"Maybe I should warm him up." I leaned forward and didn't even wait for an answer; I took his cock into my mouth.

It was cold on my lips and hot tongue, but I warmed him up quickly as he grew in my mouth. Soon he was back to his full size, and I swallowed him down my throat to the best of my ability. I worked hard on him as his hands stroked my hair.

"I love you," he whispered, and I nearly choked.

I almost stopped what I was doing, but he was so close to his orgasm, I kept at it until he shot his release down my throat. I did choke a little at that. I wasn't a huge fan of swallowing, but he seemed like he needed it. I wiped my mouth and looked up at him, doubting I'd heard what I heard.

"You should probably get dressed," I suggested ignoring his proclamation of love. He then kissed me full on the mouth, still naked. His finger coursed down my cheek before he got himself dressed again.

The ride back was nice and leisurely, and when we arrived at the stables to put the horses back, I was starving.

"See you ... um." I put my head to Midnight's forehead. "Maybe I'll see you again. If not, don't forget what a wonderful horse you are." I tapped his nose, and he made a huffing sound as if he understood. "Okay. I'm ready to eat."

"Me too," Andre said, and he looked back at Midnight. I had taken off his tack and brushed him down and bonded with him as much as I'd ever bonded with any being, and he watched me as I left the stable. Andre noticed but didn't say anything.

"So, what's for lunch, boss?" I playfully wrapped my arm around his middle, almost skipping as we walked toward his ranch house.

"I thought we might have Mexican food." He looked down at me, and there was that amorous glow again.

It was nice but really strange. When we arrived back at the ranch, we both retrieved our phones. It was about two in the afternoon, and each of us had the same horrified looks on our faces. We scrolled through the various messages, and we simultaneously slumped onto the couch.

"I'll read you mine if you read me yours," I said, in a catatonic kind of shock.

"I think I'll order us lunch first." Suddenly Andre was back to being a cold businessman.

I missed the playful guy who jumped buck naked into a freezing cold lake, but if his messages were as scary as mine, I wouldn't be so playful anymore either.

"Tacos and salad, okay?" he asked as he tapped on his phone.

"Yeah, tacos sound amazing."

"We'll have steak or something hearty for dinner, but comfort food might be a must right now." He placed the order and set his phone down. "Okay, you first. I'm afraid mine is a little more complicated."

"I don't know, this feels pretty complicated." I looked at my phone and did my best to act out the texts from Bill.

"Bitch! Don't pretend you're not getting my texts. I have money and the means. I will have someone at your doorstep in an hour if you don't call me back. You go to the police and I'll drag everyone you know under, especially Reid Prentice, your politician friend. Don't think I won't stoop very low. I have a question to ask you, Princess, and I can't put it in writing, but you know exactly what I'm going to ask about, don't you? I will remind you, stealing is a crime. You want to keep that pretty face out of jail? Text me back."

"That was sent at ten o'clock. And this was sent at twelve o'clock." I returned to my text reading performance.

"I have your address."

"This was sent at two."

"I've sent someone really special to check and make sure you're okay."

"And ten minutes ago."

"Eliza, there is some weird guy here to see you. Where are you? Text me, I'm worried. Peyton."

Three minutes ago.

"WHERE ARE YOU BITCH?"

"I'm going to call Peyton and tell her to call the police." I started shaking a little; he actually sent someone to the house.

"Yes, have her call the police if the guy is still there." Andre was really worried.

"What about your texts?" I really didn't want to focus on the problem; I'd gone into some kind of fear-induced walking coma.

"It will wait; solve this first."

I dialed Peyton's number.

"Peyton, it's Eliza are you okay?" I tried to sound casual.

"Oh, holy shit, some weird-ass guy was looking for you, but I said you weren't here. You're spending the night with Andre, right?" Oh God, she didn't tell him that, did she?

"Did you tell him where I was?" Please say 'no.'

"No, I just said you weren't here. He stayed for a minute, and Gen and

I freaked and called the police; when the cop car rolled up, he left. Are you okay? Are you in any trouble?" She sounded terrified.

"No, I'm fine. Just call the police if anyone comes by, and don't tell them where I am. I have a crazy stalker at work. I'll explain it all tomorrow when I come home. Don't worry but keep your phones handy just in case. He just wants me; he won't hurt anyone else, I'm sure."

"Okay, well, you stay safe, okay? Don't be heroic." She was sweet.

"I promise I'll be good." I ended the call and looked up to Andre. "And so, what have you got?"

"There was another earthquake in Zapata, and it's completely devastated the small community of Paradise Point. They fear that there may have been some casualties, and Bill has asked repeatedly if you are with me; he says you stole money and jewelry from him."

"I only took the files." I was suddenly angry.

"I know."

Chapter 26

Andre

We hadn't thought this through. I had to call Dylan and have him do an emergency audit of the company. Bill would be spending the weekend covering his tracks, especially because of the earthquake hours after his last drilling.

"I have to make a call. You stay here for a moment, and we'll discuss the next steps."

"Okay," Eliza said, but the poor thing looked so nervous.

I called Dylan and expressed the urgency. I told him I would double whatever Bill was paying. With the earthquake and the file and laptop that Eliza retrieved, he was suddenly very interested. A case like ours would put me in the limelight. I wanted my company spared; we would focus the investigation only on Bill. I needed to be seen as the whistleblower, not the perpetrator. Dylan agreed to be discreet, speedy, and efficient. The only reason Dylan changed his mind about auditing our company was that he finally saw there was a real bad guy to catch. This would be good for his record, and divorcing himself from whatever deal he'd made with Bill would be essential.

With that call made, I felt easier talking with Eliza about what the future would look like for us. I wasn't going to let her leave, not even to get her things. I'd have someone go and get everything out of her house, and so my second call was to a security firm where I hired her bodyguards, one for the day time, a night shift guard, and a weekend guard. She was never going to be left without protection. I was sure she was going to hate all of it, but I didn't care.

"Okay, that's all arranged. Loverboy send you any more texts?"

"Um, let's see, I have a few." She grinned at me being playful, which was sweet, but she really didn't understand the scope of what that man could do.

His ex-wife had nearly been beheaded in an 'accident.' He was not someone to toy with. Luckily, she got a good lawyer and a restraining order, but Bill was certifiable at times.

"I'm gonna hunt you down bitch, don't think you can hide from me. I'll check every

shitty-ass hotel in the state. There is no way you are going to stay hidden for long, and when I find you, I'm gonna hug you and kiss you so hard, Love, you'll just die."

"This one's a keeper.

"I'm tracking your phone."

"Can he do that?" She looked worried.

"Maybe. I'm not sure what his technological abilities are or how he knows your cell carrier, but it's best we get you a new phone. I can order one and have it here in an hour. Turn that one off and take out the battery." I didn't want to alarm her, but chances were Bill already knew she was with me.

"What if he comes here?" Her voice dropped.

"I've called in security staff; they'll be armed, and they just texted saying they are on their way. Someone will be stationed on the road at the front of the property. No one is going to get onto this lot by car, and we'll have a nightguard patrolling the house after dark. We'll be fine. He's just trying to scare you. I've already let my caretaker know that we have amped up security, but it does worry me the lengths he's willing to go to protect that information. This has to be bigger than a little border town. Either he has totally fallen in love with you, which is possible for anyone to do, or his operation is much bigger than I ever imagined."

"I'm going to go with a bigger operation; there certainly was no love between us, but I'll trust you on this. Just do what you have to do to keep us safe." She looked a little lost.

"What do you say we watch a movie and just chill out? We've had a lot of exercise, and I want you to rest up for tonight." I gave her a seductive wink.

"Oh? What's so special about tonight?" I love how lusty she'd become.

"You're going to have to wait until tonight to see." I took her hand and led her into the screening room.

I enjoyed watching a movie with her the last time she and I were in there. We cuddled, and this time, we watched an epic space adventure. It felt good to lose ourselves in the spectacle of a big Hollywood movie. My caregiver got her package during the movie and texted me the arrangements he'd made with the security staff. Though there had been no suspicious activity on my property, we were armed to the teeth and would have no less than five guards on the premises at all times. I felt very relieved that Eliza was safe with me and that she'd been able to find the files and the laptop. I was looking forward to diving into both, but at that moment, I wanted to just be with her and know that she was feeling secure.

When the movie was over, I left her to program her new phone while I went over the files and flared up the laptop. Of course, it was password-protected, but I had my IT guy opening it up remotely. He could hack into anything, and Bill wasn't creative enough to make an uncrackable password. It took my guy all of seven minutes to open the laptop and in it was gold. I immediately started sending files to Dylan, who was already at the office starting the audit. He was surprised to find Bill there, but Dylan was prepared for him. He had a team of people with him and said they were the external accountants. Bill didn't give them much attention as it was nearing accounting season and the end of our fiscal year, plus how was he going to explain his reasons for being there? Dylan had more legal credence than Bill did as Dylan was the state auditor in charge of business ethics and fraud management.

According to Dylan, Bill looked both angry and freaked and started spouting off accusations against me about how I had stolen his ideas and was profiting off them on the side.

"If there is anything illegal happening in this company, we will find it," Dylan assured him, but by Dylan's account, that didn't give Bill any solace.

I wasn't worried about myself; I did take Bill's ideas, he was our company idea guy, but I never profited personally from them. I funded the company, the entire investment into the firm was mine, and he offered his enthusiasm as per his role in the company, and for that, I paid him well and gave him several points on the profit, so he was a rich man and well-compensated for his ideas.

Additionally, I was the one who hired the engineers, scientists, and mathematicians that brought his ideas from concept to consumer, so he should have been grateful, but the fact that he was grabbing at straws to bring me down didn't surprise me. I wasn't worried. At that moment, my life felt pretty damn good. I ordered steak and potatoes with broccoli and garlic butter for dinner, and we were both stuffed when we ambled into the shower to rinse the day away before hopping into bed.

"I really like my new phone," Eliza gushed as she soaped my back. "Thank you; that was very sweet of you."

"It was very sweet of you to risk your life and get me the files I

Loving The Enemy

needed." I took the soap from her and returned the favor, soaping her back for a moment before looping my hands around her body and fondling her gorgeous breasts. "You feel clean enough?" I poked my hard cock into her behind.

"Right, I'm getting a special treat tonight." She craned her head back and smiled at me.

"You sure are," I wiggled my cock on her ass.

I actually wasn't sure what the treat would be, but a night full of sex; however, I did plan to make it all about her. I was going to make that woman cum so many times she'd be dizzy, dazed, and adoring when I was through with her. I wanted to see her face contort with ecstasy. I wanted her to lay beside me, spooning my body with my sperm swirling around her well-protected womb. I certainly didn't want children, but the idea that I'd leave a bit of myself with her made me really horny.

"Yay, me." She raised her hand and made a little victory sign, which gave me the perfect opportunity to grab her by the waist and wrangle her out of the shower.

I toweled her off while the blowers dried us and made sure to spend a lot of time on her erogenous zones. "All I ask," I whispered into her ear, "is that you let me do everything tonight. All I want you to do is enjoy me." I kissed her cheek, and she broke into a warm smile.

"That sounds amazing."

When I finished drying her, I carried her to the bed and gently set her down. "Don't bother with Fred and Ethel tonight," I teased. "Keep your focus on me."

"Yes, Master," she played. I loved how she was always ready to play.

"You know it." I kissed her warm, clean belly, then trailed kisses, one by one down her stomach to the sweet, well-trimmed tuft of hair that hid her heaven from the world.

I raked my teeth through the hair, which probably wasn't the smartest move in hindsight as it had me spitting out a few stray hairs, but the surprised reaction it gave her was worth it; also she was visually glistening from the flood of arousal that that one simple act brought on. I was tempted to do it again but decided against it. Maybe instead, I'd shave off all her hair before I repeated the teeth grazing, though I did love her little tuft of light brown curls.

"Oh my, God." She giggled.

"Knees up, legs out as far as they will go my, dear." I kissed just above her pussy as she complied.

"What on earth are you planning?" She tried to lift her head to see me, but I held onto her thighs and spread them wide.

"As I said, just sit back and enjoy this."

I continued my kisses until I reached her sweet cleft, and then I released her thighs, but she knew to keep her legs up for me as I parted her labia with my fingers making sure to stretch it just a little past what might be comfortable. She gasped, and that was my cue. I dove my tongue into her as far as I could reach while pressing my thumb hard against her clit and rolling it over her pelvis bone. Her breathing escalated, and soon she was panting, gasping for breath as she bucked into my face. One orgasm down. I flicked her little clit with my fingers as she came down from her high.

I knew she wasn't a big fan of tasting herself, so I rolled off the bed and darted to the bathroom to swill some mouthwash around in my mouth before I dove into kissing her. When I returned, she was still all flushed and pink from her orgasm. She looked so floppy and amorous; I loved her.

"That was fun," she slurred.

I pumped myself a little and then slid in on top of her. "This is gonna be fun too."

While I was just going in for a little missionary, I kissed her long and deep. The deeper my cock went, the more I loved her. It didn't take me long to work myself into her as she smiled with my kissing her nose, her cheeks, her neck, her chin.

"Andre," she writhed as I gently rolled my cock deeper into her.

As soon as I was well planted, I started to rock and roll, literally. I kissed her, my tongue tangling with hers, and I fucked her, with love, as hard as I could. I knew she liked it rough; she craved it hard and deep. I planned to annihilate her with my lust then do nothing but love and caress her hot spent body after I'd turned her to goo. I laid all my weight on her as she held on tight.

"Oh my God, Andre," she screamed as I bottomed out in her as deep as I could go. "Ah, I love this so much."

"I know, baby," I grunted as I continued my attack.

I felt her body tighten up and clench around me and her second orgasm of the evening was in full swing when her body latched onto mine, and before I knew it, my balls tightened, and I was shooting hard and fast.

My whole body shivered with the intensity of my orgasm, made more powerful by the look of love and ecstasy on Eliza's sweet face. She may have cut her hair and gotten a nose piercing, but her dear sweet soul was still untouched by the beauty modifications. As I was awash in my own bliss, I felt a hard jab to my cock that had me screeching like a wild animal.

"Holy fuck! Aye, fucking God!" I ripped myself out of her, not wanting to hurt her but desperate to know what was impaling me.

"Are you okay?" She shook off her post-coital daze to find me rubbing my softening cock where there was a tiny red spot with some swelling.

"What have you got in there, girl? Teeth?" I was kidding, but some instinctual part of me wanted to suss out what had bitten me.

I fished my fingers around in her gently and found a tiny piece of plastic wrapped in copper that I carefully pulled out of her vagina.

"Ooh, ouch." She felt the pain too.

"What the hell is this?" I held the little T-shaped plastic piece up to the light trying for the life of me to understand why I'd fished it out of her vagina.

"Oh, God no," I looked over at her, and she was white as a ghost.

"What? What is this?" I suddenly panicked, though I didn't think I had any reason to; the thing looked perfectly harmless.

"It's my IUD," she whispered.

"As in birth control?" I looked at the funny thing and realized I didn't know much about women's contraceptive devices.

"Well, no need to panic, it just came out …"

"It belongs in my uterus," she said in disbelief. "I don't know why it came out."

"Well, you like it rough, honey." I held her to me as she looked like she was going to cry.

Probably all the stress she was under was getting to her.

"What am I going to do?" She started biting her nails, which I've never seen her do.

"It's no problem. We'll go to the doctor tomorrow and get a morning-after pill. I have a private doctor. I'm sure he can prescribe the pill. We can get one over the counter, but I'd prefer a doctor administer it. We have seventy-two hours; it's no problem. I'll take you there in the morning. No worries." I kissed her forehead. "Well, this wasn't exactly the surprise I had for you. I just wanted to love on you and make the whole night about lavishing you."

"Thank you." She was still so sad.

"I think maybe the rest of the night should just be loving you." I kissed her again and brought her in closer.

"But you don't love me." Boy, she was really down.

I caressed her sweet body. "Maybe I do."

Chapter 27

Eliza

I had a hard time sleeping that night trying to figure out how my IUD had gotten dislodged, but Andre was probably right. We hadn't been very careful. I did love his hard pounding, and we never shied from rough sex, so losing my IUD was the consequence. I should have gotten the shot, but I wasn't having sex before Andre. Ugh. I tossed and turned until the sun came up and felt like complete shit. By the look on Andre's face, he didn't sleep too well either.

"Okay, let's get this taken care of." He kissed me. "Everything is going to be just fine."

"I hope so." I followed him out of the room to go to the bathroom to get dressed.

"After the doctor, we'll stop and grab some bagels; then I'll have someone go to your place and get your things."

"I can go," I protested.

"You aren't stepping one foot in that house. We already know that someone has come for you. I don't want you out of my sight."

"He came and left," I corrected, but I was too scared to argue, so I stayed silent during the half-hour drive to the doctor's office.

Andre must have been nervous, too, because he put on some soft music, and we both seemed to relax a little. "I'm sure everything is going to be fine." He caressed my leg and remained loving.

It was hard to see such a cold man who was addicted to sex become the soft loving soul I knew was hidden inside of him. I almost wasn't ready for it. We arrived at the doctor's office, and I was completely panicked, but I just kept trying to breathe. I don't know why I was so scared; I mean, I just lost the IUD. The worst-case scenario was that I'd have the morning after pill and maybe feel a little yucky for a day or two; what could be bad about that? Perhaps I was just scared that Bill was really after me. I wasn't sure.

"Okay, Ms. Piquel, before we administer the Plan B contraception, I'd like to give you a pregnancy test. Mr. Michelson tells me that you have been sexually active, so it's best to check for pregnancy before going ahead with the contraception. In most cases, when the IUD has been evacuated, it doesn't just slip out of the uterus. In fact, an IUD rarely dislodges, so it may have been in your vaginal canal or at the mouth of your uterus for some time, possibly lowering the IUDs effectiveness, so I like to take precautions. I just need you to sign a release form so that I can perform the test."

I looked to Andre, not sure I wanted to know if there was a chance I was pregnant; that would absolutely be the worst thing on earth.

"Do I have to?" I knew I was being stupid.

"Well, in an abundance of caution, I advise you to take the test. I can't give you a morning-after pill in this office if I don't have a negative pregnancy test. If I give you the morning after pill and you're pregnant, it won't terminate your pregnancy, but it also won't offer any benefit. If you are pregnant, I won't be administering a contraceptive; instead, we would be discussing options for terminating your pregnancy."

He said it so casually, like 'instead, we'll be hacking out your baby.' I felt like I was going to faint. I grabbed Andre's arm, and he led me to the little bed in the doctor's office.

"She'll take the pregnancy test," he told the doctor and gave me the papers to sign.

I signed them with my head in a blur of stress, fear, and sadness. How did I end up in this situation? I thought I was being such a grown-up getting the IUD. Here I was thinking I'd found the greatest solution to having an active adult sex life. I don't know why I didn't just go with the shot. I just figured I could take the IUD out if I needed it, and it would last for five years, not a few months, so I opted for IUD, and here I was waiting for a pregnancy test.

The doctor took my blood first and then gave me a regular stick pregnancy test, the kind you pee on.

"Just take this into the restroom and place it into the stream of your urine and hold it there for seven to ten seconds and then we'll wait. I've given you a blood test that is almost one hundred percent accurate, but those results will not be available for at least three days. If your urine pregnancy test shows positive, I'll have you take another one in an hour, and if that second test is positive, we will have to wait until I get the blood test results to discuss the next steps. Okay. Here you go." He handed me the little test, and I almost hyperventilated.

"Okay," Andre took the test from him and escorted me to the

bathroom.

"You don't have to do this," I blathered as he ushered me into the tiny restroom.

"It was my sperm that did or didn't do this, so we're in it together. Pants down, spread your legs. I wish we were doing something else right now, but squat and pee for me, darlin'." He put on his best Texas drawl, and it made me laugh.

I didn't think I could pee in front of him, especially with his hand there waiting with a stick to catch the stream, but God works in mysterious ways, and I peed. It was gross, but I really appreciated Andre being there with me. When we were done, he put the test in the little tube the doctor had given him, we both washed our hands, he kissed me, and I still felt cold and clammy like I might pass out.

We waited in the room silently for the little lines to show up. At first, there was a prominent blue line.

"Is it one line or two?" I asked in a whisper.

"I'm not sure." Now Andre was quiet as a faint second line appeared. "We'll wait for the doctor." He held my hand, and the room began to spin.

A few minutes later, the doctor came in and looked at the test. "Okay, well, we'll have you drink some water, and you'll retake the test in an hour. Sometimes we see false positives."

"So, I'm pregnant?" I blurted out near tears.

"We'll need a second test to be sure. I'll get you some water." After he left, I looked at Andre feeling my whole face freak out.

"We'll just take this all one step at a time." He was a little less confident than he had been.

The nurse brought in a bottle of water and instructed me to drink the whole thing. Then she left, noting that I had drunk the entire bottle. Andre stayed stroking my arm, but we didn't say anything. He answered some emails on his phone, and I sat there in shock doing nothing. All he did was hold me. I couldn't find the words to speak; I was terrified. When the doctor came back in, I could hardly believe an hour had passed as I had spent most of the time white as a ghost in a terror-induced state of shock.

With Andre's help, I took the second test, and within minutes, we had an even darker second line than the first. Now it was Andre's turn to be freaked.

The doctor came in and looked at the test, then addressed us. "It's rare that a pregnancy test will deliver two false-positive results. We will wait for the blood test, but I've performed many of these tests, and I'd have to say I'm fairly positive, Ms. Piquel, that you're pregnant. An IUD can take days, if not weeks, to dislodge and evacuate the body, and in that time, it is possible, given the fact that you both have told me you've been sexually active without any other form of contraception, you may be several months pregnant. Therefore, I need to confirm your pregnancy and the size of the fetus before we can look at what options you have for terminating. I will know by Wednesday the final result of your pregnancy test. At that point, I'd like you to come in, and we will perform an ultrasound."

"We can't do anything until Wednesday?" Andre asked.

"You can go to another doctor; they might be comfortable performing a DNC or chemical abortion on the spot, but I like to give couples a chance to sit and consider their options before making termination plans. I assume, since the two of you came in here looking for an emergency contraceptive, that termination will be your first choice, but as a doctor, I need to see how old the fetus is before I give my recommendation. The earliest I can do that is on Wednesday." He was a practical man, and while I hated it, I also appreciated it as he gave me forty-eight hours with my baby.

It was at that moment that I burst into tears. Andre was kind, stroking my back and answering the doctor for us.

"We'll be back on Wednesday, and we'll discuss termination plans then." My heart dropped the minute I heard him say 'termination plans.' It was as if my baby was already being ripped away from me.

I was pregnant. I had a little life growing in my body. I couldn't just throw it away. I cried harder, feeling the heaviness of the last twenty-four hours.

"I want to go home," I said quietly on the car ride back to Andre's ranch.

"Your home isn't safe for you right now." He stayed close to me, but we were no longer touching.

"You hired bodyguards; I'll be fine. I just need …" I kept bawling; I just couldn't get my shit together.

"I know. You need time, space, air. I feel the same. I'll let you go home, but only with the bodyguards, and you'll check in with me every hour." Was he for real?

"Isn't that a little excessive?" I couldn't bear to look at him, so I said that into my hands.

"It's either that or stay at the ranch with me where I prefer you be. And I'm taking you to the appointment on Wednesday, then you and I will need to sit down and discuss this."

I couldn't cry anymore; I was numb, raw, aching.

"Okay," I managed to choke out.

"I'll go home with you now." He took out his cell phone. "Then, in two days, you're coming back to the ranch." He texted something into his phone then looked at me.

"What if I want to keep the baby?" I barely said it, and I started shaking all over.

"You're still coming back to the ranch, and we'll discuss it." I was about to start crying again when he put his hand on my knee. "We'll discuss it. Nothing has been decided."

His voice was remarkably calm, for what I was expecting from him. Perhaps his anger would come later like my abject sadness or despair, but at the moment, we were both numb and immobile.

It took over an hour to get to my house, and since I had only brought my purse with me and left my one change of clothing at his house, I had nothing to bring inside but myself.

"I'm going to come in until the security guard gets here; he's on his way, but it will probably be another thirty or forty minutes." He was so matter-of-fact.

"Sure, come on in. I don't know if my roommates are home or not, so just giving you a heads up." It felt good to go into robot mode.

We walked into the house, and Genevieve was sitting in the living room with her laptop on her legs, feverishly typing.

"Oh, my God. Eliza, you're home. Are you okay? Hey, Andre." I appreciated how relaxed and not freaking out she was. Since someone had come looking for me, I thought she'd be a little more stressed, but she was even keel, and that settled my nerves a little.

"Hey, Gen. Did anyone else come by after that guy left yesterday?" I crossed my fingers, praying that it had been quiet.

"Nope, no one. Nothing. You're all good. Crazy stalker, huh? Andre, you gotta nip that in the bud." She returned to her computer, not even noticing that she was placing responsibility for my safety in Andre's hands.

"Already nipped it. She'll be having twenty-four-hour protection. They won't come in the house, but you will be having people surrounding you for a while. I hope you don't mind. Just consider it free security." He flashed her a handsome smile, and my knees almost buckled.

"Cool." That's all she gave him.

"We'll be in my room," I announced for no understandable reason.

"Great. Since Thanksgiving is on Thursday, we're having turkey tonight. Hope you don't mind. Peyton's heading out to a thing in Houston with some friends she met in her art class, and I'm going to Mom and Dad's tomorrow, so you'll have the place to yourself. Do you guys have Thanksgiving plans?"

Shit, I hadn't even thought about Thanksgiving. I wasn't going back to DC, and I had no one but my roommates who were going to be gone and Andre in Texas.

"We're going to have a quiet evening in, just the two of us," Andre told her.

"Ah, so romantic." She scrunched her face into a funny smile, and I thought I might be sick.

"Yes, very." I took Andre's hand and shuttled him into my bedroom down the hall.

I couldn't bear any more roommate banter about things that weren't real. We wouldn't be having a romantic evening. We'd be talking about ending my pregnancy, my ex-boss stalking me, and Andre's plot to kidnap me and keep me on his ranch. I closed the door as soon as we entered my modest little room.

"You want some tea?" I needed tea, or something stronger actually.

"I'd love tea." He took a seat on my bed, and I slipped out of the room, not really wanting to start whatever conversation he wanted to have.

As I left, he took out his phone, so I figured he'd be significantly occupied, so I left him in my room as I started the kettle.

"He really is dreamy," Genevieve said, not looking up from her computer. "I can totally see why you're spending so much time with him. And of course, he's also one of the richest men in Texas ... there's that."

"Stalker," I teased.

"Seriously though, you are so lucky. Not that you don't deserve him, you're the most adorable freaking thing." I'm sure she meant that as a compliment right?

"Um. Thanks." Ugh, everyone was weird.

"Is he staying for dinner? He can stay. I'm sure we have enough. Peyton always overbuys. Oh, speaking of, there's a grocery bill on the fridge; you owe a third. Cool?"

Right, roommate life. I had almost forgotten I had another life outside of Andre and the office. I had a term paper due at the end of the month and classes the next day. I wondered how the whole bodyguard thing was going to go down in my lecture class.

"I'll ask him, but I'm pretty sure he's heading out tonight. It's a really long drive to his place, and he has a lot to do. Don't get to be crazy rich without working a ton. And yeah, no problem. I'll Venmo you the grocery bill." I smiled as soon as the kettle whistled, and I poured hot water in two cups of earl grey tea. It was all we had. I liked it with a splash of milk and sugar; Andre took his harsh and black. He liked everything to be intense. "What are you working on?" I asked as I blew the steam off the cups and grabbed a tray from under the sink.

"A new song. I'm stuck, though, blah. I wanted to have this done before I was body-snatched by the rents, but that isn't gonna happen. I'll keep jamming until I have to leave, but I'm just not feeling this."

"I totally understand what that's like. Good luck." I left her to her songwriting and brought the tea to Andre, who was not sitting on my bed playing on his phone but pulling clothes out of my closet and packing my suitcase.

"Hey there, I haven't agreed to anything yet. Unhand my clothes!" I offered him his tea, hoping he'd change directions.

"You need something to wear at my house. I'm picking my favorite things. Don't mind me. Carry on." He took the cup with the darker liquid in it and raised it to the air in salute.

"Ugh, you're infuriating." I plopped down on the bed and sipped my tea.

"I'm infuriating? Did I ask you to cut your hair? No. Do I like it, yes. But I am in charge of all things in my life, and in the few short months I've known you, you've made my sheets smell like you, you've consumed most of my waking thoughts, and now …now I'm …" he took a deep breath.

"You've changed my life a lot too," I said quietly.

"I know," he confessed, but I couldn't have 'that' conversation yet. "The bodyguard is here. He's going to stay in his car tonight. He's the night shift, so he'll be up all night, but before he begins settling in for the evening, he's going to set up surveillance cameras around the house. So, you might want to let your roomies know while I pack up more of your things." He gave me an evil grin, but I didn't have the energy for anything snarky.

I left my tea and told Genevieve and Peyton about the surveillance cameras, and they both thought it was crazy billionaire overkill but loved that Andre was that caring. I didn't have the heart to tell them what was really going on.

Chapter 28

Andre

I wasn't sure why I was packing up most of her things. I just didn't want her to be there. After making the drive with her, I realized how far away she was, and I just wanted her with me. The news of her pregnancy was shocking. In fact, at that point, I was still in shock, but strangely I wasn't as angry as I thought I might be. She was using protection; she never lied. It was just one of those things. Now we had an issue we had to resolve. Since she was the one who would have to suffer the abortion, I promised myself I'd be kind and loving. I would have hated to be in her position.

Bill had contacted me but didn't ask directly about Eliza, only said that he was worried that she might not be a good fit for him and the company, and he told me that there were state auditors in the office. I addressed both of his concerns, letting him know that Eliza would not be back to the office, and I'd get him another intern. I explained that the auditors were doing a state-mandated audit, and I wasn't concerned because our company wasn't doing anything illegal. I explained that it was routine because we did business with state agencies, and often they audited business and financial records of companies they paid. I told him not to sweat it, but I could tell he was sweating it, which gave me a lot of joy.

"Dylan is doing the audit!" He was livid.

"Dylan is the state auditor. You two should go out to lunch and catch up." I played it off as if none of it was a big deal.

"We're both too busy," was his gruff reply.

After my conversation with Bill, I called Dylan and checked in on his progress while Eliza was with her roommates and the security guy installing the surveillance. Dylan wasn't too forthcoming and spoke in cryptic bureau speak, which was a little concerning, but I did know for a fact I wasn't in the wrong.

"You should make a show of going to the Zapata and donating some money to the relief effort. You own a lot of the county, and most people work for you in some capacity or another. It would be good if you were seen down there for many reasons," he advised.

"I'll go after the holiday. And yes, I'll be making a significant donation to their relief efforts, of course." The call unsettled me, and I was on edge when Eliza returned to her room.

I had her suitcase all packed and was almost completely resolved not to let her stay. I'd just bring her back to the ranch. I didn't care about the time or expense expended to install the surveillance cameras; no doubt someone would be returning to the home. Best to keep her lovely roommates protected as well.

"I don't want to leave you," I said as soon as she walked in.

"I need you to go. I want to just have dinner with my roommates and be a person in grad school. I have my lecture class tomorrow, and I need to work on this research paper that's due at the end of the month. Also ... I need time to think, as I've said."

"I can't leave you here; I'll worry the whole time."

"That's on you, Andre. You can either worry or don't." She was getting stronger.

"And I can't have you going to school tomorrow. Doesn't your school offer an online component? I recall you joining classes from your computer." I didn't want her to leave that house if she was going to be apart from me. Being in crowds of people was not going to work. If he had a hacker get her address and her phone information, he certainly had her school schedule.

"I prefer going to school in person." She knew the minute she said it that she was making a pointless argument.

"That was before Bill threatened your life."

"Okay." She heaved a heavy sigh. "I'll contact the professor and get the login info for virtual learning." She looked like she might cry for the third time that day.

"I promise." I reached out to her. "This won't be forever." I kissed her cheek, and she just sat there. I so wanted to make love to her, as we weren't always very good with our words and were much better at communicating with our bodies. However, she needed some time, and so did I, frankly, so I held her hand and surrendered.

"I don't want to leave you, but since we will be seeing each other on Wednesday to go to the doctor, I'll let you have the day to yourself, but I want you back at the ranch Tuesday night so we can talk. Please." That gave her Sunday and Monday night to herself, and I would check in with her often.

"Okay." She looked at me, and the two of us called a truce.

We were both still so numb, but I kissed her goodbye, and she walked me out.

"Thank you for understanding," she said as we walked to my car.

"I know this is tough," is all I said as I kissed her again, then turned to the bodyguard to implore him, yet again, to keep her safe. "Please, any sign of anything, and you call the police, me, and get her to safety. She is your top priority!" Of course, Eliza was his top priority; it was literally what I was paying him for.

"Yes, sir. I will make sure no one gets near her or the premises. I have a backup on standby.

Well, he knew how to make me happy, and so I reluctantly said goodbye to Eliza, called my valet service, and ordered a driver as I'd sent the other driver back home. I spent the whole ride back to the ranch texting Dylan about Bill, but he was tight-lipped and said he was conducting his investigation. I'd be getting the report when he had his findings. He had a stick firmly lodged up his ass; he'd make a great public servant. Instead of doing any more work, I googled abortion, and my stomach dropped out. While it was the best choice for us because I had no desire to be a father, the act seemed really heartless. Hundreds of people did it, and most likely, our fetus was only a few days old, but it did seem like a tough thing for Eliza to go through. I then looked up adoption, and that seemed even harder. I then looked for nannies, and for whatever reason, that seemed more doable until I considered the fact that I'd have that child for the rest of my life. It was at that point, I just closed the phone and my eyes and tried to shut out the world.

I went to work the next day and went to HR to tell them about Eliza deciding to stay at school and canceling her internship. "She's going to be doing independent research for me instead of working in the office. I approve of her getting the credit she needs for school. This is much more valuable to me than having her file papers."

"Great. I'll leave the internship as it stands then; she'll just not be in the office." Carol, the HR manager, didn't seem to care much, which was fine with me.

On Monday, I called Eliza six times, and she was busy working on her paper. No one had shown up at the house, and the bodyguard, a different one from the night before, was standing outside her window. She was more creeped out by him than by the fact that Bill might have had someone casing her.

I texted her a few times and thought of her all day. Not once did we mention the baby or the fact that she no longer was working with me. Life was a blur, but what I realized in her one-day absence was that I couldn't really handle being away from her. I had only brief conversations with Bill on Monday as he acted like nothing was wrong. I'm sure he was nervous, but the more he blew it off, the better he deflected the blame. That night I went to Dylan's office and gave him the files Eliza had stolen from Bill's house. I had a sleepless night on Monday and came into the office feeling like shit on Tuesday. I literally just tracked the hours until I could drive to Eliza's house and pick her up.

"Hey, Andre," her roommate Peyton, a gorgeous supermodel of a woman casually said as she opened the door. "So does our hot security guard leave with you guys? Can you let him stay here on the DL?" Her eyes glanced over to a very tight muscled, tall plainclothes security officer, and I could see what she was referring to; if I were a woman, I'd be smitten.

"Sorry, he comes with us, but I can get his number if you want it," I said realizing that befriending the roommates was the best course of action.

"Oh, my God, would you?" Wow, she was serious.

I gave her a kind smile. "I'll see what I can do."

"Great. So, Eliza's in her room; you want me to go grab her?" She cocked her hip to the side.

"No, I'll get her; it's fine." I gave her a wink and walked in to find Eliza sitting in a chair, with a suitcase by her side, staring out the window.

"Hey," I walked in and sat on her bed. I could tell by her red face and puffy eyes she'd been crying again. It was a very sad state of affairs.

"Listen all we are going to do tomorrow is find out more. We are not making any decisions, okay? We are just getting more facts," I tried to assure her.

"But we will have to make a decision." A slow, silent tear slid down her face.

"Eventually, yes." I sighed.

We had a quiet car ride, and when we got back to my ranch, it was still daylight. I showed her to the guest room, and she seemed relieved that she had a place to go to be alone. I then smiled and kissed her sweet face.

"I'm happy you're here." I wanted her to know that she was beginning to mean so much more to me.

"I'm just …"

"We'll take this all one day at a time." I kissed her again. "Midnight is waiting for you. I don't want you riding him until we decide what we're doing with the baby, but he's here until Christmas. I own him until then." I gave her a warm smile, so she understood I just wanted the best for her.

"The person who bought him didn't want to pick him up 'til Christmas?" Her face was veiled in happiness, but I saw the sadness in her eyes.

"Yes, he's a Christmas present, so I won't be transferring ownership until Christmas Day. So, let's enjoy him now." I took her hand and brought her out to the corral.

Of course, a genuine smile lit up her face the moment she saw him. There was a deep affection between the two of them, and I loved watching Eliza's mood lift. She walked the horse around the property as the sun set. I let them have time together alone as I sat and did some work from my phone, just watching her have time with Midnight. When she came back, we returned to the ranch, and I had my caregiver's wife, Jane, make us a light meal of salmon and salad. We had tea on the porch before retiring. We never once mentioned the baby, and any time I thought it might be a good time to talk about it, she segued. When bedtime came, she asked to sleep in her room. I was disappointed but understood.

"Let's just see what we find out," I said, stalling her as she was about to go to the room.

"Why don't you spend the night with me?" I asked her.

"I don't think that's wise," she said, looking sad again.

"I know it's hard to resist you, but we do need to talk. I'd rather be by your side tonight, and we need to have the difficult discussion we've been avoiding." It was time.

She didn't say anything, just bowed her head and followed me to my bedroom. I had her pajamas laid at the end of the bed. They were a new pair of sleep shorts and a soft T-shirt. While I hoped I'd make love to her that night, I wasn't banking on it. I was going to be there for support to help her cope with the tough decision we were about to make. She changed into her pajamas and left to put her dirty clothes in her room. When she came back, she was already crying.

"I know," I said as I brought her into the bed.

She didn't say anything, just continued to cry. I stroked her skin and kissed the top of her head. "What are your thoughts? Let's be honest with one another."

"I don't want to hurt the baby. I already feel like I know him. I think it might be a him, and I just … I want to love him and care for him and just give him the world, and yet, I can't. I'm still in school. I don't have a home to raise him in or any money." She started to cry more.

"Okay, and what does the reality of parenting really look like? You said both of your girlfriends have children. How has it changed their lives?" I was hoping she'd start to see reality and not just the concept of a child.

"They are busy, tired, their lives changed completely, but it wasn't all bad. They love their kids, but they have their husbands. I mean they are invested …" Her words trailed off.

"That baby will be awake every two hours at first; he'll need your constant care and attention. You'd have to drop out of school, and if you chose to raise him, I'd help financially, but I'm not father material. I couldn't really be present for you. I have to be honest; a baby is way far out of my wheelhouse. I'm willing to love you and make you a bigger part of my life, but a bigger part doesn't mean a wife. I'm sorry." I had to tell her the truth that had been welling inside me as I knew she was leaning toward the idea of keeping our baby. But as I labored over the scenarios in my head, I couldn't ever see myself being a father, and she needed to know I wouldn't be a part of this even if it meant losing her.

Chapter 29

Eliza

Those were the words I knew he would say, but I never wanted to hear. He would support me but wouldn't be there for me. If I choose to keep my baby, I'd be keeping him on my own. I'd have to drop out of school and give up on the idea of a career and just focus on being a mom. I wasn't like Harper or Ophelia; I didn't have a burning desire to be a mom. I never really considered it. I was fine just having a casual relationship with Andre. In fact, I had begun to really enjoy it, and if I chose to keep the baby, he was telling me it was over. I'd lose him if I decided to keep his son. I knew it deep down inside. He was honest and never pretended to be anyone different. He never wanted a wife and certainly never wanted kids.

"I can't make the decision right now. I have to …" God, I couldn't stop crying.

All he did was curl his body around mine. "You don't have to make the decision right now." He kissed me again as his hand coursed over my belly.

His hand was warm, and I welcomed his affections. As his caress slid up to my breasts, I felt how tender they already had become; no doubt that was because of my pregnancy. He kissed my shoulder, and I could feel his hardness on my back. I angled my body to better accommodate him as I wanted him to take me from behind. I couldn't bear to look at his face but wanted the comfort of sex to help ease the horrible feelings swirling inside of me. Andre seemed to understand my needs and focused on loving me from behind as I continued to sniffle and cry.

"I wish I could make this all better for you," he said as his hands left my breasts and focused on rubbing my sex, preparing me for him.

He lifted my leg and set it across my body so that he had better access to my vagina as he smoothed his fingers along my puffy pussy lips. I was wet and highly aroused despite my sad emotional state. He dipped his fingers into my body, and I shivered with the anticipation of him. He moved his head in closer to mine as his finger slid in and out of my body, making me want him more and more.

"I love you, Eliza, whatever happens, I want you to know that." With that admission made, he pressed himself into me, and I winced from the invasion.

I didn't realize how tightly I had held every muscle in my body until he struggled to enter me. I breathed and tried to relax so that he could have better access, but it was so hard. I was fighting a tough internal battle, and I just couldn't relent. Somehow knowing this, he kissed me again.

"Relax, and let me love you." His hand swung around to the front of me, where his fingered played with my clit until the stress and worry I'd been carrying around for two days started to vanish.

In its place was the warm swell of emotions that always accompanied our lovemaking. I was so hot for him, and as his fingers pressed and pinched me into a euphoric state, his cock found its way into the sacred space I held for him. Having finally entered me he laid his weight upon me, making me feel surrounded and protected by him. Even though he was part of the problem, that night, he was the solution. I loved his body, his sex, and I was coming to discover that despite everything, I was starting to love him.

If he wasn't ready to be a father, then I wasn't going to force him. That night as he gently bucked me into two earth-shattering orgasms, I fell asleep after he came inside me and just let his body stay on top of mine as we both succumbed to the weight of the world. In the morning, we took a shower but didn't play with one another. We were both quiet and reverent. We didn't have to say any more about what would be happening; we just had to let it happen.

We drove through Starbucks on our way to the doctor, and I ordered a chamomile tea with honey, and he got a triple espresso. Clearly, we were drinking our feelings. When we entered the doctor's office, I started to shake, and so he took my hand.

"Whatever we decide, we do it together," he whispered to me. "I've given this a lot of thought, and I promise, whatever happens, you will not do it alone."

I did my best not to cry again. My eyes hurt from so much crying, and I was pretty much in shock again, and I just sat there and waited for the doctor to enter the room.

"Okay," he said. "I have your lab results, and I'm ready to discuss the results with you and perform an ultrasound. Regardless of your decision today, giving you an ultrasound is my practice, and it's the law in Texas. So,

I will be doing an ultrasound, and you'll hear the fetal heartbeat. The blood tests have confirmed, Eliza, that you are, in fact, pregnant. So, I'm going to perform the external and transvaginal ultrasound to confirm the age of the fetus and its viability. After I perform the test, and we discuss my findings, we can talk about your next steps." He was clinical and cold.

I laid back on the table as the doctor put cold jelly on my belly. I hadn't even realized it, but Andre was still holding my hand.

"Okay, so I'm just going to check and see the size of the fetus, and that will help me confirm the age as the age of the fetus determines the types of termination procedures this office uses." After he said that, I thought I was going to truly be sick as my stomach tightened.

As my body grew clammy with stress and nausea, Andre's grip got tighter, and his hand stroked my hair, which was already damp. I was sure I was going to pass out, and then I saw that little blip on the screen. It had a tiny heartbeat. There he was, my son. I would probably never know him or even know if he was a him, but there he was growing inside me. I should have been horrified; I should have screamed, but I simply laid there and stared at him, marveling at his little cellular body.

Andre's grip loosened the moment the baby's body came onto the screen. It was now his time to fight his own inner demons. We saw his little head and the beginnings of his tiny body.

"Okay, well, as I suspected, the fetus is over two months old. I'd say you were nearer to three months pregnant. Have you had any morning sickness?" the doctor asked, which just sounded like curiosity.

"None," I answered, thinking for a moment that meant the little thing with a tiny beating heart on the screen wasn't a baby.

"Lucky. Most women are experiencing nausea at this point in their pregnancy."

Ah, nausea I had, but I hadn't been throwing up.

"I'm nauseous now," I quietly confessed.

"That's normal," the doctor dismissed. "So, I can't tell the gender of the fetus definitively this early with just the blood test, but I'm almost ninety-nine percent sure that the fetus is male, but the ultrasound isn't revealing anything yet. I have to now let you hear the heartbeat, and then we can discuss your options."

At that moment, despite having cried for days and thinking that I had cried myself dry, I started to cry again. Andre took my hand, but this time there wasn't much emotion in it. We were both facing a lot that day. The doctor turned on the speakers on the computer before he put a device on my stomach. He then prepared a wand with a condom and lubricant.

"I'm going to have you listen to the baby while I perform one last ultrasound; this will give me a better look at the heartbeat."

I could barely make it through the last part of the appointment. I heard the baby's heartbeat and saw his little head, and all I could do was cry. I stayed staring at the picture, watching his little heart go up and down as the rest of the world became a blur. All I cared about was my little baby. It was probably the only time I'd ever have with him, and I knew it. Andre was drifting farther away from me and was actually sitting in a chair. I had hardly noticed him move. I was transfixed on my baby, my son. How could I take his life? How could I raise him alone? I had no answers.

"Okay." The doctor clicked the mouse around the screen, then slipped the wand out of me, and within an instant, the picture of my baby was gone; our moment was over. I could hardly bear it. "From what I can deduce from the blood test results and two ultrasounds, is that the fetus is strong, probably male, and at about eleven weeks gestation. If you want to carry your baby to term, I suggest we start monthly prenatal visits and make sure that Eliza is getting the right nutrition for a pregnant mother. If you choose to terminate this pregnancy, I recommend you do it within the next few days because if the fetus grows too much more, the abortion procedure becomes a little more traumatizing, and I can see here that Eliza is struggling as most women do with this decision. We do have availability today, and since you have already completed half of the procedure, it can lessen the emotional impact not to have to see another ultrasound. I can give you medication to calm you and prepare your body for the procedure if you choose to terminate your pregnancy today."

Again, I was about to be sick; in fact, at that moment, I was pretty sure I was going to be sick.

"Can I go to the restroom please?" I asked, feeling frantic.

The doctor helped me off the table and directed me to the restroom, where I just made it to the toilet to throw up. As soon as I was done, I sat on the toilet and cried. After a while, I heard Andre outside the door.

"Eliza, are you okay?" I couldn't answer him; I was completely drained, hurt, and gutted. "They have a room for us if you want to sit and talk this out. They are booking a procedure room."

I was swimming in a sea of weird, fully freaked out and unable to do anything. After a while, I did stand up and open the door to find Andre sitting on a chair in the hall.

"Hey," he stood up and approached me. "They have a room for us this way." He guided me down the hallway and through a few corridors until we came to a room that had a big 6 on it.

Inside the room, there was a bed, a chair, and a desk with a lamp. "The doctor will be in here any minute now to talk to us some more, but I wanted to know, what are you feeling? I want the absolute truth."

"I don't know what I'm feeling," and that was the truth. "What are you feeling?"

"Sad, scared, unsure," he said as he held me. "I'm going to leave this choice up to you. I can support you if you don't want to go through with this today, but I'm still very sure I don't want to be a father. I'm sorry I can't be a better man for you. I know that you didn't do this intentionally. While you were in the bathroom, the doctor explained how your IUD may have become dislodged, and it really fits the profile for us, vigorous sex, horseback riding, stress. I'm larger than your body might be used to; they are all contributing factors. Some women have severe cramping while others don't feel anything. You either have a really high pain threshold, or yours didn't cause you any issue. He thinks it has been partially out of your uterus for a while and finally just slipped out of your body. Either way, my sperm must have really wanted to make that baby because getting past an IUD is a feat of heroism no matter where it is in the body. I learned a lot today." He laughed, a strange emotion to be having at the time, but maybe that was how he was coping.

I was beyond laughter; everything was horror from my point of view. Whether I kept the baby or terminated the pregnancy, everything my eyes saw and my ears heard was something scary.

"The doctor also mentioned adoption, if you wanted to maybe find the little guy a family." At that point, Andre's voice trailed off.

I could tell by the way he mentioned it, adoption wasn't something he wanted to consider, and it wasn't something I could do either. If I carried the baby to term, I knew I'd want to keep him, and so it was time to decide. Either go through with the procedure that day or come back and have to go through all of this again ... or keep him. I took a deep breath and imagined life with a tiny baby, trying to study, find and keep a job, and no longer have Andre as I knew he wouldn't be able to handle it. It was too much. I knew what I had to do, but I needed his confirmation.

"If you were to have exactly what you wanted, and it be the outcome that works best for your life, what would you do?" I asked him in a dull monotone.

"I would terminate the pregnancy," he barely said.

I knew that was what he would choose, and to be honest, my son, at that point was just a tiny mass not able to withstand the procedure that would end his life. When it was over, he would be gone, and maybe one day in the future, I'd have a child with a husband.

"I want to have a baby with someone who wants a child. I don't want to bring an unwanted child into this world. I want him; I want to have him, to smell his little head and tell him I love him, but I … I don't know if I can do it alone." I did my best not to cry.

"You wouldn't be alone; I'm not a monster. I'd support you the best way I knew how. I'm just saying, I … this …" he sighed, unable to say the rest.

"I know."

At that moment, the doctor came in. "How are we doing here?" he asked, definitely in procedure mode.

"I'm going to go through with the procedure," I said, having made my decision.

I couldn't think anymore. I didn't want to think or feel or do anything. I just wanted it all to be over. I wanted to cuddle into Andre's arms and just have him be big and strong for me because at that time, I just couldn't be big and strong for myself. I think Andre hugged me. I think he told me he loved me; it was all a blur. I was given some medicine and told it would relax me. The doctor explained the procedure, and I blocked it out of my mind, and when I was asked if I wanted Andre in the room, I said no.

I was then walked to a cold room with what I thought was a metal table, but it probably was a little more comfortable than cold, stark metal. I had been given a relaxant, and he was just about to give me a pill that would dilate my uterus.

"This will relax your cervix and dilate your uterus so that the suction device can be easily inserted. You might feel some cramping, and you will probably continue to feel cramping for the next few days as your uterus returns to its normal size. So, I'll give you the medicine, and then you'll need to stay here and rest for about a half-hour before we start the procedure," he said in a calm, methodical voice.

"Will this medicine hurt the baby?" I asked before taking the pill in my hand.

"Well, yes. It's meant to prepare your body for fetal extraction." And then it all came crashing down on me.

If I put that pill in my mouth, if I went through with it, I'd never meet him; he'd never know me. Our baby, our little boy, would die if I put that pill in my mouth. I didn't know why I had agreed to do it. Perhaps I wanted to make it better for Andre. I was worried I couldn't be a single mother, but sitting there holding that pill in my hand, knowing that the moment I took it, I would end my son's life, I couldn't do it. I wouldn't.

"I'm sorry. I handed the pill back to him. I can't do this." I stood up out of the chair, not even caring that I was wearing a hospital gown.

I was ready to put on my clothes, find an Uber or a cab and go back to my roommates and just never see Andre again. Not because I didn't care about him or had lost interest in him, but more because I was ashamed I couldn't end my pregnancy, and I was choosing to have his child.

Chapter 30

Andre

The doctor walked her out of the room, and that was the end of it. Within the hour, our baby would be gone. I had seen his little body in her womb. I had felt the spikes of terror about what it would be like to be responsible for another human life, and I doubted I would ever have enough empathy and love not to permanently ruin a child's life, but Eliza had all the love in the world. She had enough love for both of us, and she was strong and brave. I knew she was making her decision because I refused to step up and be a father to my child. Hell, I did my part in making him, that's for damn sure, and if I didn't want children well, I could have worn a condom. No, I left birth control up to her, and by the laws of nature, the fail-proof IUD she used failed her.

I sat there and watched the sun start to set as the days were getting darker earlier. The next day was Thanksgiving, and I had made no plans. Usually, I ate with my caretaker and his family, and I'd order a huge meal, but they were going to her mother's for the holiday, and in a strange twist of irony, Jane was also pregnant. It would just be Eliza and me for Thanksgiving. I ordered a fancy turkey dinner for us and some expensive wine. I'd already gotten her a Christmas present I knew would make her the happiest woman on Earth and was tempted to give it to her on Thanksgiving, but it wasn't the right time.

I then realized that what she was doing was truly against all that she was, and for a brief moment, I thought of being a father. Maybe I wouldn't be the best, but if he had her eyes and her heart, I'd love him, and perhaps he'd learn to love me, warts and all. He was my son. I almost busted into the procedure room and told her to stop, but she had her reasons too for not wanting a baby at that moment. Maybe we could consider it again in the future.

Suddenly, I was emotional. I hadn't cried since my parents died, and there I was with big fat tears rolling down my cheeks. I almost didn't hear her and the doctor walk in. I looked at Eliza, and I was happy to see she wasn't crying. In fact, she looked better than she had since we got the news of her pregnancy. She wasn't happy, but she looked relaxed, content. I was still having pangs of grief, but I assumed if she were happy with the decision we made, I'd soon be happy with it too. I just needed a longer emotional lead time than she did because I was still feeling a lot of grief over losing the little guy.

"I'm sorry, Andre," she started, and I interrupted her.

"No, it's what you had to do, we had to do. I'm just glad you're okay." I reached out to hug her, and she stopped me.

"I didn't do it. I couldn't. I'm going to keep him; I'm sorry." She bit her lip. "I know this isn't what you want, but I discussed it with Doctor Singh, and he says there's a form where you can opt-out financially, and when the baby is born, we can go to the court to terminate your rights. Also, I won't put your name on his birth certificate."

She was rambling so fast; I was just doing my best to understand what she was saying.

"You mean we're having a baby?" I suddenly felt elated.

"Yes," she looked at me confused. "I'm keeping him."

I threw my arms around her and held her tight. "Oh, thank God!" Sure, I'd be a shit father, but I'd be that little baby growing in Eliza's belly's shit dad. "Let's go home. Thank you, Doctor. I'm sorry if we caused you any stress. Just bill us for the day." I didn't even know what I was saying, and I didn't care. I felt an incredible amount of relief.

"I just couldn't do it," she said quietly in the car. "When he told me he was giving me a pill that would open my diaphragm, I just thought that was going to hurt that baby, and then I realized I was there to hurt the baby, and I couldn't do it to him. I just couldn't." She didn't cry, but she wasn't as happy as a new mom should have been, more she was apologizing to me.

"I know, I wouldn't be able to do it either," I confessed. "We'll make this work somehow, I promise."

She stayed quiet on the drive back to the ranch. We had a lot to think about because as all of it sunk in, we both had to realize we were going to become parents in not that much time. We didn't even know each other that well.

"Maybe I should just go back to my house," she said quietly.

"No. I want to spend Thanksgiving with you. I'm not going to let you get away that easily. We still have to worry about Bill, and now that you're pregnant, that makes everything even more vulnerable. I'm not letting you go that easily, at least not yet. Let's just not be reactionary about all of this."

Suddenly, I was so kind and rational that I hardly recognized myself.

"But maybe I need to be around women and people who will understand what I'm going through?" She looked up at me, questioning.

"At the moment, you're not going through anything much different than you were two days ago; you're pregnant. You're still pregnant, and you will remain pregnant until our son is born. You have more than six months to hang out with your friends and get their advice. Tomorrow is Thanksgiving, and I don't have anyone else I'd rather share the day with than you. Please indulge me. I'll let you see your friends, but right now, I want it to be just us. I'm not committing to partnership or fatherhood, but I am committing to tomorrow, and let's see where that leads us, okay?"

"Okay." She reached out her hand and took mine, then laid her head on my shoulder.

The gesture was warm and loving. I needed it more than I thought I would. The next day we had a quiet Thanksgiving at home. The gourmet kitchen delivered the food hot to our door, we had sparkling juice instead of wine, and she spent a lot of time with Midnight. When we sat down to our meal, we prayed. I wasn't much of a prayer kind of person, and she didn't strike me as one either, but she did take the time to thank God for things she was grateful for.

"And thank you for Andre's understanding and offering his home and his heart when I know both have been so solitary. Thank you for the surprise blessing of our baby boy and for all the strength I know you are gonna give me for the future."

I wasn't good with words, and I certainly was worse with prayers, but I gave it a shot.

"Dear God, boy that sounds weird." I laughed. "Thank you. Damn."

"You don't have to say anything," Eliza said, giving me the grace to bow out.

I looked at her cute pixie cut hair and her sparkling nose piercing, and I knew this incredible human had my son in her body, and damn if I didn't have a lot to be thankful for.

"No, give me a minute; I can do this." She smiled, and I loved her a little more. "Dear God, thank you for Eliza. I didn't know I needed Eliza and baby What's His Name in my life, but damn if I do. Thank you for helping me realize that because this was all on you. We wouldn't be having a baby if it wasn't for you, that's for damn sure. And so ... for this sweet woman and for this soon to be a loud and poopy baby, I thank you." I raised my eyebrows and gave her a look. "Well?"

"It was perfect." And I got the first genuine smile I'd seen all day, full of love, no fear, and there she was ... the mother of my child.

That night, I was afraid to make love to her the way we had been. For some reason, I thought if rough sex jostled the IUD out, what about the baby? The doctor did explain to me that perhaps my size was what really caused the IUD to be dislodged; it did have a little string that came out of the uterus and could be accessed through the vaginal canal, and maybe we just rocked the sheets a little too hard. I was a little too much, and it probably was improperly placed at the women's clinic where she had it inserted, but I wasn't going to take any chances. Until little baby What's His Name was bigger, I was going to slowly rock Eliza's world.

Here I was thinking about protecting the child that just hours before I was ready to eliminate from the world. I kissed Eliza on the neck and held her close; I didn't ever want to lose either of them. She turned her head back to me with a look that said she knew and understood and, I believe, felt the same. I hadn't ever felt as content, comfortable, and loved as I did at that moment.

In the morning, I got a text from Dylan saying the audit was going to take a month, that his initial findings showed there were a lot of discrepancies in Bill's department that he would be digging into. All of what he was saying started to make me very nervous. He also said that we were in deep with Zapata County and that making a public show of support would be crucial. He also said that Fasco was responsible for the fracking and new oil wells that caused the earthquakes. Our company owed their community compensation from what he saw in the books and how many oil wells we'd drilled with hydraulic power before our green charter. The fact that Bill was funding Fasco with Michelson Energy Corp money meant he was embezzling, and Dylan was getting to the heart of that.

When Eliza woke up, after sleeping more than she usually did, I pitched an idea to her.

"How would you like to take a little road trip with me?"

"Where?" She wiped the sleep out of her eyes.

"Zapata. It's on the Mexican border, and there are some nice beaches we can chill on. It's about two hours away. I need to see what's happening there and try and offer my help if I can. I feel like our company and Bill's negligence has caused this community to suffer. I know I've been a horrible person at times in my life, but I can still change. I want to do better," I confessed.

"I'd love to go with you." She kissed my lips and got out of bed.

I watched her as she walked toward the restroom and just marveled at her beauty. I knew her body would change with the baby, but it wasn't really her body I loved as much as I did the woman inside it. When she came back into the room, she was showered and dressed. Usually, we showered together, so it made me a little worried, but we had made love twice the night before; she could have been sore.

"So, I didn't have morning sickness at all, not even a hiccup before I knew I was having a baby, but now, the day I decide we're doing this, I get sick!" She sat down on the bed. "Little What's His Name has quite a sense of humor." She rubbed her flat belly, trying to talk to the tiny baby inside of her.

"Well, that's definitive proof he's my son." I kissed the top of her head and went to take a shower myself.

"Oh, this is gonna be so much fun with the two of you. Hey, while you're getting ready, I'm going to keep working on my paper."

"Sounds good." I headed off to the shower, and everything felt wonderful and natural; my contented state of calm remained.

After getting ready, we got in the car and started our journey. Eliza sang at the top of her lungs, and her voice was not great, but it was amazing because her singing showed me how happy she was. The drive was easy until we reached Zapata, and she stopped singing. The first thing we saw was a toppled grocery store with broken glass and food items strewn about a crumbled street. Looters may have ransacked most of the store, but the roof on one side was still hanging on, and it was dangerous to be near the building. That side of the street had been taped off, and all lanes of traffic had been diverted to the other side of the road.

The rest of the town was in complete ruins. People had tarps covering large holes in their homes, and many were living in tents. The community had been completely devastated. While not large, everyone who lived there had been affected.

"Can you take pictures, please?" I asked Eliza as she pulled out her phone to start snapping photographic evidence of the devastation. "I caused all of this." It was a huge wake-up call.

I may not have been great with people, but I loved the earth, and I would have never knowingly done this to anyone. It was my association with Bill and his abysmal ethics that brought this devastation to so many lives. I realized there was more to the world than money. In my pursuit of wealth, I put these people at risk. I put Eliza's life in danger, and I was jeopardizing my reputation. I could no longer control Bill. I could no longer turn a blind eye. I had to go public.

I had Eliza take pictures, and I made an appointment to meet with the county commissioner to discuss what I could do to help their devastated community. We stayed in a hotel three towns over, and I spoke with my publicist about how I could raise awareness and help. He suggested I post Twitter, Instagram, and Facebook posts with the pictures, my condolences, and my offer, which I decided was to give money to help rebuild the community and provide clean energy storage to each home and business. The price would be around a billion dollars when all was said and done, and so included in my offer was the sale of my company. I had been hounded over the years by many larger corporations offering to take us over to the tune of billions of dollars. I always hung on, wanting to run my own show. Now I wanted nothing to do with it.

If the storage units became mass-produced and readily available in the next few years, my goals would have been accomplished. I could retire, work on community projects like the one I'd be embarking on, invest in other things, and not run a company where my integrity and world view wouldn't be at stake. I was very comfortable with my decision, so I contacted Dylan and my investment firm and started to make my way toward the sale.

It was risky with Bill still on board, but Dylan assured me he was amassing what he needed to get Bill out of the company and perhaps slapped with criminal charges. By late that afternoon, with my publicist's help, I sent out the social media proposals of support with pictures and started the ball rolling on my company's sale. Eliza and I stayed and worked with the community for a week. We met the community commissioners and devised a way to help fund the rebuild. Most of the money came from my own private investments until the company could be sold; however, I did give them the energy storage units at cost. The community was small, but our efforts made a massive impact.

Going to bed in our crappy little hotel room felt great after a long day cleaning up debris and working out ways for everyone to have housing again. We were teaming with local contractors to build modular homes which, in some cases, were better built and more luxuriously appointed than what the residents had previously. As I laid there looking at my beautiful partner in crime, I couldn't help feeling grateful.

"Who are you?" she asked gently. "I've never seen this side of you."

"Yeah, I didn't actually know I had this side of me until now. Perhaps you and baby What's His Name are having a positive effect on my life." I snuggled her in closer. "Imagine that," I teased.

"Imagine that," she spooned in and started to rouse me in a way that only she could when her phone went off several times. One text after the other. "That sounds important. You should see who it is."

Her face went white as she read off each successive text.

I know you're with Andre.

I know you're trying to get me fired from my own company.

I know where you are.

I have a hit out on you. Watch your back. LOL.

She stared at me with tears welling in her eyes. "It's from an unknown number."

"He's covering his tracks. Here, let's call the police."

We immediately dressed and got out of bed. I was stupid to leave our security team behind. I called them before the police, who met us at the hotel to take our report, and from that moment forward, our life was on lockdown.

Chapter 31

Eliza

It had been an exhausting few weeks. We visited Zapata, and Bill threatened my life, so Andre was in hyper-vigilant mode. He wouldn't let me out of his sight, and honestly, as much as I wanted it to annoy me, I kind of loved it, only I was starting to feel like he and I and the baby growing inside of me were the only people in the world. We did have his caregiver Beau and his family. Jane was about to be a mother again. I got to talk to her some, but Andre wouldn't really let me leave his sight for long enough to have a real conversation. I think she also felt weird talking to me since Andre was her boss. I was starting to get a little lonely, even though I was falling in love with Andre and he, me. I just needed a little more interaction with people.

My roommates, who I barely knew, were sort of freaking out that I was gone. I explained that I was giving it a trial run with Andre and that he wanted me with him because my stalker was sort of upping his game. They understood but were still weird about it. It was also the holiday season, and I was cooped up on a ranch with a man who didn't care for Christmas. As much as I appreciated all that Andre was doing to keep me safe, it was still a little intense. I missed Harper and Ophelia and my life back in DC. Baby What's His Name was kicking my ass in the morning sickness department, but we finally figured out how to curb all that. Andre gave me saltines in the morning with a little ginger ale, and I felt gurgly and swirly, but I didn't spew. Yay me.

So, it was on a morning in December. We'd just won the morning sickness battle, and as I headed into my second trimester, I was feeling triumphant as I had read that morning sickness pretty much was gone by the third trimester. Still, my morning sickness hadn't been as bad as many people got. Harper was hospitalized and could no longer have any more children because of her severe morning sickness. I certainly didn't have to deal with the same kind of drama. Life was pretty good, if not just a little boring. I spent a lot of time with Midnight while Andre worked on the deal to sell his company. I was going to school online and about to finish my first semester. Andre was working from home most days, and Bill hadn't sent me any more texts because the police showed up at the office and asked him questions, which pretty much had scared him into not threatening me anymore.

Andre had given Dylan all he had on Bill, and they were about to arrest him on embezzlement charges. Or at least that's what I understood of Andre's rambling about the inner workings of company audits and infractions. It was all a bit mind spinning. So, Andre and I had just made love when the doorbell rang. I freaked, but he kissed me and told me not to worry.

"It's okay, love, I've got this. You should probably get dressed." He jumped into jeans and a T-shirt, and I sat up, curious.

Maybe it was a delivery? I decided to get dressed regardless because it was time to get up and get a move on. I had nothing really planned but wasn't going to lounge around naked all day. I passed Fred and Ethel and thought to myself that if I were really going to live there in Andre's house for any length of time, I would have to eventually warm it up. Especially if he decided to have me and the baby stay with him. His house was nothing but museum artifacts, sparse leather furnishings, and open space. I loved using his gym in the basement, and his screening room was fun. Outside of the stables and those two areas, his house was a sophisticated recluse's wet dream. It was three weeks until Christmas, and there wasn't a hint of holiday cheer anywhere.

I was thinking of confronting him on the lack of his Christmas when I heard voices.

"Where is she?" Harper's voice said. "I am dying to see her!"

"Now, she doesn't know, you know, so let her tell you," I heard Andre instruct.

"I promise we won't say a thing!" That was Ophelia's voice, and my heart started to race.

He had called my girlfriends from DC. I couldn't just sit in his room waiting; I rushed out to the foyer to see them standing there.

"Shut up!" I screamed.

"Pickle!" they yelled, and there were hugs and squeals, and I completely forgot about being stalked by a killer, unwed, and pregnant.

The lack of Christmas didn't even bother me anymore; I had my girls.

"Did you call them?" I looked at Andre with nothing but love and adoration.

"I did." He kissed my cheek. "I set up the media room as a guest room; there are two beds in there. You show them to the media room, and I'll get us some tea and snacks."

I didn't think I could love him more; he had changed so much.

"Yeah, no problem. This way, ladies, tell me what's up!" I started in on the girls.

"First, you tell us what's up. You have new hair? A nose piercing and …" Harper bit her lip.

"I'm pregnant!" I blurted out, knowing they already knew.

"Oh, my God! This is such great news!" Ophelia threw her arms around me. "I'm pregnant again too!"

"Are you kidding; how many is that?" Ophelia already had a mess of kids. "Only baby number four. Asher and I like making babies." She winked.

"And Reid and I are happy with our little Angel. She's almost two; the time flies, and you have to just enjoy it. I am so excited for you, Pickle, you're having a baby!" Harper squealed.

"I'm scared, but I know you guys are pros, so if I need any advice, I'm going to come to you ladies for sure. So, what have you guys been up to? I want to hear all the gory details."

Andre brought us snacks and sodas then disappeared. We talked about their lives. Ophelia still wrote for her human interest magazine, and it was doing very well. Harper was running for a spot on the school board and was starting her journey into politics, and they seemed well and happy.

"So, tell us about Andre?" Harper finally asked.

"Well, we were pretty much just physical at first. He wasn't even anyone I liked very much as a person, but he's warmed up, and I've cooled down, and now, well, I don't want to jinx it, but we are enjoying this. I mean I do have a deranged business partner threatening to kill me, but Andre hasn't let me out of his sight, so we're making it work."

"That's super dangerous." Ophelia looked freaked.

"We have security everywhere, and I haven't left the ranch. There is no way anyone is going to get to me. I'm never near the front door or any windows. I think Andre is having his business partner arrested tomorrow, so I only have one more day of this, and then it's back to normal." I was actually more nervous than I let on, but truly, it would only be one more day, I hoped.

The police had scared Bill with their questioning, so hopefully, it was all coming to an end. I had a wonderful time with Ophelia and Harper, and we talked about them coming back after Christmas. I took them to meet Midnight before he was sold, and Ophelia offered to buy him, but I told her Andre had already had a buyer.

"He's the father of your child, so surely he can back out on the sale if you love this horse that much," she said, petting his nose. "I'm going to talk to him about it." She seemed completely angry, and I did see her approach Andre later that night, but we never mentioned it again.

We watched a movie in the screening room, had a late-night dip in the jacuzzi, and I headed off to bed as soon as we were too exhausted to talk any more. When I entered Andre's room, he was already in bed waiting for me.

"That was one of the nicest things you have ever done for me," I said, getting into bed. "Thank you for bringing my girlfriends here; I needed to see them." I cuddled into him.

"I don't know what it's like to have friends," he confessed. "But you had mentioned several times that you needed them so," he curled his arms around me, "I figured I should fly them out here. Unfortunately, they both have to go back the day after tomorrow, but I promise I'll fly them out again after the holidays. Their husbands warned me that I was lucky to get them for two days."

"Yes, it's the holidays, and they both have little kids. Their husbands are amazing with their kids, but little ones need their mother." I yawned as I snuggled into his warmth.

"I'm never letting you leave the house when the baby comes," he said in a pretend panic.

"Well, at least I'm getting practice not leaving the house." I was too tired to make love, and he knew it, so he just held me. "Maybe you'll be a better dad than you think you'll be."

"Maybe," he didn't sound too convinced as he held me, and I fell asleep in his arms.

The next morning, I bounded out of bed and met Harper and Ophelia in the dining room for breakfast. We spent more time with the horses, took a walk to the lake and had a picnic there. When we got back to the ranch, Andre had a nice candle-lit dinner all prepared outside on the veranda. He spent time with us at dinner, which I appreciated, and seemed much happier and more animated than usual. I noticed his effort to be a better man, and it warmed my heart.

"So, tell me, what's the worst thing about being a parent?" he asked.

"The poop," Harper chimed in. "But Reid thinks it's the snot. He hates when they drool or have snotty noses. He can't even deal. Sorry, Andre, but men can be such big babies." Harper laughed.

"No, I'm willing to admit, I can't handle snot. I'm even gagging a little just thinking about snot." Andre pretended to gag.

"For me, it's the sleep. I just want to sleep all the time. Asher is good at living on nothing but coffee and air, but I need my sleep." Ophelia smiled while rubbing her belly even though she wasn't showing yet.

"And you want more?" I asked her.

"Sure, I love having kids. We have two boys and a girl, so little miss here will even the score." She just glowed with joy. "And your little dude and my baby will be cousins/friends. They'll be the same age; it's going to be perfect. We'll have to have a Legende party just for the little ones pretty soon. I am so excited for you two. Really, you are going to love being a family."

And that's when it all hit home for both Andre and me. We were going to be a family, something neither of us really had much of. He took my hand. Life would be brighter as a family, and I looked over and smiled at him. The next morning, I watched as Ophelia and Harper left. My heart sank a little, thinking that I'd be back to being alone again. I had Andre, but he was also so busy. I waved at them as the driver rolled out of the driveway and down Andre's private road. A red pickup truck passed the entrance to Andre's private road, and for some reason, both Andre and I froze with worry. The truck slowed a little but picked up speed seeing the town car come down the drive.

"Get inside," Andre barked as he whipped out his phone. "Get out to the front of the property; we have a suspicious vehicle. Red Ford F-150." Andre came back inside the house and continued to look stressed. "I don't want you to fight me on this; just get into the shower now. There are no windows in there. Please, just do it." He looked so scared. I marched my ass straight into the shower room without even saying a word.

I knew he had to be overreacting, but I worried he wasn't appropriately dealing with his stress, so seeing him freak out actually was a good thing; at least, he was having emotions. I sat on the little bench in the shower and just played solitaire on my phone, not worried in the slightest. I felt like I was in there for hours, but it was probably no more than one hour when the door finally opened.

"Okay, is this little scare over?" I stood and looked up to see a man wearing black with a gun pointed at my head.

My heart leaped into my throat, and I begged, "Please, I'm pregnant!"

I knew telling the man I was pregnant wasn't going to help, but it's what I thought of first, protect the baby.

All I did was say over and over again, "Please, I'm pregnant! Please, don't hurt the baby."

Chapter 32

Andre

I knew the moment I saw the red truck slowing down that we were in trouble. Bill had the audacity to do this in broad daylight. I called security, and two men took off in Beau's truck to trail the red Ford. Beau and the other two security guards started casing the property looking to see if the truck had dropped someone off. I grabbed my gun and went with another security guard to search the house. My home security system had been hacked while we were saying goodbye to Eliza's friends. Something horrible was definitely happening; I could feel it in my bones.

With the security system nonfunctional, who knew if someone was listening in on our conversations? My system was also the intercom I used to communicate with my caregivers from anywhere on the ranch; it was always on listen mode. Beau had Jane hide in their garage, and I felt safe with Eliza in the shower until I realized that there was a remote chance someone had gotten into the house.

"The red truck is circling back," one of the security guards said over the speakerphone. "We're gonna blow out the tires."

"Fine. I'll compensate the driver if our instincts are wrong," I told the guard.

"Mr. Michelson, we have another suspicious vehicle slowing down at your driveway. A black Lexus."

"Keep an eye on it," I said as I finished my search of the house.

I looked in every room, each bathroom, and I was about to open the storage cabinets when I heard Eliza's voice, faintly in the distance. *Please, I'm pregnant.*

I took off running. I knew they'd found Eliza. When I ran down the hall, I saw the shower room door was open, and a figure wearing black was standing inside.

"You should have thought about that before you stole Mr. Blascoe's files," the man said, and I heard his gun click.

I didn't think; I just started shooting. I shot the walls, the doorway, and in an instant, the man spun around, and something bit my thigh. I didn't care; I kept shooting and shooting, aiming haplessly, praying I made ontact with the intruder. When I heard a grunt and a heavy thud, I knew my mission had been accomplished. The security officer ran up to me.

"Fuck, I need back up!" he screamed into his earpiece. "Michelson and an unidentified are both down. Call the paramedics; there's blood everywhere."

"Eliza!" I screamed, thinking she'd been hurt in the spray of gunfire.

I didn't care that I'd been shot; I didn't hear her. I didn't know if she was alive or dead. I tried to get up and go to her, but the hallway wall was blocking my view. I hadn't even made it into the shower room.

"Easy there, Mr. Michelson, we have someone on the way. They'll be here in a few minutes."

I could hear the sirens in the distance, but soon everything became heavy, and it felt like my head was underwater.

"Eliza?" I called out again, but soon there was nothing.

***

I woke up in a cold room with a light sheet covering my body. I could hear machines beeping, and there was a sterile smell in the air. It hurt to open my eyes, but when I did, I recognized immediately that I was in the hospital. I sat up frantically, but my head hurt so badly I had to lie back down on the pillow. An alarm went off, and a frustrated looking nurse came running into my room.

"Okay, Mr. Michelson, just lie back down. It is way too soon to be getting out of bed," she scolded.

"Where's Eliza?" I didn't care if I looked desperate; I was.

"Detective Anderson will be in to speak with you in just a moment, just lay back, Mr. Michelson."

"Bitch!" I screamed. "Tell me where Eliza is!" I knew I was in bad form, but no one would tell me anything.

"I'm sorry. You have to talk to the detective. I don't know where she is. Now lie back down." With that, she left the room, and my heart raced.

Where the fuck was the detective, then? Within moments an officer wearing a police uniform, a badge, and a gun walked into my room and shut the door behind him. I started to panic. Was this going to be it? Was this the moment they told me that she was dead, and my whole life was over? I swore in that second that if the detective did tell me she was dead, I'd become the most hateful person alive, and I'd make sure that Bill would suffer. If he killed Eliza, I vowed I'd kill him.

"Good morning, Mr. Michelson." The detective took the chair beside my bed and dragged it over so that he could sit next to me. "How are you feeling?"

"Cut the crap; where's Eliza?" I didn't want anyone's bullshit.

"Ms. Piquel is safe. We have her in protective custody. You can relax."

I almost started crying. She was safe; she was okay. She survived.

"Was she hurt? Is the baby okay?" I still felt like there was something he wasn't telling me.

"She's completely safe and well, and the baby is fine. She wasn't harmed. Luckily, you arrived when you did. The man who was in your house is also in our custody. You shot him in the shoulder, and we're getting him to talk. He got off a round in your leg and your head. The bullet in your head just grazed the surface, which is a miracle because just a few inches more and you and I wouldn't be having this conversation." I could give a shit about myself; I was just so happy that Eliza was alive.

"Can I see her?" I didn't care about anything else; I just wanted to hold Eliza.

"We can arrange for you to see her at some point, but we do need to keep her safe until we can apprehend Bill Blascoe and assess what happened. The man Mr. Blascoe hired to kill Ms. Piquel has confessed. He told our detectives that he couldn't continue his mission when he saw how she begged for your child's life. He said it touched him, but he probably would have mustered the conviction to finish the job. Then you came in shooting, and now we have him in police custody, and he's talking after we offered him a plea deal. He's a professional hitman who has a lot to lose, so he told us about Mr. Blascoe hiring him because Ms. Piquel stole some top-secret files. I need you to clarify events for me so that we can start collecting evidence. But I do have to know, and it would be best if you tell me. Were you involved in this hit? Perhaps you wanted your pregnant girlfriend to go away?"

"How dare you! I love Eliza. I'd die for her. Fuck, I almost did die for her. Don't you dare insult me with such questions." I was so pissed; everything on me hurt.

"I'm just doing my job, Mr. Michelson. The evidence will eventually speak for itself."

"What the hell is that supposed to mean?"

I spent a few hours with the detective going through every detail until I was beginning to feel nauseous and couldn't continue. He told me he would launch an investigation and confer with the police department that had been working with Dylan on the embezzlement charges. He explained that Eliza would be in a safe house until they could find Bill and any of his accomplices.

I discovered that the bullet in my femur lodged into the bone and shattered it. I'd need reconstructive surgery, and the bullet that grazed my head took out a nasty gash that had been stitched up. They shaved my head for the procedure. So, I was bald and would soon be in a full leg cast and a wheelchair, then later on crutches. It was worth it knowing I'd saved Eliza and the baby; I would have chopped off my leg if it would have saved their lives.

I was in the hospital for a little more than a week. During that time, they found Bill hiding out in a dilapidated house in Zapata. There, he had hired local hitmen in the decimated community and devised his plan to kill Eliza for finding Fasco, his secret company. Dylan discovered Bill embezzled nearly two hundred million dollars from Michelson Energy Corp and would not only be going to jail for embezzlement but also attempted murder. He'd never be getting out of prison. As for my company, the scandal made the sale almost impossible as the offers were too low to take seriously. It was a time when I really needed Eliza's advice.

The police were still not allowing me to speak with her, and I had conversations with detectives and answered their questions every day. I assumed they were gauging my level of involvement in an attempt to find if I too engaged in any criminal activity. When I felt I'd been finally cleared of suspicion, they let me send a text to Eliza at a number I didn't recognize. Though they had Bill in custody, they were still being cautious, ensuring all their loose ends were tied up before letting me talk to her.

I love you - A

Was the first thing I texted.

I love you too. Thank you for saving my life, Andre. I miss you every minute of the day. - E

I would have died for you. I can't wait until this is all over! - A

As it was less than two weeks until Christmas, the police and the hospital had pity on us and let me go home with a nurse. We still had security guards on the premises, and I had gotten word from Beau that Eliza had returned to the ranch just before I was transported from the hospital. Soon I'd be home with my sweet lover, and we'd work to rebuild our lives. I was still very immobile and confined to a wheelchair for another few weeks, but just having her near me, I knew would speed the healing process.

The first thing I noticed while riding in the hospital transport van up my private driveway were three huge lit-up signs in the front yard that read PEACE, LOVE, and JOY. I then looked up to the rafters and saw lights hanging like icicles from the roof. It wasn't as shocking as finding a man in your shower holding a gun to your lover's head, but it was unsettling in a different way.

The nurse wheeled me into the house, and as soon as I entered, I smelled peppermint and cinnamon. As I looked around, there were tasteful Christmas decorations everywhere. In the corner was a big tree all trimmed in silver and white lights, and there were tiny lights draped around my statues. A few white poinsettias were carefully placed about the living room, and four packages were wrapped in silver paper under the tree. It felt like Christmas, glorious, glittering, and minimal. Dearest Eliza must have done it, and I couldn't have adored her more for it. As I was wheeled in, Jane was the first to see me. She was looking much more pregnant than I'd last seen her.

"Oh, Mr. Michelson. You're here." She seemed shocked. "I wasn't paying attention." She gave me a nervous smile as she whipped out her phone and dialed.

"Yeah, Jane?" I heard Eliza's voice.

"He's here," Jane said.

"Oh. Okay, Oh, my God ... okay!" Eliza's happy and surprised voice made me tingle with excitement.

"What are the two of you cooking up?" I asked, looking at Jane suspiciously.

I wanted to get out of the damn chair, but the nurse put her hand on my shoulder when I tried. "I'm afraid you're not ready to get up out of the chair until we can get you some physical therapy," she scolded.

I was being overrun by strong, confident women.

"Andre!" Eliza ran to me and every worry and stress I'd been battling just melted away the moment I saw her.

She, too, looked more pregnant. She had a tiny baby bump. Oh, my God, it was our little baby bump, our dearest tiny baby inside of my beautiful lover.

Chapter 33

Eliza

"I have been crazy missing you!" I hugged him as best as I could with him in the chair.

I hated seeing him in that damn wheelchair, but I also knew he had to recover. They had to do a lot to dig the bullet out and reconstruct his femur bone, and he had a nasty scar on his head from where the bullet hit his skull. Most of it would eventually be covered by his hair, and the bullet didn't mar his handsome face.

"I love you. I love you. I love you," I gushed as I held him.

"Get me out of this damn chair, so I can hold her please!" he barked at the nurse who had come in with him.

"Sure, Mr. Michelson. Let me just call for some help," the nurse said, and within moments, Beau was there to help transfer Andre to the couch.

"Thank you," he said kindly when they set him down and apologized for being gruff.

"No worries, Mr. M. I'm sure it's gonna take some getting used to," Beau said softly.

I had befriended Beau and Jane and their kids Michael and Madison while Andre was in the hospital. They didn't let me talk with him until the police had released him from custody. I don't think he even knew he was a suspect. They didn't tell him I was back at the ranch until he'd been completely cleared.

That first night after the shooting, I was held in a safe house with other women and locked in a room with a personal guard until they caught Bill the next day near the Mexican border. He was about to leave the country, but they got him at border patrol. When the coast was clear a day later, I was returned to the ranch. I thought about going back to my roommates, but I knew Andre would have wanted me at the ranch with the security staff and precautions he'd already put in place. Not that they really stopped the bad guy. Bill's hitmen were smart; they sent out a decoy truck to get the security's attention, then the hitman came in on foot from another vehicle parked behind the neighbor's house. The hitman didn't know that the neighbor was a sheriff, so he was apprehended within minutes. But Andre was the one to save me. He had the gut instinct to know I was in danger, and it was his bullet that stopped the hitman from firing at me.

The man dressed in black had hesitated as I begged for my life and the life of our son, but ultimately I could see he had decided to shoot me anyway. There was nowhere to go; I was literally trapped in the shower room. It was then, when the gunman took precise aim that I heard shots being fired. I ducked into the shower and tucked myself up against the wall to make myself as small as I could, and it protected me from the stray bullets. The police arrived while he and Andre were still shooting, and everything was a blur of motion after that point.

I snuggled up beside Andre the moment they got him onto the couch and loved being near his warmth again.

"I love you." I took his hand and just held it, happy to have him back.

"Let's let these two have a minute," Beau said as everyone disappeared out of the room.

"You decorated," Andre noted quietly.

"I hope you don't mind. I tried to think of you and what you'd want Christmas to look like." I stroked my thumb over his skin.

"It's perfect." He turned to me and kissed my lips.

It had just been too long. I craved the taste of him, and so we sat there and made out on the couch like love-starved teenagers. When we broke from our kiss, he was in tears.

"I almost lost you," he barely whispered.

"But because of you, you didn't." I touched his cheek to wipe his tears away. "And now you're stuck with me." I kissed him softly.

I knew he wanted to say a lot more, but he didn't, and I'm glad he didn't. None of it was worth saying. I loved him, and that's all there was or ever needed to be. He struggled with being physically limited, but he got stronger every day. I asked if he'd be okay if I invited Peyton and Genevieve over for a little Christmas Eve dinner as they were both away from their families, and he agreed that having them around would really bring the Christmas cheer. He admitted that we could use a little lightness and fun in our lives as he laughed and looked over at Fred and Ethel wearing their Christmas hats.

I called my mom as I'd missed a few Sundays and finally told her I was pregnant.

"You're what?" My mom was horrified, which wasn't a surprise. "What are you going to do?"

Andre was listening in to the call. His face grew red when he saw the shame on my face, but I bucked myself up.

"It's okay, Mom. The father and I are on very good terms, and we're going to raise him together. We're fine. I just wanted you to know that you're going to be a grandma. Merry Christmas and give Dad and Richard a big hug for me." I couldn't bear any more of the conversation, so I ended the call.

"I'm sorry," Andre said as he kissed my shoulder.

"It's okay. At least I told her." I kissed him back.

Sex was a little tricky those days as he still had a lot of pain, so we just stuck to oral stuff. I pleasured him, and when it was time for him to return the favor, I just straddled his face so he didn't have to maneuver around too much. We made it work and were still able to send each other to the moon. One day he'd be well, and we'd be back to our old tricks, though I'd be quite pregnant by then. I was already starting to show a little, and I could feel the little guy inside me.

"Woah," I smiled as I put my hand on my belly. He was starting to make little flutters.

"Was it What's His Name?" Andre asked, looking over at my tiny baby bump.

"Yes." I smiled at him adoringly. "And my love." I stroked his face. "What is his name? We should probably think about that."

"Chris Kringle?" Andre teased.

"Saint Nicholas?" I played along.

"Zachery?" he said softly.

"Zackery." I smiled. "I love it. Zackery Andreas Michelson."

Andreas, I'd discovered from Andre's medical release papers was Andre's full name. Andreas Victor Michaelson. Victor being his abusive father's name.

"Are you sure you want that to be his name?" Andre asked with a little worry in his tone.

"I think it's a beautiful name, and unlike you, he'll be proud to have his father's name. I'm sure of it."

"You are the dearest woman," Andre said out of the blue. "When I'm healed, I promise you, we will spend an entire day in this bed. I won't let you leave until your world has been rocked so hard all you'll see are stars."

"All I need to see is you. Now, let's get you up and at 'em. We have people coming in a few hours, and I'm not gonna let them see you in your birthday suit."

I helped with Andre's bathing and general care, though he did have twenty-four-hour nursing staff on duty at all times. He was getting much stronger and hardly needed help standing up anymore, just the occasional shoulder to balance on, which was pretty remarkable having only been shot two weeks before. We got ready for the Christmas Eve dinner, which was delightful. During the time Andre had been home, he bought lavish gifts for everyone. He bought a 75-inch television for Peyton and Genevieve's living room and gave each woman a beautiful pair of diamond earrings with a matching necklace, and each of them got the newest iPhone and a small residential energy unit. His gifts were crazy and lavish, and both were thankful beyond words.

"You have a keeper there," Peyton gushed as she put on her diamond necklace.

I looked at Andre and smirked. "I sure do."

Andre had also given crazy expensive gifts to Beau and Jane and their family, with more big-screen TVs, phones, iPads, and new computers for the kids, and a new truck for Beau. Jane had confessed that outside of a Christmas bonus, which they both appreciated, Andre had never given them gifts or celebrated Christmas. The fact that he had turned into Santa Claus had brightened everyone's holiday. By the time everyone left that night, we were happy and exhausted.

"Thank you," I said when Andre and I got back into bed. "What you did for everyone was so thoughtful and kind. You really have unleashed your inner superhero." I kissed him.

"It was all because …" I put my finger up to his mouth to stop him.

"Because you wanted to be more. I had very little to do with it. People don't change people …" I snuggled into his embrace and played with his cock as I usually did.

"I think I'm feeling well enough for you to hop on board if you want to. There's no more pain, and having sex with you always helps." His smile was wide and beautiful.

"If you feel up for it, I'm so ready for this." I yanked on him a little, and he slapped my ass as I moved to straddle his erection.

He was almost back to his sexy self again. We made love twice that night and went to sleep happily in each other's arms. The next morning was Christmas.

While Andre was in hospital, the community councilman for Zapata had reached out to me, saying that the citizens wanted to thank Andre for what he'd done for them. Since they knew he funded the rebuild himself, everyone who received financial help wrote him a letter for Christmas explaining how much his support meant to them and what they intended to do to honor his generosity. I decided that morning that we'd open those letters first.

With a little help from me and his nurse, we got him dressed and out of bed, which he almost resented because he was getting so damn good at doing it himself. I wheeled him into the living room to find there were a lot more presents under the tree. We were both baffled by the additional presents but pretended they weren't there as we focused on the wonderful breakfast spread laid out on the dining table. There was fruit, coffee, tea, pastries that were dazzling and delicious looking, bacon, and sausage. It was quite a little feast for the two of us. There was a handwritten note on the table.

Merry Christmas, from Beau, Jane, Michael, Madison, and baby Mary born this morning at 2 am!

Jane had had her baby. We quickly discovered that the gifts under the tree were from them. Most were things for the baby and a hand-painted sign that said, 'Family', which was made by one of the children. The spread was from the same place Andre had ordered Thanksgiving dinner. Beau must have had them deliver it while he was with his wife helping her deliver their baby. Everything felt so miraculous.

"Wow, for a man who's never really celebrated Christmas, this is pretty much an entire Hallmark movie," I commented, gushing. "However, there's more," I said, wheeling him over to the box of letters I'd wrapped.

He opened the box and read each letter, and with each one, he got more emotional. The final piece was a framed picture of all the families surrounding a plaque in front of a beautiful park with brand new grass, benches, and children's play equipment. The bronze plaque said: The Andre Michelson Blessings Park, and that's what did him in. Tears rolled down his face. I knew in his heart he was dealing with what it felt like to be the good guy. All I did was hold him as he let his emotions sink in.

"I have just a couple more gifts for you," I said gently as I put another box in his lap.

"Another gift?" he asked in surprise.

"Well, these two are from me." I sat beside him and watched him open the first box. He pulled out a pair of red Christmas pajamas and then a second pair, which was my size, and a tiny pair big enough for the baby. "The only thing I remember loving most at Christmas time was having matching pajamas with my brother. So, now we have matching Christmas pajamas for next year."

He blew me a kiss and laughed. "I love this." His smile was warm and genuine. "I just have one more for you." I got up and picked up the box and handed it to him. "I spent all of my savings on this, so if you decide to kick me out, make sure you give me a heads up so I can get a job at Starbucks or something." I really had spent my very last dime on his gift, but I knew I wanted it. "When I found this, though, I knew you needed to have it."

"This box is huge," he said, wrangling into his lap. "What the hell did you buy? It's heavy too." I helped him stabilize the box because the last thing I wanted him to do was to drop it.

He managed to get it open, and inside was a tiny Paige Bradley statue of a baby boy. "I thought Fred and Ethel might like to have this." I raked my hand through Andre's short fuzzy hair.

"Fred and Ethel will love this baby …" is all he said as he choked up. "Paige Bradley … This did cost a fortune. Thank you so much. He's perfect." Andre turned to me and rubbed his hand on my bulging little belly.

"Okay, time for your gift." His smile could not have been wider. "For this, you'll have to wheel me outside."

"You've already given me my gift," I said as I patted my belly.

"Well, yes, but I have another gift. Now, this is a little awkward, but I want you to put on this blindfold." He brought a strip of black cloth out of his pocket. "And hold onto my wheelchair. You'll have to just trust me and don't let go of the chair." I had no idea what he was doing, but I played along because it was fun.

"Okay," I said with a note of skepticism in my voice.

We walked for a long time and took twists and turns, and at times, I thought he was just messin' with me, but we finally made it to our destination; however, he didn't let me take the blindfold off.

"You'll have to wait until the baby is born to use your Christmas gift, but I think you'll like it, even if I won't let you use it yet." The only thing I could think he was giving me was a car.

He'd be the kind of man who was crazy enough not to let me drive while I was pregnant. I was curious to see what he'd gotten me since all of his other gifts were so lavish and over the top. As soon as I heard Midnight whinny and smelled his familiar scent, my heart stopped.

"Okay, love. You can take the blindfold off." I did, and standing before me in the middle of the pasture was Midnight.

"You can't," I said. "You spent so much money rebuilding Zapata; how can you have the money to keep him?"

"I would never sell him knowing how much you loved each other. And don't worry about money. I've made a deal for Michelson Energy Corp to mass-produce the clean energy units and sell them retail to the public. My partnership with Tesla has come with a steep price tag, and soon, you and I will have more money than we'll know what to do with. You will definitely never have to work at Starbucks." I just gave him a confused look. "Midnight is yours, my love. Enjoy him ... after Zachery is born. I don't want anything happening to you or the baby, so I plan to bubble wrap you both."

"Thank you," I threw my arms around him and just held him; I couldn't say anymore. "I just have one more gift for you," he said after I held him for a while. "I'm going to have to do this a little differently but bear with me." He then locked his wheelchair. "Now, don't help me. I need to do this on my own." He then struggled and used all of his strength, but he could stand up and take one step away from the chair.

I rushed to him, but he put his hand out to me. "I can do this, love. Just give me a minute." He took one more step and was at his full height, and I remembered what a tall and impressive man he was.

"That's amazing, Andre, you can do it," I cheered thinking that was the gift, the fact that he was healing so quickly.

He laughed. "I love that you think this is what I'm giving you. No." He put his hand in his pocket and brought out a tiny black velvet box. "This is." I froze, staring at the box. He slowly opened the box and presented me with a ring with a massive diamond. "Will you, Elizabeth Piquel, please be my wife?" All I could do was stare. "Is that a yes?" he asked, sounding a little worried.

"Are you really asking me to marry you?"

"Honey, I took a bullet for you. I think you should know that I am."

I just started crying. "Yes, yes! Oh, God, yes! Are you sure you want to do this?" I looked up at him.

"I've never been more sure of anything in my life. You did it, Eliza; you broke me." He kissed my forehead, and we spent the rest of the day in bed just like he had wanted us to. It was one of the most glorious days of my life.

Epilogue

Eliza

It was April and time for the Legende Ball. I was seven months pregnant and married to Andre Michelson. We got married on our ranch in a small ceremony, which was just perfect for us. Though his ranch was big, we had plenty of space to expand. I knew he'd need his quiet, minimalistic, man-cave if he was going to survive parenthood, so instead of a honeymoon, we added onto the house. We expanded and created another wing with four more bedrooms, a nursery, and an indoor basketball court. I thought it was completely frivolous, but Andre's dream was to play one on one with his son, so we had an indoor basketball court and a huge playroom that would eventually become a teen lounge. Andre had big dreams for our kids. We decided that after Zachery was born, we wouldn't mess with IUDs. I'd get the Depo shot until we were ready to make baby number two. Andre was an only child, and he didn't want Zachery to grow up lonely.

"Besides, I like making babies with you," Andre said as we walked through our finished house and dreamed of the kids who might fill the halls one day.

My mom and dad got really excited when I told her I was married, and we planned on visiting them as soon as the baby was old enough to travel. I had to warm Andre up to the idea of meeting my parents and brother, but he'd braved so much already, he was sure to be able to survive them. We invited Peyton and Genevieve to come with us to DC to the Legende Ball since they had become our regular guests at the ranch for Friday fun nights where we played games, watched movies, and ate way too much food. Andre usually stayed away and just let us girls hang out, but I knew he was happy I had friends.

When we reached Legende, it was great to see Harper and Ophelia, and we laughed as Ophelia and I were both hugely pregnant.

"Must be something in the Legende drinks because every year, one of you ladies is pregnant!" Asher commented.

"Maybe it's because you keep knocking up your wife," I teased.

"Yeah, we do like to make babies." He kissed her, and Andre smiled.

"I know the feeling." He laughed, and I could see that Andre was slowly making friends of his own.

Our world could not have been more beautiful. It was also that night that Genevieve met Johnny Cresta, one of the five singers in the band Dangerous Liaisons. He was about to go solo and was doing a publicity tour, so he ensured that the press was there to see him enter the legendary Legende Ball. Genevieve went right up to him and introduced herself, and he was a typical rock star only there for the publicity. She didn't care; she was a crazy fan, so she risked embarrassment to shake his hand and snap a selfie. During the Karaoke portion of the night, she got up and sang, just having fun, and that's when he crossed the room to get her phone number. It was one of the best nights of her life, and she gushed about it for days.

Andre

I wasn't the world's worst father, but I had to admit diapers really weren't my thing. I helped Eliza as much as I could, especially when little Zachary was a tiny newborn. Eliza was so tired, and I wanted her to get all the rest she needed. We had hired a nanny for the night-time feedings while Eliza recovered from childbirth, but I tried to do as many diapers as I could stomach. I was completely healed from being shot and only had a tiny sliver of pain every once in a while when I stepped on the leg wrong. My injuries, however, could not be used to explain why most of the diapers either ended up sliding down Zachary's leg or not really doing the job a diaper should. The poor guy was wet and poopy so many times after I'd diapered him, I was officially taken off diaper duty. I felt simultaneously triumphant and regretful.

Michelson Energy Corp quickly became a Fortune 500 company, and we were rolling in money, but Eliza couldn't have cared less about the money. She was happy we were successful because it made me so happy that we were providing clean energy to the world that she loved. We decided that while she was raising our children, she'd stay home and finish her master's degree online, and when she was ready, and the kids had grown, I'd retire, and she'd go into the world and make her mark. She was happy with this decision and excited about being a mother and wife for a few years before working in environmental ethics, which she loved just as much as me, and mothering was the work we did with communities.

After seeing what we accomplished in Zapata, we decided to work with other communities, getting them clean energy at cost and helping them strengthen their infrastructures. We loved working on those projects together, and more than that, we loved being together. After almost two years, I was still as desperately in love as I'd ever been. After she evicted little Zachary from her womb, we were back to our old selves in bed, and boy, was that amazing. Loving her was the most fun, but having sex with her was a very close second. We had a beautiful family and a wonderful life together. I didn't really think it would ever be possible, but Eliza introduced me to the man I never knew I wanted to be, and we lived happily ever after.

THE END

Dear reader,

thank you so much for reading my book, it really means the world to me! If you liked it and want to do me a little favor, please leave a short review on Amazon – that would be too wonderful!

XOXO
Mia

Printed in Great Britain
by Amazon